The

By

Sandy Berlin

To Don & Lydia

Love from

Martin

xx

This is the story of the rise of King Edward IX of England.

A journey from the modern world to a different place, of war, starvation, disease, Death, and the ghoulish light of perverted science.

Edward Gaunt is descended from the bastard line of John of Gaunt, mixed with French and Algerian royalty. Dr Henry Bryant is a brilliant military chemist with a taste for young girls. Colonel Alex Rheinhart is one of Britain's most decorated female soldiers.

Together they form a psychological ops unit based around the most secret of all weapons. The Americans want it, Gaunt sees a way to become the last Plantagenet King and fulfil what he considers to be his destiny.

Through devious and divers means he sets in train a savage, violent Armageddon. He destroys the modern world and creates a new world over which he is King. He seeks immortality and total control.

THIS IS HOW IT BEGINS.

I
The Village in the Mountains

It was hot. The wind blew curls of yellow dust into the air. The very air shimmered in the heat A tall man with a long stride paced along the road with an air of purpose. A woman walked behind, also tall and maintaining an easy pace in her stride. Her black robes, faded in parts and stained with dust, billowed out revealing her worn leather sandals and pale feet and ankles on which was a small blemish which looked vaguely like an upturned ship's anchor on a green background.

The man's robes were dark grey, perhaps brown once. Under his cloak he wore a white robe. On his head a dark turban, with a red cap, barely visible. He was exceptionally tall. Perhaps more than six and a half feet, and his wide shoulders complimented his height, but what caught the attention was his face. Stern, with fierce dark grey eyes that stared straight ahead from skin browned and hardened by the wind and the sun. A large brown beard covered most of his face, like a schoolboy image of a stone-age man. Perhaps the best description.
Apart from her feet, the woman's eyes were her only other visible part. Blue grey, or maybe a hint of green.

In the rear distance a great cloud of dust

signalled the approach of a vehicle, but neither walkers paid it any attention. It caught up and overtook the two. A bleached red pick-up with no windows in the cab, containing six serious looking young men in black turbans and sporting a black flag tied to the roof of the cab. On the flatbed a mounted anti-aircraft gun, probably of Russian manufacture from several decades ago.

The truck drove on up the mountain road covering everything in dust before turning a bend. The wind quickly blew the remains away. To one side of the road lay a gully, a small mountain stream which supported a ragged collection of fields in which there were assorted crops of wheat and some rice, but mainly poppies. A few sheep and goats together wandered about a pasture, fenced off with pieces of rusting barbed wire, sticks and stones.

The village came into view around the bend. A poor place. A typical subsistence level village. Small groups of people scratching a living from the poor soils and worse weather. A collection of shanty huts formed around what might be called a village square. It had been there forever. The British may have found it in the 19th century, or perhaps the Mongols in the 12th century. Maybe it had never been seen by anyone except the sorry collection of peasants who had reproduced from generation to generation over the millennia. It may have had a name but no one from outside knew, nor cared.

The truck was parked next to the only building that had been cared for. The Mosque. A small square building with a concrete roof and a small brick built tower on which stood a familiar metal sickle. In front of the building was a small walled courtyard with a flowing water fountain driven from the stream, together with a circular trough filled with clear water. Attached to the side was another smaller room. The women's room. Corrugated iron covered the roof of this, there were no windows and the doorway was a simple frame leading to the dark interior.

The tall man and woman walked across the village square. The woman broke away and headed into the darkened doorway of the women's area. The man proceeded into the fountain courtyard. He removed his sandals, bathed his feet in the trough, and ran his wet hands briefly over is face and beard. He stepped onto the rush matting which lay at the entrance to the shrine, leaving his shoes by the door along with the mound of shoes or sandals that were already piled up there.

The cool interior was a small relief from the sun and the wind. The tall man raised his arms with his hands out, palms inward. He held them there while he walked forward to the front of the congregation. The presiding Imam looked on at him. He was reciting his chant but then stopped as the man passed in front of him. His face became a blank stare. The village men and boys were kneeling down in prayer. The six men in black robes from the truck were also there. Each looked up and said nothing but simply stared ahead.

The tall man spoke in perfect Persian.

"Who is your head-man?"

No one spoke. A small, dishevelled man in ragged pyjamas and a filthy puggaree wrapped round his head stood up. He had no teeth and his beard was grey. He said nothing.

"Where are your weapons and explosives?"

The man replied that they were under the schoolhouse, the Madrassa, at the back of the mosque. The tall man signalled that he should lead him there and the old man led the way. No one moved or said anything. There was only the sound of the wind outside and the muted crying of a baby in the women's room next door.

The headman stepped outside, down a small stone alley and then into a small room with a threadbare carpet. He bent down and pulled back the carpet to reveal a loose trap door in the floor. He pulled on the ring at one side of the trap and lifted the wooden door. Piled up in the centre of the hole was a small cache of weapons, mainly old Kalashnikovs, RPG's, and crates of ammunition. A few modern rifles and a couple of old English double-barrelled shotguns.

The tall man told him to return to the mosque.

He knelt down and took a package from under his cloak, set the timer for five minutes and placed it on the cache. He closed the trap door leaving the carpet rolled up at the side.

He walked back into the Mosque where the old man had returned.

He spoke to them

"Men, I have spoken to God and he wishes you to lay down your arms, return to your fields, raise your families, and grow your meat and crops. Cast aside your troubles and live in peace"

The congregation stared at him but said nothing.

He walked out of the mosque, recovered his shoes, and stepped out into the hot and dusty square. The tall woman appeared a moment later from beyond a dung heap that was piled up against one of the shanty houses. She came towards him.

The man turned and walked past the truck. As he did so he dropped another packet into the flat bed.

The tall man and his woman walked back out of the square and round the bend onto the road that had brought them.

As they passed the fields next to the stream the man reached into a pocket in his gown pulling out a handful of small seeds, which he threw casually into the field and the stream. They were *planta genista* seeds, the common broom.

Moments later there was a large explosion, followed quickly by more large explosions. A gout of flame shot up, followed by great clouds of black and grey smoke, mingled with flying lumps of rock and dung.

The pair continued to walk down the road to another bend where they veered off into a small dry nullah. A British Army Land Rover in desert colours stood there. As they approached the engine started. They clambered aboard and the car rolled out onto the road, back up through the village and the smoke, and on a few more miles through the hills towards the next village.

II
Westmoreland

The yacht lay off the western coast of the British Isles just beyond the mouth of the river Lune in Morecambe Bay. Its hull was painted dark blue and its sails were bleached with the salt and the sun. Several repairs had been expertly stitched indicating that these sails had been through rough weather many times.
However everything was clean. The teak decks had been scrubbed and oiled. The cockpit was marked but clean. The lines were tight and in good order, the halyards tight and un-frayed. The boat's wheel gleamed in polished chrome.

A tall woman stood behind the wheel. She was perhaps late thirties, maybe early forties. She was lean and fit; her strong hands were coarse from hard work .Her brown hair was pulled back into a short ponytail, the only sign of femininity. Her face was strongly sun-tanned. She wore a cream Arran sweater which was slightly crunchy with salt, and a pair of faded regular jeans with signs of repair. On her bare feet, a pair of good quality leather boat shoes with sliced rubber soles, also salt stained. On her wrist an expensive seaman's watch, her only adornment.

She checked her watch. It would be high tide in less than an hour. The boat bobbed in the slack water with only a very slight swell and a light breeze, which she had turned into.

She leaned across and unclipped the foresail lines then lowered the sail leaving it in position. She did the same with the mainsail. She stepped up and onto the starboard deck towards the bow and threw out the sea anchor, a large orange parachute drogue attached to one of the bow cleats. She held onto the tripping line until the bag filled and slipped under the surface. She measured out and secured the slack tripping line then tied that back to a separate cleat before returning to the cockpit.

She looked about her for any other vessels. Visibility was good and there was nothing in sight.

She slipped below deck to gather a small grab bag of clothes and essentials. Everything was tidy and stowed away. She locked the chart table, together with the sat nav.

She checked the locks in the galley and the forward hold. All stowed away tight. Long life tins of food were stowed in several holds and secure cupboards. She checked the fuel level and the fresh water levels then went back up to the cockpit with the grab bag and waited.

Through her binoculars she saw a blue flag being raised at the boatyard. Clearly an indication that the lock gates were being opened. At this she went forward and tripped the sea anchor, pulling it aboard and stowing it with two nylon straps on the forward deck. She flipped the fenders out on both sides as she returned. Then she raised and trimmed the sails, turning the boat towards the river mouth and sailed in. The lock gates were open so she swung the boat around using the sails with one hand on the wheel and the other holding the mainsail line round a brightly polished capstan. The boat slipped through the lock gates. She let fall the main sail and foresail and the boat cruised slowly to the main dock of the yard. A man was standing on the dock who signalled for her to throw the stern line to him which she did, then stepped forward and did the same with the bowline.

"No engine,... very impressive" said the man on the dock without smiling. She was quietly pleased at the recognition. The man stepped back to look cautiously at the boat, his hand holding a large boathook with what looked like a sharpened point.

"Anyone else with you?"

"No just me."

"Can't be too careful these days unfortunately, we have to be a bit cautious, sorry to be rude but I need to check the boat."
"Be my guest." As she waived her arm, "Come aboard."

The man stepped down into the boat, still armed with his boathook. He used it to poke through the open hatch that led down to the galley. He listened, then stepped warily through and down into the boat's interior.

After a couple of minutes he returned.
"Sorry, but we've had a few robberies. Gangs that come in by sea or land, they think boatyards are the hangouts of the wealthy and come here to steal what they can get."

"I understand." She said. She'd seen it elsewhere in the world, particularly the western world where law and order had more or less broken down.

"Who do I talk to about some work on the boat?"

"Have a word with old Tom over there" He pointed towards a large boat shed. " how long will you be staying?"

"Not sure, quite a while, it'll need lifting out and put in dry standing, there's a floating compost heap growing under the water"

"Ok, I'll pull her out now if you want to gather any things?"

"All sorted" she said holding up the canvas grab bag. She climbed out of the boat. As she stepped onto the dock he noticed a small tattoo on her ankle, what looked like an upturned anchor on a green background? He wasn't sure and the moment passed.

She noticed the steel fencing around the yard and the cameras facing both in and out.

"I'll get the hoist, leave it to me and you can have a chat with Tom while I pull her out". He walked off to bring over the large boat crane. She walked over to the larger boat shed. She could hear the sounds of an electric sander. An older man was sanding off the hull of a small boat. When he noticed her watching him he switched it off and walked over, dusting his overall's off. He smiled. She noticed a shotgun lying on the workbench.

" Hello ducks can I help you?

"I'm looking for Tom,"

"Well, that would be me" He looked over her shoulder and saw the younger man swinging the canvas straps under the hull of her yacht.

"That's a fine boat, Aussie?"

"Yes it is, not my first boat though, I lost the first one in a storm on the southern ocean. Insurance paid up so I got the steel one" she said pointing backwards with her thumb.

"Come a long way here then?"

"I've been afloat over four years. Started in

Portsmouth, and ended here via the Med, Suez, East Africa, India, Malay, China, Americas, North and South, Oz and NZ then back up the East coast up to the Arctic, and round the Baltic before coming back via Scotland and Ireland. A long way round" she smiled and he nodded with some appreciation.

"On your own?,"

She gave a swift smile but he noticed a slight shift in her stance and her grey blue, maybe green eyes remained fixed on his like an animal ready to strike.

"Any firearms aboard?.

"No," she lied. The guns were all wrapped in waxed polythene, stowed in the bilges, and concealed in concrete boxes to look like regular ballast.

"So Tom" she said " I need a few things. The hull needs scraping and re-finishing. A check on the inside for any rust and removal if needed, I need the engine serviced and checked over for any wear or leakage on the bearings. The sails need replacing with new but you can stow the old ones in the sail locker. The electronics need an update. The gas fitting needs replacing...and no doubt you will find other things. Then into long-term storage as I'm not planning to go on the water again for a while. Can you do all that?"

"Well, it'll take some time, and I'll need some cash upfront, it'll be expensive , it's this inflation business, everything's gotten so expensive, plus there'll be storage etc but yes we can do all that". " Happy to do all that" he added with a smile "Er Miss...?"

"Alex, Alex Rheinhart, just call me Alex, here's the contact details for my solicitor, call him and tell him the Colonel asks him to send you some money. Give him your bank details and he'll send you the cash" she handed him a small card from her back pocket. "Meanwhile..." she slipped her hand into her shirt and pulled out three Krugerrands "..you can hold these as security until you've been paid in full."
It was the same everywhere now. Governments all over the world had been printing excess money for years creating price inflation. That together with an ever-increasing population had meant more people chasing fewer and fewer resources. Population around the world was now estimated at over fifteen billion and continuing to rise. Even old Britain had well over one hundred million people now living there creating wholesale rifts in society, and a thriving criminal black market. A near impossible position to control.

" I can give you a quote..."

"It needs to be done and I'm sure you're not going

to rip me off" she said and her steel eyes looked straight at him. He had an uneasy feeling, but just nodded "Ok Miss..er Alex"

"Send any invoices or quotes to him if you like and he'll agree or otherwise for me" she said slightly softer and gave him a smile. " and if you need to contact me, go through him until I've sorted out a place to live. Talking of which is there a hotel or pub nearby where I can get a room for a few days?"

"Ah well, we haven't got a hotel but there's a pub in the village, The Golden Lion, Some rooms there I think. Landlady is Sue Pine, tell her old Tom recommended you to her...good food too".

"Is it far?"

"'bout a mile down that way" he pointed.

It began to rain. She pulled out a rolled up dark green nylon waterproof from her grab bag and slipped it on, pulling the hood over her head.

"Thank you Tom, good of you, I'll be in touch, look after her" she pointed at the boat that was now sitting on a steel stand dripping seawater from an impressive assortment of marine life.

"Just a couple of things yet, ... Alex, so many regulations and whatnot, I need you to fill out a few forms, border documents and customs declarations, and I'll need a copy of your passport. They're very hot on things these days"

"Of course, nearly forgot" she said and followed him to the yard office. Once completed she headed out of the yard.

"I'll need to let you out ducks, don't touch the fence, its electric.."

"Er Alex" Tom said, "my daughter is an Estate Agent, maybe she can help you find a place if you're looking longer term, I'll give you her number" and he walked over to a table and scribbled her name and number on a piece of paper.

"Thanks Tom I'll give her a call" and with that she turned out of the boat shed. Old Tom let her out and into the rain.

III
General Gaunt

Board meetings at the National Trust are dull affairs. A national charity with nearly six million members who want to visit the many great historic country estates and walk over parks, moors and hills maintained by the charity. Even though the charity is supposed to be apolitical the agenda items generally include the latest views of one or other of the political parties, social media trends, and assorted groups with a particular agenda to push. This was reflected in the make-up of the committee members. More recently this had included the more radical elements of the conservation movement and a distinct left-wing bias.

The Chairwoman sat down at the end of the conference table. Her LGBTQ plus credentials were impeccable leading to her being called on to head up this particular organisation. She was a lifelong member of the Labour party, a trustee of Greenpeace and Amnesty International. She had been one of the Greenham Common women who stood outside the perimeter fences of the Greenham Common USAF air-force base where their nuclear missiles were kept until the protest succeeded and the Americans moved them out of the country. She looked at the board members and the trustees assembled around the table. She had a stiff air and her facial features were pulled

tight with a tight forced smile and clenched teeth. All others around the table had similar expressions except for one man who sat in the middle. A huge man dressed in a dark blue naval uniform. His long dark hair hung down over his neck and the sides of his face. A thick brown beard obscured most of the bottom of his face but his eyes were bright and he looked relaxed. He looked like a stone-age man come to life.
He sat passively as he sensed the hostility of those around him.

She spoke "Ladies and Gentlemen, welcome to this months board meeting. I want to start by welcoming our newest member General Edward Gaunt who you see has joined us today"

A few turned to Gaunt, one of the polite ones smiled and nodded at him but the others chose not to look and stared straight ahead, or at the Chair.

"General Gau....." but she was interrupted as Gaunt stood up

"Thank you Madam Chair" his voice a deep rolling thunder. "Don't let the uniform fool you " he said with a smile "NATO liaison works with all the armed forces so I have an equivalent rank as Admiral of the fleet, and Air Marshall in the Royal Air Force. I have coats of many colours." He bowed slightly with a smile and raised his hands, before moving around the table still holding his hands out as if to say he was unarmed.

The trustees fell silent and looked at him with a mildly curious stare, then their expressions turned blank.

Gaunt moved to the head of the table and spoke to the Chair. "I would like you to nominate me as the new Chairman....and the Chief Executive of this Board, and I would like you all to vote me in with a show of hands." His voice courteous, his smile sincere. Then he bent slightly towards the Chair and spoke "I nominate General Gaunt to preside over this charity as chairman and chief executive, all those in favour..."

She repeated the words and each member raised their hands.

"Good" he said standing up straight " Thank you all. Now I know you are all tired of your duties here and wish to spend more time with your families.
You may tell your staff that you have resigned and that I am appointed. Now leave. Return to your homes and your families."

All members stood without a word.

Gaunt opened the doors out of the boardroom. "Thank you for your service" he smiled as they passed.

Outside the room several men in dark grey uniform were waiting and they now filed in.

Gaunt sat at the head, tossing away the papers that were spread across the desk.

“Gentlemen please sit. We have a lot of business to attend to.”

IV
Politics

" It's all very suspicious" Stephanie Walker, political secretary, was sitting in an armchair in the offices of the Department of Culture Media and Sport, the DCMS as it was known.
Across the coffee table Christopher Spens, the Minister sat cross-legged looking at his polished black Oxfords.

"I mean somehow he's managed to gain control of both the National Trust and the Forestry Commission, and now he's also taken over at Historic England. "We " She emphasised the 'we' "need to do something, we need to raise a question over this, it's too much control of the nation's premier assets"

Spens looked up " As I see it, 'we' can't do anything. The NT is a private charity, nothing to do with this department, the board voted him in, likewise the Forestry lot. As for Historic England, the PM suggested it on the recommendation of the Defence Minister. I'm not going to challenge the PM on what is such a small matter when I have all the BBC stuff on my plate right now. One shit at a time don't you think?"

"What about a leak to the Press then? I can have a quiet chat with one of the women at the Guardian, they can do some digging, there's bound to be dirt somewhere?"

"No! absolutely not. I don't want any suggestion that the DCMS are concerned over a decorated general sitting on a few charity boards. It would potentially embarrass the MOD, and on top the PM gave his recommendation. I will not be sitting in here for too long I have my eye on the defence brief myself. Let it go Steph, there's no mileage in it, ...and potentially some danger, and for what? No, what harm can it do. Leave it alone. I want the BBC thing to be my crowning glory here, someone else can deal with Gaunt if he steps out of line. Let it go"

Walker pulled a face. "I don't like him, this Edward Gaunt. He's far too right wing in my view."

"Steph," Spens laughed " everyone connected to the military is too right wing for you, but most of the National Trust assets have a military connection in some way or other. The Forestries were set up after WW1 specifically to replenish timber supplies, and Historic England, well they're all castles! You can't get much more military than that, actually, it'll keep the Army lot happy with Gaunt in the chair, God knows they need something to cheer them up after all the cuts. Do you know Blenheim Palace? Do you know why it's called that?"

"Some sort of colonial tragedy, and home of the big warmonger Churchill I believe? Not my cup of tea at all."

"Steph, your lack of knowledge of English history is appalling! " He laughed again. "look it up" He frowned "....meanwhile don't let your views on Churchill pass out of this room or I'll disown you"

"What was Gaunt anyway?" She wouldn't let it go " a Colonel in Afghanistan, what... 15 years ago? With that woman, what's her name, Rheinhart? And that business at Porton Down? The paedophile chemist. Then suddenly he's a General and NATO liaison, and she's goes to Military Intelligence as Colonel?"

"I don't follow people's military careers Steph" Spens sighed, "...only met them once or twice in the past and as far as I know they're both retired or semi retired. Now enough. Let's go through this new charter, tell me where the mines are!"

V

Death of the West

And the old Queen died.

She had reigned for over seventy years but now she was gone and the facade which was the system of hereditary monarchy began to crumble.

In her lifetime she had seen England change from the largest empire that ever existed through incessant humiliations to a small battered island being eaten alive like a rotting corpse by her many enemies and so called friends.

Her many achievements had been reduced to being unspoken for fear of upsetting assorted collections of fastidious, easily offended people who could rage on social media, cow whichever government happened to be in situ. Be nice to the fringes, embrace multicultural Britain. Don't fly the flag of England in case it provokes hostility to our neighbours. Allow Washington, or Paris, or Berlin to run the place, and feed off it.

She had become the pantomime stereotype of Britain with it's tea towels, and bobbies, its changing of the guard, a full English breakfast, and afternoon tea at the Ritz.

Let the hedge funds own the buildings. Let the great English cities descend into religious and mafia anarchy. Don't dare to speak out or you'd be hung out to dry by a media intelligencia who could move to California, or Brussels, and come back now and again to give the English another kicking.

The oily tributes to the old Queen subsided after many long weeks of overblown coverage of her somewhat childlike, silent reign. Seen but not generally heard, she did her duty to her parents when she had to step up to the throne after her father's untimely death and after his own reluctant acceptance of the kingship after his brother decided he didn't want to do it either.

The facade of this attempt to maintain a royal lineage was an extraordinary suspension of disbelief , a trick of the mind which had been sustained by the establishment forces in Britain way beyond its original purpose. To have the royal seal of approval, however tacit, gave an almost unassailable quality to the many people and institutions who gathered behind the queen's skirts....and cashed in.

The mob, represented by the press and assorted media were kept mostly in check and preened themselves against this facade whilst occasionally stooping to convey what they thought the mob might like. She must pay her taxes like everyone else, she must cry in public, She must lose her Royal yacht.

While the reptiles offshored their own companies to make sure they can keep their large bonuses and protect their status.

And so the Queen was gone.

Long live the King.

He had waited for more than seventy years. Made his mistakes. Suffered at the hands of the press. Finally, in his eighties, he could wear the crown of England, at least for a short time.

The reptiles gathered. The Scots demanded their own say in the matter, and a Scottish President. The Welsh would want a Welsh Prince. The Cornish wanted their kingdom returned, south of the Tamar.

Retired politicians stepped forward to offer their advice, and to suggest a new role as President of Britain.

As if by divine intervention, the death of the old Queen would coincide with equally seismic events around the world.

The European currency died when the southern states of Europe had finally had enough of their transition to poverty and humiliation decided to restore their own currencies. This event alone created a systemic default on the huge loans which had been made to them by the Northern states and the global banking industry.

Suddenly, and across the world, commercial banks would become insolvent overnight. Cash machines would become unavailable, credit cards would cease to work, asset prices collapse.

The daily lives of the people around the world would change from surplus to shortage.

Food would become a currency. Riots broke out at supermarkets. 'Stockpilers' were killed and their homes looted. Murders would become commonplace as people fought to find food.

The government employed the army and food rationing returned, not seen since the aftermath of the second world war.

The black market flourished.

Hyper inflation returned to the western world.

In North America the vast paper printing exercise of the dollar would finally come home to roost. The cost of food rose dramatically. People would begin to starve to death.

The wealthy began to barricade themselves into their estates, or move to New Zealand, grow their own food, sink their own wells, rear their own cattle.

VI

Modern Policing

Detective Chief Inspector Rob Manning of His Majesty's Leeds Constabulary stared out of the rear window of the police BMW heading south to Wakefield. He was born in Kent, first of his family to go to University where he graduated with honours as a BA Ppe.

He went on to take his Masters in Philosophy, Politics and Economics, then joined the metropolitan police force going straight to the officers training school in Hendon.

He rose quickly through the ranks. He was nominated for the programme at Common Purpose where rising members within the Police, Local and National Government, the Civil Service, The Courts, assorted Institutions, and the Church are taken as like minded future leaders.

He wasn't far off Assistant Chief Constable if he played his cards right. He had fostered warm relations with MP's and the heads of local councils. He had had some good media coverage. He could count on a few influential journalists and University fellows.

And then...a constabulary of his own...hopefully not in the North...Scotland Yard perhaps, the Met, or counter terrorism?

"Tricky business Sir" he was interrupted by his detective sergeant who was driving the BMW.

" The local plod say that two women have been stoned to death in one of the parks, and they've raped six young girls sir"

"Big riot in't place"

"Yes Sergeant, a tricky business. How many men have we got?"

" 'bout two hundred, And the GMP are sending another. We're bringing in the Special Unit boys sir,"

"I'm putting them at all the mosques in the City sergeant, the local NF gangs are going to get a nasty surprise I think"

"It's not right sir, they should be the subject of our laws, not theirs"

"You're entitled to your opinion of course, but we need calm not violence. First rule of policing sergeant?"

"Aye sir but it's getting beyond a joke sir"

"They have their laws and we have ours, and there are a growing number of them so we have to compromise."

"Still not right sir"

"Well as long as you're happy to remain a sergeant, Sergeant"

" How many have been arrested so far?

"Word is sir, they've caught the boys who stoned the women and the local Imam's are pleading for them to be released. The families are going ape, say's it sharia or something"

“ First thing is to restore calm sergeant, as I said, first rule of policing sergeant....what’s the media doing?

“TV crews from all over sir, who’s handling the PR?”

“The PR unit are there in a mobile command centre sir”

“OK get me to them will you Paul”

Something caught his eye as they drove fast through the hills. On the top, in the distance it looked like horsemen, many of them. They wheeled away and were hidden behind the ridge.

“What are those horsemen doing up there?”

“Oh them, quite a big camp, so the lady wife tells me sir, she runs the local pony club for the girls but that lot have bought up all the breeding horses for miles around. She went to see if she could buy a couple of ponies but they weren’t very nice about it. She says they’re up at Nostell Priory, and Marsden moor, and several of the farms round here. ‘Says they’re National Trust men. Bringing back the old skills sir, they’ve got blacksmiths, and farriers, saddlers and armourers, carders and weavers, bowyers and fletchers, stringfellows, thatchers and carpenters that sort of thing. There’s a flag sir, black lion on a white background, re-enactment stuff I believe. Actually I do a bit of that myself sir. Sealed Knot and the like.”

“It’s the past sergeant. The future is what’s

important now. Nevertheless I'll send a unit up there when I have the time. I don't like the sound of it. It could offend too many parties, upset the peace, and as you know...first rule of policing sergeant"

"Aye sir"

VII
The Farm at Rawston

Old Tom was right. The food was good. Sue Pine's Golden Lion was a friendly place. Not too much trouble in such an out of the way place, and it was good to be back on dry land after such a long time at sea. She still swayed a bit when she walked but was getting her land legs back slowly.

She met some of the local farmers, quiet Westmoreland men, hardy stock who manage the wind blown rain swept landscapes of the moors, fells and gills. Strangers were noticed, and watched.

She needed transport and bought an old diesel Land Rover Defender from one of them replete with sheep muck and straw jammed into every corner. But the chassis was solid despite being near the coast and the salt. She knew Landies back to front, and, just as well, she was handy with a spanner, a regular requirement.

Rheinhart leant against the side wing of the battered old Land Rover Defender watching the Cumbrian rain fall in a gloomy drizzle over Rawston Valley Farmyard.

Her thick brown hair soaking up the rain and falling over her waxed jacket onto her black Wellingtons.

She turned to see a small red Fiesta coming

up the gravel drive. The Fiesta pulled up and a brunette woman of about middle thirties stepped out.

"I'm so sorry I'm late" she said in an excitedly apologetic voice. "Some sort of violent protest going on in Morecambe. Hardly any police either. Someone blockaded the main road so I had to come round over the moors."

" No problem, I got here early so no harm"

The brunette dragged a pair of green wellies from the boot "Just got to put these on" slightly breathless.

"Hi you must be Miss Rheinhart?, ..I'm June Fording from Allsops, Tom's daughter"

" Call me Alex" The two women shook hands.

" Not great weather I'm afraid but ..well this is it…let me show you around. shall we start with the outside first seeing as we're booted up and then we can dry off a bit inside the farmhouse?"

June Fording led Alex across the farmyard to a big solid oak barn .

"It's an old farm…started way back in the 19th century. Apparently a Captain Rawston and his men came back from the Napoleonic wars, he acquired the land and set up the farm, most of the village as well. Not that it's much of a village, more a hamlet really. Built the church and some of the cottages too ..hence Rawston Valley, Rawston village and Rawston farm…the church has been de-commissioned but the old vicar still lives in the vicarage , and there's a retired lady vet living in one of the cottages...other than that...well you're pretty cut off from the world, especially in winter. Not such a bad thing these days I suppose."

They entered a large timbered barn that appeared to have been well maintained except for a few missing pieces of timber cladding to one wall and a clutter of bits of agricultural equipment some of which seemed to have been here since the barn was built. A collection of odd side barns and storage sheds clustered around the side including an old glasshouse that was half derelict and overgrown.

"There are about 400 acres of land here though much of it is up the side of the valley and really only good for sheep. Herdwicks really. But there's a natural gill spring up there which feeds the house, and there's an open coal seam on the land which I understand the farmer used for heating."

Beside the main barn was a small milking parlour which looked like it had been refurbished recently. June hit the light switch but the power was out.

" That's the thing these days...power outages are common I'm afraid, they blew up the local old power station a few years back, solar and wind are just a joke, but I believe there's a standby generator in one of the outbuildings by the house"

They opened the door to one of these and found a large diesel generator and behind this an old steam boiler which must have supplied power before the diesel was installed.

June looked at the generator for a moment before Alex stepped forward. She pulled down a battery switch then hit a green button next to the switch...nothing happened. She picked up a spanner, wrapped an old oily rag round the middle and then touched both open ends to the battery terminals. Nothing.

"wait a minute..." and she disappeared into the Land Rover returning with a set of jump leads and a spare battery.

"If you have a Landy you need to carry a spare battery" she announced

She connected the jump leads to the old battery from the spare, checked the oil level and the diesel tank then switched on, waited for 30 seconds then hit the starter button.

The diesel coughed into life.

The lights came on.

"I've done it before" Alex said as June looked at her with a surprised smile.

The farmhouse was a very old small cottage covered in moss and lichens with a leaking roof with several small stone outbuildings clustered around the side and back.

Inside was a large farmhouse kitchen and living room with a parlour and a separate study/ office. An old Rayburn oven sat at one end of the kitchen. Also a boot room leading outside and a toilet and bathroom. Upstairs two large bedrooms and a small bathroom.

"I'm afraid the old farmer let things run down quite a bit in here since his wife died a few years ago. Poor old man couldn't manage the farm and eventually sold off the few cattle and sheep he had here. He died a few months ago"

"The owners are the sons of the late farmer, one's a solicitor in Newcastle and the other is something in finance in London. Neither want the farming life so it's up for sale"

Alex stepped outside.

She pulled out a sheet of paper and wrote a figure on it.

" I like it " she said " here's my offer...I won't pay a penny more...also I want to know if it's accepted within 24 hours, and tell them I want to complete the purchase within seven days ..that shouldn't be a problem for the solicitor. Here's the address and contacts for my solicitor. He's already got my money sitting on his clients account with my instructions to complete"

She handed the paper to June.

" Er...I have to advise you that you should have this properly surveyed before you commit you know"

" I can see what I'm buying and you'll see in my letter that I waive the usual niceties so you won't get sued" She smiled.

"I've also put in my current contact details at the pub near the Lune marina where I'm staying. The landlady is Sue Pine so if I'm out you can leave her the message if I'm not there, either yes or no."

"well ok I'll speak to them today and call you as soon as I know"

Alex went back to the generator shed and switched it off. Then they both shook hands and climbed into their cars.

Alex sat for a moment looking out at the rain swept farm sitting in the wilds of the Westmoreland hills and valleys. "yes it's perfect.." she smiled to herself.

The following day she received the call. It was the solicitor son in Newcastle.

Yes, he and his brother would sell at that price and yes they could complete in seven days. He wished her luck with the farm and was glad to have got rid of it, even if they hadn't got quite the price they were hoping for.

She moved in a week later. The power was back on for now and spring was in the air, even though it was still raining.

She looked at the farmhouse that would be her

home now. The first job would be the roof. Start at the top and work down she told herself, start outside and work in. Many slates were cracked, the chimney needed re-pointing, and the guttering was rotten.

She drove to Kendal, the nearest town, where she bought the supplies she would need. Fortunately the old farm had a collection of tools and machinery stretching back over time so she had the roof ladder fixed and up in no time. She re-pointed the chimney, slid in new slates from a pile of spares lying in one of the derelict barns using folded lead straps and galvanised nails.

There was a very old Ferguson tractor in the large barn. She recharged the battery and bled the fuel bowl then re-filled it with red diesel which came from a large tank in the yard. It fired up almost immediately. In a separate machinery shed were several implements for the tractor including a saw bench which ran off the tractor's PTO shaft.

She ripped off the iron gutters but saved them for re-use. The soffits and fascias were gone and she worked for a week shaping and fitting new ones into place. The roof joists and rafters were solid oak and although there was a bit of rot in places they were typically solid.

She sanded off most of the rust and accumulated paint on the big iron gutters, brackets and down pipes. She repainted the lot in red-lead then black paint that she found in the barn. She reinstalled them over the freshly painted fascias.

Then she went to work on the windows which were all rotten. She bought lengths of pine timber and a router for the drill. She pulled all the old windows out one by one taking care not to break the old glass. She replaced each one and painted the frames a dark grey then glazed them with the old glass panels and fresh putty.

It was dirty exhausting work but it came with immense satisfaction. She was no stranger to hard work. Once a farm girl, always a farm girl. It was in her blood, even if the farm she was born on was a long way away in a different world.

The farmhouse was constructed of limestone blocks that had been painted over. The paint was either peeling away or had given up to the algae and moss which covered most of it. She scoured it off and coated everything in a petrol based sealer. She bought gallons of good quality off-white stone paint and painted the whole of the house with it.

The porch and boot room were scrubbed as clean as could be done then she began on the farmhouse kitchen.

The principal component of the kitchen, indeed the house, was an old coal fired Rayburn stove which provided the cooking facility as well as a boiler for the hot water. The house had no central heating but provided the Rayburn was lit the house was always warm.

She had let it run out and now that it was cold she dismantled the great cast iron beast. The enamelled outer case was scrubbed and cleaned to a fine brown shine. The internals were wire brushed taking off years of crap and hardened tar. She cleaned and tested the valves. Then she re-assembled it and re-fitted the water pipe which was gravity fed from a pipe that ran from the small gill stream that ran past the back of the house before disappearing back into the limestone underground. She re-attached the chimney pipe after sweeping it out and then lit the fire in the coal grate.

It was a fine spring day so she dragged out the few pieces of furniture and set to scrubbing the quarry tiled floor until it returned to the original fine burnt red colour.

The old elm kitchen table was scrubbed and sanded then re-waxed. The two old leather chairs and a small sofa just needed a wipe over but the cupboards were a stinking mess and it took her two days to bring them back to some kind of order.

The walls were painted the same as the outside and things began to look cared for after years of neglect.

She found a 12 bore shotgun in one of the cupboards along with a few boxes of cartridges. It was too much of a temptation so she went out across the lower field and shot a couple of pigeons. She cut out the breasts with her knife leaving the rest of the carcass for the foxes and assorted wildlife. Then she fried them on the stove with some potato and onion cakes, and a few parsnips. She sank back into one of the armchairs, which turned out to be super comfortable, and admired her work and her new home. As she sipped her tea she made a mental note to buy wine.

A few days later she heard a car coming up the drive. She stepped out of the barn where she had been repairing some of the slats. An old blue Subaru Estate. Out of it stepped a woman, probably in her sixties. Shortish dark grey hair and a practical look about her. From the passenger side an older man, most probably late seventies, perhaps older. He was wearing a dog collar, and a charcoal grey suit that had seen better days. Two Labradors followed them out and bounded over to Alex.

The man spoke first.

"Hello, hello" he smiled " Welcome to Rawston my dear, I'm Cedric Bell, one-time vicar of this parish, and this is my good friend Colette Green who was the one-time local vet round these parts"

The woman came over and they shook hands. " Hello dear, welcome to our lovely part of the world, I'm so glad we have someone who can take care of the farm, and what a grand job you've done dear"

Alex introduced herself and invited them in for a cup of tea.

She had forgotten about dogs. At one time she had three. Ridgebacks, and puppies as and when. But you can't have dogs when you're away so much, and they don't work on boats.

The vicar was in full flow.

"I'm so, ...we're, so glad you've taken the farm. Poor old Jim Gallagher, he's with me now....in the church cemetery...with his wife Rose, a lovely woman but died far too young and poor Jim struggled to keep going for years on his own. My, my, look at this place it's a wonder, so, ...so clean and tidy...and warm!"

Small talk, tea and biscuits with the vicar and the vet.

"I'm sorry that we are all that's left of Rawston, the three of us now, well I suppose that's a fifty percent increase" The vicar laughed. "Very sad really. When I came here it was still small but there were about forty people, and children. We had a pub and a garage with a village shop, and a village school. A few small cottages. But the supermarkets killed the shop and the garage, and the smoking and drink-drive thing killed the pub. They're all in the towns now, and I don't like going into town anymore, and the buildings are in a terrible state, what's left of them."

"Old Jim had a decent number of milking cattle

and sold his milk and country produce but it didn't pay and he had to close most of it down. Lived off his old age pension, wouldn't take any money from his sons of course. Too proud."

Alex interrupted the vicar's flow.

"What about you Colette?"

"Oh, I was in practice in Kendal, moved out here as Cedric said to get a bit more air, the towns have become very unpleasant places for most ordinary people, and to keep chickens and dogs and all that. I was one of a handful of vetinaries who helped the local Westmoreland farmers, including here. It's always been a hard life for hill farmers and as Cedric has said, it's very hard to make a living from it now. Are you planning to develop the farm?"

"No, I'm retired now, I just want the peace and the space, and to try to be as self sufficient as possible" She quickly turned to Cedric before they asked more questions about her past.

"So Cedric, are you still the local vicar, you said 'one-time' earlier...?

"Ah well, although there's no official retirement for a vicar, except the full one provided by God one of these days. The Bishop decided that the church should be closed bearing in mind the lack of congregation. Part of the inevitable 'modernisation' you know. So it has been what is termed, 'released', that is, it's no longer funded or maintained. I have my pension and the Bishop has allowed me to stay on in the small vicarage. My dear wife died a few years ago too so I potter about, make ends meet and try to keep the church and the ground from the slow decay of nature as best I can. Colette has been wonderful to me, she brings me dinners every week and keeps an eye on me. I'm her flock, and she is mine, so to speak."

"And what of this place? The farm, do you know much about its history?"

"Don't get him started on that dear he can talk all day" Colette smiled at Cedric.

"Well very briefly" said Cedric in a mildly mocking tone, looking across at Colette, "The place is named after one Captain Rawston, officer with Wellington at Waterloo. He and his surviving men and their wives came here in the early 19th Century. Built the farm and the church and all the rest too over time. They're all in the churchyard now of course. They cut the coal seam that's up the side of this hill "he said waving his arm out towards the yard. "and they built the barns, raised their cattle and grew a few crops, mainly potatoes and hardy wheat. Kept quite a few Herdwick sheep up the hillside, and brewed their own ale. They built the school and all was going well when the smallpox arrived and killed most of them including the children. So very sad but not uncommon in remote rural villages like this one at the time.

A few new people moved in. So when my wife and I arrived many decades ago it was still a very nice place to live. It's only in the last twenty years or so that it has slowly died away. Still here we are. Things are always changing and perhaps the pendulum will swing back one day?"

"Meanwhile nice and peaceful for you. We won't keep you but come along to the village on Sunday and I'll make both of you some Sunday lunch?"

"That would be very nice Colette, thank you"

"And call in at the Church on your way down and we'll say a prayer for you"

"Thank you Cedric, I will"

They both said their goodbyes and left.

She was feeling hungry after talk of Sunday lunch so walked up the hill with the shotgun and got another pigeon and a rabbit for supper.

On Sunday morning she walked about a mile to the church. She heard a choir singing. It was Ave Verum Corpus, one of Mozart's many hymnals. She stepped through the door into the old nave where she saw Cedric on his knees at the altar. It was a beautiful piece, sung by the King's College choir. She recognised it. One of her father's favourites. Unprompted. a tear ran down her cheek. Thirty years passed in a moment. She knelt in one of the pews at the back of the church. The floor was wet from one of the many leaks in the roof. She put her head down and closed her eyes. When she opened them again Cedric was standing quietly by her.

Neither spoke for a moment. Miserere Mei, Deus, was coming from a set of old speakers in the chancel. The music echoed round the old stone walls.

" I keep Sunday service alive through music" he said. "and I remember to pray for all the suffering in the world, and for my own if I'm being totally honest, I'll pray with you" and he knelt down in the aisle next to Alex and they both knelt in silent prayer while the music played.

"Come along Alex, let's go to Colette's for some lunch , she's a marvellous cook you know" and Alex smiled and felt refreshed as she hadn't felt for years.

A few days later Cedric found Alex up a ladder on the church roof.

"It's just a few of your slates" she said. " The oak beams are fine. I'll bring some spare slates and sort it out for you"

"The Lord does work in wondrous ways" he said and she laughed.

The days passed into summer. It still rained now and again. The south-westerlies that ran over the Atlantic picking up moisture would roll over Ireland and on into the peaks and hills of Westmoreland depositing their rain. But when the clouds lifted it was relatively warm and lush.

Alex had bought a couple of cows from one of the distant farms, several Herdwick upland sheep, two pigs, and a few chickens and geese.

It looked as if old Jim Gallagher had bought a new milking machine so once the milking shed and equipment were cleaned out and sterilised she had her own supply of milk and cream. She set aside a small outbuilding and bought a cheese vat. What spare milk she had went into her own cheese.

She cleared out the brambles and thorns that had taken over the large glass-house and planted a range of vegetables, a few tomatoes, and assorted experiments.

She ploughed part of the hay field and planted some late wheat which began to grow fast in the mild and wet weather. She also planted some root crops and rows of potatoes.

The chickens and the geese gave her eggs....and the occasional sacrificial chicken. She got a cockerel and soon had a few chicks.

Some feral cats moved into the barn, and the foxes patrolled at night, but the geese are very fierce guards. Even the foxes found themselves in trouble, so all was well.

The cow slurry was building up in the yard so she adapted an old mangle by attaching it to a belt driven by the tractor's PTO pulley. An old flux-cored arc welding kit was another barn find that she used to make a metal feeder tray. She shovelled the slurry into the feeder and the mangle separated out the liquid from the solids.

She called it the 'shitzsplitter'. The liquid fell into an old bath which acted as a tank for the spreader on the tractor, and she spread this over her fields where she could. After a few days the remaining solids became the most wonderful fine compost which fed the glass house plants, and also grew big mushrooms when bagged and left in a darkened shed.

A farming year came and went.

Colette came by occasionally to check the animals and help with cutting and baling the hay which went into the hay loft in the barn, ready for winter. But Alex got told off when she shot the pigs in order to salt and dry-cure or freeze the meat. She was supposed to have them taken to a registered abattoir for humane slaughter. Nevertheless Colette (and Cedric) gratefully accepted the bacon and the hams when offered as an apology.

Autumn turned to winter and the roads became impassable for weeks. She walked to church each Sunday, and her two villagers came to the farm for Christmas. Thankfully Colette offered to do the cooking and a big goose provided the main fare.

Another year passed. The coal seam continued to supply the fuel for the house. Alex had the steam generator's boiler rebuilt and tested. On a cold winters day when the mains power failed she set the fire going. When the steam pressure was right she lifted the valve lever and gave the flywheel a quick turn. The whole thing sprang to life creating her own electricity from her own coal, and a great sense of satisfaction.

VIII
And so it begins

Captain Peters, 2nd Signals Regiment, entered the private chapel in the old Treasurers House inside the walls of the walled city of York. He saw Edward Gaunt kneeling at the altar with his eyes closed, but he wasn't praying, he was thinking. "...And so it begins..."

Sitting quietly to one side of the chapel was a man dressed in near black naval uniform. He held a walking stick. His hair was thin and grey although his age was not clear he seemed younger than he looked. He wore a skull cap. Commander William Levine, Naval Intelligence who accompanied Gaunt.

Peters gave a slight nod to Levine who reciprocated.

"It's time sir" Captain Peters watched the giant form of his General rise up and turn towards him. God he was a big man, Peters thought.

"Very good Captain, are the men ready?"

"All in position sir"

"Then give the word, send the signal, and light the beacons."

"Very good sir" Peters made the salute and spun round on his heels to give the command to his field force.

Across the country, from Lands End to John

O'Groats a chain of fire beacons had been made ready, including one on the top of York Minster. It was a clear but frosty New Years Eve. There was snow in the air. The beacons were lit, spreading rapidly across the country, as they had done over previous centuries.

Small units from the camps, under trusted County Commanders, comprising four men each, rode on horseback into remote countryside fields and forests towards the great steel electricity pylons that carried the Nation's power supplies from the power stations. Whether coal, oil, gas, solar or wind, it all had to be transmitted via long lengths of aluminium and steel cables before descending into a cascade of sub-stations and then underground into cities and towns to power modern life.

As the fireworks shot up into the sky across the country in celebration of the New Year other larger, more deadly explosive fireworks tore through the steel supports of the pylons bring them crashing down to earth. The force ripped the cables apart in showers of high voltage sparks.

In the National Grid control centre in Basingstoke, the giant screens began to flicker red as the shutdown spread rapidly across the country. Then everything went dark, the big backup generators cut in, but almost immediately blew their circuit breakers. The power requirements of modern buildings such as this are immense. Someone had a torch and was shouting that everyone needs to switch off unnecessary equipment. "Just the lights, just the lights!" The breakers were reset but blew again. "Turn off the aircon " someone shouted. It wasn't until most of the racks of computer servers had been switched off that the emergency lighting finally stayed on. The evacuation began.

The duty manager tried to call his boss at home but the phones were out. So he used his mobile phone, but there was no signal. Hurried conversations were being held amongst a few senior engineers.

IX

No Power

Christopher Spens spent New Year in his Parliamentary apartment in Lord North St, Westminster, paid for by the taxpayer. He could have gone home to his Leicestershire Manor but his wife would not want him there. They only stayed together for appearances sake. The children had long gone on to begin their own way in the world. His daughter was in the USA on a scholarship to Yale, and his son was backpacking in New Zealand.

He spent a jolly New Year's Eve with some of his fellow Ministers and parliamentary colleagues who were also suitably unhooked. Fine dining in Rules, followed by drinks back at his apartment with his favourite rent-boy to see in the New Year. He had had the electricity removed from the bedroom so that they could fuck in candlelight. It gave him a sense of being back in time when things were a lot simpler. No media to worry about.

Some time before dawn he got up to use the bathroom. He pulled the light switch and screwed up his eyes in anticipation of the bright light, but nothing happened.

"Damn!" the concierge would not be available until 8am to replace the bulb.

He returned to the bedroom and lit another candle. His smart watch said 5.30am. He checked for any emails or texts that might have come in from his children but the wifi was down. He climbed back into bed and snuggled up against the boy.

He was woken around half past eight by the concierge knocking on the door to tell him the power was out in the whole building. He was trying to raise the electricity company to find out what was going on but the phones were out too.

Spens went into the kitchen taking one of the candles with him. He switched on the kettle without thinking then realised he couldn't make any coffee. He took the candle into the bathroom and stepped into the shower. No water came out of the showerhead.

He tried the sink taps with the same result.

"Christ! And this is supposed to be the 21st century"

The boy came into the bathroom "I need to take a shit so..."

Spens left and heard the bolt click.

He slipped on a pair of jeans and a polo shirt. It was cold so he went to get a sweater but he'd not brought one to the apartment. Only suits, shirts and ties were in the wardrobe so he put on his Crombie overcoat which looked faintly ridiculous with his jeans and trainers. His hair was sticking up all over the place which he couldn't plaster down. He stank.

"Christ I need a shower" he muttered. The RAC

club wasn't far. As a member he could go there to freshen up. The boy came out of the bathroom.

"Oh my god, the flush won't work, don't go in there, it's a mess, and I can't wash my hands either, there's no water, god it's cold in here, don't you government ministers get a heating allowance or something? god you stink..."

"Fuck off back home then,...and Happy New Year to you too" Spens said as he went in to get his toothbrush and toothpaste to take to the RAC along with a disposable razor, and his comb."

They left the apartment together, the boy heading to St James St tube station. Spens looked for a taxi but there wasn't one around. He tried his phone for an Uber but there was still no signal. So he slipped through the alleyway and decided he could walk across St James's park to Pall Mall. It was bitterly cold so he jogged to get warm. No-one was around at that time in the morning on a bank holiday but even so the place seemed eerily quiet. There was no traffic in the Mall. The traffic lights were out. Suddenly a police car came screaming down the road. He tried to flag it down but they ignored him and it quickly disappeared under Admiralty Arch.

When he arrived at the RAC the doors were shut. Someone had stuck a hand written note to say that they had a power cut and they regret that for safety reasons they can't open until the power is back on.

"Fuck!"

"He jogged across to Golden Alley to get a coffee from the little Italian café. One of the few whose plate glass windows had survived the rioting. It was open but very dark inside. The owner was boiling water on a propane gas stove.

"God I could murder a coffee!"

The man looked up. "I can only do instant for you mate. The power's off and I haven't had a delivery yet, so no milk either"

"Got anything to eat?"

"Just what you see. We've been closed since Christmas so there's only crisps and biscuits at the moment, sorry"

Spens grabbed a packet of wrapped shortbread biscuits. He put his hands round the mug of black instant coffee. At least it was hot, and the biscuits could be dunked in the coffee.

"Just give me a couple of quid mate" said the owner. Spens had no cash on him but pulled out his debit card.

"Won't work mate…nothing's working. But forget it, you can have those on the house seeing as you're my first customer of the New Year. " Felice Anno Nuovo!"

"Kind of you, and a Happy New Year to you too."

He retraced his steps back through the park, past his apartment and the silent, darkened Home Office building heading for his ministry in

Victoria street. They kept a skeleton staff on duty over the holidays. Maybe they had power, and a staff shower.

He saw several police cars, and a policeman stationed outside the main entrance along with a few more dotted along Victoria Street at the various Ministry buildings.

"Sorry Sir but you can't go in there" said the policeman at the door.

"I'm the fucking Minister officer, it's my ministry"

"Of course it is sir" The officer looked him over. "Can I see your ID please sir?"

"Look officer, I don't carry my ID around, I'm known here, just ask the receptionist and he'll verify me"

"Security is a 'She' sir, but I'll ask, just wait here please"

The officer returned "She says she's temporary contract staff and doesn't know you so if you'd kindly move on sir"

"Christ! there must be someone in there who knows who I am? My office is on the tenth floor, just go up there and get someone to come down will you"

"There's no-one else in the building. It's a bank holiday sir and there's no lights or heat so if there was anyone in there they will have left. I have orders not to let anyone in sir. There's been a major power outage sir. We've been given orders sir"

Spens realised that there was no point arguing. He turned away in frustration and headed back to his apartment block. He met the concierge outside who was in conversation with another copper, and one of the other residents.

"Minister" he said. "We're being told that there's a major power outage so I can't get the water and the heating back on, before you ask" He seemed somewhat flustered. "I can't get hold of my boss either as the phone's not working. The police say we should all just stay put for now"

Spens turned to the Police Officer "How widespread is this, do you know?"

"All I know sir is that while we were on duty, just after midnight, I'm night shift sir by the way, everywhere went dark. Police comms is being rationed so I don't have much information sir. Scotland Yard is asking us to guard the main government buildings and to send everyone home until this is cleared up."

"Are the trains working?"

"Don't know sir but unlikely if the power's out"

Spens had a thought. If this is an emergency, and most of the other Cabinet Ministers were not in London it would look good for him if he turned up at Downing Street. He wasn't on the COBRA Committee, but nevertheless.

So he walked around to Parliament Square towards Whitehall. A large RAF Chinook was sitting on the tarmac at the main junction between Whitehall and Westminster Bridge. Two armed soldiers were stationed at either end of the aircraft.

He walked up to Downing St. Two armed soldiers were stationed at the gates. Fortunately there was also one of the Policemen on duty at the gates who was a regular and recognised Spens.

"I must see the Prime Minister" He said in his urgent but not too threatening tone.

"Of course Minister, do you have your ID card with you? I know who you are of course but I have to follow the rules"

"I'm afraid I don't " He was about to say 'exigent circumstances' but the officer produced a hand held radio. The result of the radio communication was that he should be let through, and straight to the Cabinet Room.

This was altogether better he thought as he rushed up the short street. The door to number 10 was opened by the head porter and he was ushered straight into the Cabinet room. There were some lights on so at least the emergency power was on here, to some extent.

The Prime Minister was on his feet and turned to Spens with a smile. At the other side of the room was a very large man dressed in an Army General's uniform. He was a sizeable man with long hair and a big beard. He gave Spens a piercing look as a snake might eye up its prey.

"Chris, come in, you've beaten the Home Secretary and the Defence Minister....this is General Gaunt, I believe you might have met once or twice?"

"On a couple of occasions I believe"

Gaunt reached out a huge hand and shook Spens hand but said nothing.

The Prime Minister continued in a slightly heightened and breathless tone. His health was suffering from the many burdens of office. Spens made a mental note to keep his voice measured and calm.

"The General has told me that at the moment the whole country has been affected, or so it would appear. He says we do not yet know if this is an attack or not. We've just been to see the King to advise him and he has asked General Gaunt to take charge of the situation pro-tem until we can restore the power. The Army has it's own power and communication network so it makes sense"

"I'll get a car and see what the BBC is doing" said Spens. "We should try to make an announcement, if only on the radio via the emergency transmitters"

"Yes that's a good idea Chris, we need to tell everyone to remain in their homes until further notice, not to be alarmed, and that the Government is working fast to find a solution"

Gaunt turned to Spens with his snake eyes and spoke, seemingly for the first time. His voice was deep and loud.

"Who has a radio these days?"

"Well in their cars perhaps" said Spens feeling pleased.

"Only if they know how to tune it, but go ahead."

He turned back to the PM

"The King appears to want to proceed with his Coronation next Thursday?"

"Yes he's very keen to get that done for, I suppose, obvious reasons. He's waited a lifetime for this moment. Unfortunately it's proving very difficult to get messages out to the invited Heads Of State to advise them about all this"

Gaunt said "My men will secure the Savoy and the Ritz, we'll get a power unit in there so those that arrive can stay there. I will liaise with Brize Norton as I understand Heathrow's power station is not operational. The fuel lines have stopped because of the pumps."

"What about the Palace and the Abbey?"

"Same applies, I have already stationed men at both locations and our generator trucks are coming in now.

As soon as he left Downing St, Gaunt made his way back to the Chinook along with the four soldiers and it took off heading north.

X

Consequences

DCI Rob Manning was suffering from stress.

It had been a week since the power died. The batteries for the phone and the radios were dead. The motor pool was running out of diesel. The constabulary couldn't function as there were no lights in the great modern suite of offices in which it was housed. The Chief Constable had driven to London to gain information leaving Manning in charge and had not returned. He was sleeping in his car. His wife and daughters had been attacked in their own home so he had brought them with him and they now sat in his car. The toilet facility in the offices was rancid without running water.

Officers and men who turned up were reporting huge food riots at darkened, cold supermarkets. Anything with a remotely longish shelf life had been taken in the first day. People were eating defrosted food. A few had already died from food poisoning. Many of the elderly were dying from hypothermia. Disease was spreading from dead animals and pets which had escaped into the wild. A black market was forming, run by organised gangs of thugs. People's homes had been broken into, the occupants assaulted and beaten, their food stolen along with any valuables that might be traded for food.

Some of the Fire Brigade had turned up to report several fires, and subsequent deaths in people's homes where they had tried to convert barbeques into wood fires, the wood hacked from local trees, which had either suffocated them in their home or set it on fire by using petrol to get it started.

Christ, it's only been a week he thought. If only the power guys could restore the electricity things would start to return to normal. He had just met with a senior grid engineer who had told him that most of the pylons running across from Ferry Bridge and Drax power stations had been destroyed. It would take months, not days, even in normal circumstances to re-build, and re-string them. Even then he had discovered that many of the large substations which act as nodal points in the distribution chain had also been sabotaged. Nor could he get hold of many of his men, nor suppliers to even make a start.

His wife and their two daughters came up to him "Dad, we're freezing and there's no food, we're hungry."

"Rob, I know you're doing your best love" His

wife smiled at him "but the girls need some supplies, I need some supplies, I need to go to the shops"

"I don't think you'll find any food now" he said trying to find the right calm expression.

"Not food love, other bits"

"Look I'll see if a couple of the men can take you, but if there's trouble they must bring you straight back here"

He called over one of his officers who had just returned from Bradford and who had brought his own family with him.

"Colin, do you have any food with you, for my daughters?"

"No I'm sorry sir, we had to get out quickly as there was a starving mob of people coming at us when we tried to protect a local corner shop which was still trying to ration supplies. I haven't eaten anything in two days sir, and we've only got a bit of bottled water left for our girls."

Manning looked up. In the distance a strange sight. A policemen on horseback dressed in his uniform including his policeman's helmet, a large police issue cape over his shoulders. He was leading several other horses on which were a woman and two boys. Over his arm was a shotgun and slung down the side of the horses were several dead birds, mainly pigeon and a couple of rabbits.

As he drew near Manning recognised Sergeant

Henderson, his driver.

"I've brought you men some food, thought you might be needing something" he said with a smile. He pulled off several dead pigeons, a couple of bleeding rabbits and a few crows and handed them to Manning.

"If you want to get the kids to start plucking them I'll get a fire going and we can cook these beauties. I've also brought a couple of billy cans up from the Calder. Proper Yorkshire water sir."

"This is my spare old gun sir, and some cartridges. There'll be something flying over so you can catch it and cook it as needs be" as he handed the gun to Manning.

"This is the wife and kids sir by the way" he said pointing to the riders behind him.

"Good God Henderson, I've no idea how to pluck and cook a dead pigeon, let alone the kids. And as for this, he waived the gun, I haven't got a shotgun licence."

"Exigent circumstances sir, my lads'll show your girls what to do with the birds. I'll get a fire going. Meantime some of the lads can gather up some dead wood over there" He pointed at a nearby line of trees. "You have to eat sir, can I suggest you get all the cups and mugs out of the offices so that we can use those, oh and any tea or coffee that's in there so we can have a brew"

He handed the reins of his horse to one of his sons.

"Might I also suggest that we bring the men and their families here, all together like, so we can work as a group and keep the gangs at bay at the same time. It's gotten mighty nasty out there and it's probably going to get worse."

"Well Sergeant I've sent all the civilian staff home and the place has no lights. They'd be better off at home don't you think?"

"With respect sir, No. Order has completely broken down. No-one's going to be safe in their home.

If we can gather together as a group we can try to survive as best we can until things have sorted themselves out. That will take time so best if we band together here. There's a small gill behind the offices which has good water. Seen it before. Unlikely that it will get contaminated as it's coming up from a spring."

"Contaminated?"

"Cholera, typhoid…from the dead bodies sir, it'll get in the rivers and the ground water, not to mention the stink. All sorts of disease. Best to arrange for each family to collect some personal warm clothes and stuff from their homes. Bring it here. We can use the rooms with windows as sleeping quarters. We can set up a camp bathroom and toilet outside. You know, a dry pit and a wet pit. Use some of the tents from forensics as a cover. A cook tent for the food. There's an allotment down the road. Best send some people there to gather what they can. Potatoes would be best sir. "

"How do you know all this Sergeant?" said Manning

"Common sense really sir, bit of local knowledge, and I was in the Scouts a long time ago and you never really forget this stuff."

"oh and the ladies should bring their sewing kit and some muslin type stuff, send one of the lads to the garden centre and see if they can find some bags of dry moss,

Right, let's get organised sir...."

XI

Winter at Rawston Farm

Christmas came and went again. She had been to Colette's for a dinner on New Years Eve, and Cedric had performed the ancient offerings, going outside before midnight and leaving a piece of coal, and some bread and salt and a silver sixpence on the doorstep. As the New Year arrived he knocked on the door and would be the 'first foot', bringing the offerings inside and taking a glass of whisky from the host. Ideally he should have had dark hair, but it had been many years since Cedric had had any hair. However, no-one minded as the power had gone and the whole place was plunged into darkness.

They all laughed, Colette found a couple of candles before wishing everyone a happy New Year.

It wouldn't be.

There was no moon, but the snow on the ground reflected what little light there was.

Alex helped Cedric back to the vicarage then found her way back to the farm through the snow. There was a distant glow in the sky. A fire? Too far away to see. Usual fireworks she supposed.

There was no point firing up the generator so she lit a candle and went to bed.

She woke in the pitch dark. Rain was lashing at the windows driven by an Atlantic gale.

She could hear the cows stamping in the barn. She switched on the bedside lamp but nothing happened.

"Shit"

The power was still out. She fumbled about for the matches and lit the candle. It was just before five in the morning according to her watch. She swung out of bed. Thankfully the Rayburn was still hot so the house was warm enough. She splashed some water on her face and pulled on her jeans and sweater.

Without any light she couldn't see the rain but she could hear it. A powerful storm. No wonder the electric was out. She put a shovelful of coal in the Rayburn's grate.

She pulled on her big waxed jacket and boots, flipped up the hood and stepped outside. The wind and the rain lashed at her as she made her way around to the generator shed. She fired up the diesel generator then switched the power over from the steam boiler. The lights came on.

She stumbled over to the barn, still half asleep, maybe too much wine last night. The cattle were lying down except the two milkers who followed here to the milking shed.

She went through the usual procedures, pulling out the teat suckers from the bucket of sterilising solution, and a cloth which she used to sterilise the teats. She clamped them on. The cows were happy enough munching on some of the hay in the feeder rack. The milk began to flow into the vat inside the milking machine. She bypassed the pasteurising feed pipe. It only took a few minutes. Then she pumped out the milk into the cheese vat taking a jug for herself. When the machine was empty she sloshed the sterilising liquid into the machine and switched on the self sterilising program.

The cows went back to the barn. She swept out the cow slurry with the rubber yard scraper. Swilled down the rest of the floor and went back into the farm kitchen.

She cut herself a thick slice of homemade bread and butter. Fried up some bacon and eggs with a tomato and sat down to eat, washing it down with a strong cup of tea.

She could go back to bed, but she was awake now so she ran a shower and put on clean clothes for the New Year and switched on the TV. There was nothing, just static. All the channels. She'd bought an old transistor radio from a car boot sale. She switched it on but there was still nothing. She turned the dial, but nothing.

The phone was dead too, and no internet on the laptop. Her mobile lit up but there was no signal.

The hairs on the back of her neck tingled. Something wasn't right.

She waited until full daylight, watching the grey dark dawn slowly rise. She watched the sleet and the snow gently piling up on the roofs of the outbuildings and across the yard. She dozed off on the couch.

She woke around eleven am. She checked the TV and the radio again, still nothing. So she pulled on her coat and boots and walked down into the village.

Cedric was sitting by the fireside in the vicarage, watching the meagre flames from a small coal fire. He was wrapped in his coat and hat.

"Hello Cedric" she kicked off her boots in the hall and went into the tiny snug that doubled as a living room. It was true that local vicars were often poorer than church mice.

"Ah hello dear, are you alright?" He said.

"Yes I'm fine. Have you had any breakfast?"

"Oh just a bowl of cereal you know. The toaster won't work, there's been another power cut you know"

"I'll go and see if Colette is alright, then if you like we'll all go to the farmhouse. It's much warmer there. "

"Well that's very kind of you Alex. I won't say no"

So Alex walked over to Colette's house. She was wrapped in a fur coat.

"I thought vets didn't approve of that sort of thing" Alex smiled

"Oh bugger that, there's nothing like real fur to keep you warm. And I'm sure they were dealt with humanely as I bought it from Harrods a long time ago."

"I'll leave the cats here but can I bring the dogs?"

"Of course, and better bring an overnight bag just in case. It looks as if this might not be fixed for a while"

The three trudged back to the farmhouse and were grateful for the warmth and the light. By evening there was still no indication that the power was back on. Alex made Colette take the spare bedroom. Cedric took the couch with a spare duvet and pillow.

Colette made a ham hock and pea soup with warm bread, and they finished off a warm apple pie and custard, left over from the previous night. Alex gave them a glass of her homemade rhubarb wine, which was very good.

The dogs slept next to the Rayburn and snored with Cedric.

The snow continued to fall. The world at Rawston was a silent one except for the occasional sounds of the animals in the barn, or the chickens happily scratching for the bugs whilst roaming the glass house where Alex had put them.

The next day, no change, so Colette went out to feed her cats. She brought some food back for the barn cats that were huddled together at the back of the barn, but they were well fed. The mice had also retreated to the cattle straw.

On the third day they discussed what could have

happened but there was no conclusion. They were safe and warm enough, with plenty of food.

XII

The Crown of England

An army Vauxhall Senator, painted in drab olive, pulled off through the Buckingham Gate at the side of the palace. The entrance to Buckingham Palace used on a day to day basis by official visitors. The more familiar gates at the front of the building were generally used only for state occasions.

The car pulled into the yard by the steps leading up to the palace where waited the King's private secretary, Jonathan Strutt.

He watched the car come to a standstill. From the rear door came an Admiral of the Royal Navy, followed by a Marshall of the Royal Air Force, and accompanied by the Archbishop of Canterbury, Head of the Church of England.

The front passenger door opened and out stepped the now familiar but nevertheless large, menacing figure of General Edward Gaunt.

A following truck pulled in behind from which six armed soldiers climbed out. They assembled by the steps to wait.

Gaunt led the official party up the steps. Strutt held out his hand to Gaunt who shook it, at the same time noticing the strained smile on Strutt's face.

"Hello again General, good to see you even though I hope you can persuade his Majesty to call off tomorrow's coronation and to wait until this crisis has been resolved."

Gaunt nodded casually but said nothing as Strutt led the party into the palace and into one of the small reception rooms.

Strutt continued " Hardly any of the Heads of State who were invited have arrived, obvious reasons though. Somehow we've managed to get most of the House of Lords, and the MP's together...with your help of course, but it's really not the way it should be for this most fundamental event of the King's reign. His Majesty is determined, he can't wait but even so..." He let the sentence fade away. "The French Ambassador called this morning to say that they would not be attending...at least they had the courtesy to say something, but I'm sure they find all this highly amusing, damn them"

"Please wait here gentleman while I fetch the King"

The room was silent. Strutt returned, "His Majesty the King" he announced.

The old man who would be king stepped into the room. He was smiling as he came over to the group. No-one bowed. This was slightly odd. "General..." but before he could finish speaking , Gaunt raised his hands, there was a very faint sound.

All the occupants stood silently.

The King stepped back fractionally as Gaunt reached out his large right hand and grabbed his throat and squeezed hard. He looked up in astonishment, his face frozen as his eyes bulged slightly but he said nothing, nor could he.

Gaunt spoke" I am Edward Gaunt, descended from John of Gaunt of the Plantagenet Kings ...... I take your crown and your country...."

Gaunt watched him die, holding him upright by his giant fist enclosed around his throat and then slowly lowered him to the floor.
The others looked on, their faces frozen in a sombre stare.

Gaunt stood upright still facing the body of the old King and without turning to the others he said

"The reign of King George the seventh is ended.... I am King Edward the Ninth, King of England and all realms both current and future"

The Archbishop stepped forward,.
Gaunt knelt down on one knee with a slight bow of the head and the Archbishop spoke

"By the grace of God I pronounce you King Edward IX, King of England this day of our Lord, and of all her realms in Scotland, Wales, and Ireland, and of those realms which will fall to the King...God Save the King!"
The others repeated "God save the King"

Edward stood back to his full height.

"Gentlemen, this is the day of our judgement in the eyes of God, and of the world. You all know what is now to be done, …….. begin the operation, the word is 'Cheltenham Gold Cup'… inform your captains and commanders."

As he spoke a VSTOL jet screeched overhead and made it's landing in the rear of the palace grounds in front of the wide steps leading from the great reception room. In addition, two Sea King helicopters appeared overhead and landed along side the Harrier.

Edward left the room down the steps and climbed into the Harrier's rear seat behind the pilot. He put on the flight helmet. The harrier's cockpit canopy closed and with a roar the plane lifted vertically into the sky and headed north. The remaining men took their allotted seats in the Sea Kings and slipped into the sky, one East and one West.

A cry was heard in the palace and then a silence descended.

Along the Thames at Greenwich the sightseers heard a roar of a strange low flying jet engine and turned to see a flash of grey steel shoot past at high speed.

A tourist gasped " God! That's a …" but he never finished his sentence as there was a blinding flash , followed seconds later by an ear destroying explosion. The Thames boiled, and before the man had turned a blast wave took the lives of everyone and everything standing in a 30 kilometre radius.

Had anyone been alive to see it, the entire city of Westminster which had stood for a thousand years was gone in a micro-second, leaving a crater over 10 kilometres wide and over 100 meters deep. The Thames slowly draining into it filling the open exposed tunnel networks that criss-crossed London below ground.

At the same time one of the Sea Kings touched down on the deck of a large British warship that had been standing to off the south coast. The ship turned and began heading out into the open Atlantic.

XIII
The World is Overcome

In the US radar tracking station known as NORAD, a shout went up from several of the desks.
"Cruise missiles launched!, They've hit London sir"
"Sir there's more....wait...more missiles,..ICBM's... inbound across Britain, the major cities. The Brits are under attack sir"

"Get me the President...!"

In the Baltic Sea, deep underwater, and off the Russian port of Archangel, a huge submarine rose silently up from the depths.
One of its missiles launched upward and broke the surface, flying into the air as its rockets ignited and the missile shot up into the clouds heading across the pole for Washington.

The operator shouted " Missile launch detected in the Baltic, tracking west towards... Washington.!"
The NORAD colonel shouted " I need positive confirmation..!" to the room as operators took up their posts at other radar screens.

He grabbed the telephone.

"General, we have incoming missiles , launched

from the Baltic, course being confirmed as Washington, repeat, Washington"
"My God, stay on the line..."

A shout " more incoming...approaching multiple strategic targets ...."
In Washington,
"Sir we've gone to DefCon One, repeat, DefCon One ..you must give the code!"

"What are you saying? The Presidents voice straining, his face contorting with stress.

"We have incoming missiles aimed at US soil sir...we have less than 4 minutes....we must launch ...." Desperate voices

Confusion, Fear, Chaos.....
"God help us!"

Launch, Launch....'Gettysburg' repeat 'Gettysburg!'"

In the Kremlin

"Is this some kind of fucking joke!"

"No ....Mr President we are under attack,... the Americans have launched multiple missiles on us...we have less than 4 minutes!

Fear, Confusion, Chaos....

We must launch sir...now sir!...

"'Oktober 17', repeat, 'Oktober17'..!"

In Paris.

“Attack! Attack!... Mr Presidente..we are under attack, the Russians have launched multiple warheads ...we have less than 4 minutes we must launch now or France will be destroyed!”

In Tel Aviv
“God in heaven...we are tracking multiple ICBM launches across the world!...thousands of them! ....we are under attack ...we must launch ...

In Beijing
Several missiles are on track for our cities, we must launch our counter offensive, we have less than 4 minutes...!

In India, in Pakistan, in Iran, in South Africa the same confusion, panic, shouted orders.

...and the world that was, was gone.

XIV

Catterick, and the Kings Own Horse

In Rawston a week passed, cold and largely silent.

However on the eighth night something unsettled the animals. The dogs started howling and wouldn't settle. Alex went out to the barn. The cows were stamping about with wide eyes. The cats were arching their backs and spitting if she went near. The sheep did nothing in the way that sheep do except sit and chew their cud, with the occasional bleat thrown in.

The night was very dark but the snow had stopped and it was a frosty clear night. There was no sound, bar the animals, but from the edge of her eye there seemed to be a glow in the sky far north, and also to the south and south-east.

She tried the radio again but even Radio 4 was silent.

Her training gave her a particular insight and she had a feeling that something dreadful had occurred. She said nothing to the others for now but they all began to realise that this was something abnormal.

Morning dawned blood-red. The sun lit the sky with great patterns of dark red and amber. It was beautiful but ominous. It cast a red glow over everything turning the snow on the green fields and slopes of the valley into a sad pink. All edges of the buildings were pin-sharp. There was a smell in the air of what could only be described as cooked steak.

The only sounds were the wind catching and the animals moving about on the straw in the barn.

Alex lit the steam generator as the diesel was starting to run low.

She went into the paint shed and took out some of the white emulsion that she had used for the farmhouse walls. She mixed a bit of water into it then sloshed it over the roof, bonnet and sides of the Land Rover. She brushed out some of the thicker parts and wiped any spills that had run down the glass.

Cedric came out of the house with a cup of tea.

"Dazzle paint....that looks like winter dazzle paint for camouflage."

"Yes, that's what it is, I'm going to make a trip and I want to blend in as best I can while I'm on the road"

"But first some breakfast..."

The three sat quietly around the kitchen table. Alex wolfed down her bacon, eggs tomatoes and mushrooms, thick sliced bread and tea.

She disappeared upstairs.

At the bottom of her wardrobe was a leather trunk. It had military markings and stickers on it. It hadn't been out for a long time. It had travelled with her all around the world on the boat. She had gone back to the yard recently to retrieve it and a few other possessions, now that she was firmly established on the farm.

Colette and Cedric were still at the table when she came downstairs. They both looked up in surprise.

“That’s a full Colonel’s uniform!” Colette’s brother had been in the Army and she had met him on enough occasions to get to know the officers and their different insignia’s.

“Yes it is. I’m going over to Catterick. If anyone knows what’s going on it’ll be the Army, and the best way to speak to the Army is in uniform. Catterick was my main base when I was commissioned so there’s bound to be someone who remembers me.”

“I knew there was something more to you than your ‘farm girl’ talk” said Colette,

“My, my, a full Colonel no less, but what do you think has happened?”

“A retired colonel actually. I don’t know, but I don’t think its good, nor short term. I want you both to stay here for now. You’ll be warm and there’s plenty of food. You both know how everything works and, Colette, hope you don’t mind sorting out the animals for a couple of days”

“Of course not, but how will you get there, the snow looks pretty deep”

“I’m working on the basis that there’ll be some traffic on the old A66 so once I’m out of here it should be ok. If not I'll find a way, should be no more than two or three days"

Colette and Cedric stood, Cedric said " Go with God's help and bring her back safely"

With that she left the farm, filled the Landy with diesel with what remained in the tank and set off through the snow.

The roads were bad but passable. When she got to the A66, the old route across the Pennines, the snow was thin and clear in parts. The wind had piled up the snow in odd places but the road was passable. Nothing else was moving. There were a few cars abandoned by the roadside. One or two looked as if they had been forcibly pushed into the drifts at the side of the road.

Nevertheless it was slow going and it took her over four hours to reach Catterick, a longstanding large Army base located in North Yorkshire.

It had seen better days and was now being slowly wound down. Less and less operations were run from it as the Army had consolidated further north and south.

She avoided the main gate, so drove round the side. The metal fencing led her round about 2 miles to the rear entrance that she had used so often in the past.

She pulled in to the short drive of the rear fence slightly back from the guard-house.

A figure appeared from the hut dressed entirely

in a green rubber hazmat suit including a hood with a Perspex window. An automatic weapon was held across his chest with his gloved finger just outside of the trigger guard.

She stepped out of the Defender.

"You can't park that heap of shit there miss."

She looked at the soldier in the suit for a moment then smiled.

"I recognise that voice" She walked towards him "Sergeant 'Nobby' Styles unless I'm very much mistaken"

The man removed the hood and grinned from ear to ear.

"Hello Colonel, good to see you again, thought you'd retired"

"I have but what better way to break into an Army base than in uniform…How're the legs these days?"

"Good question M'am, no rust as yet" and he tapped his legs which made a metallic sound.

"What's a senior sergeant doing on gate duty Nobby?"

"All the lads have been moved up to the Cheviots m'am. Just a few of us poor NCO's left here to make up the numbers. We take it in turns to wear the 'noddy' suit and do this"

"It's Alex, remember, less of the m'am please….and why have you got that thing on anyway?"

"Haven't you heard? We're at war. Not sure who, but some bugger has nuked us. London's gone, along with a few other towns." He stopped "Oh and we have a new King"

"Nuked?"

"Yes ma'm"

"Best you have a word with the CO m'a..Alex. Major Phillips is in charge and he'll update you properly…I'll let you through…know where it is?"

"I do thanks, unless it's all been moved since I was here last. What's the 'rad count? Should I be worried?"

"It's all normal. Hasn't moved from background levels but I guess it depends on the wind"

Nobby, whose real name was Norman, but known as Nobby because of the old football player, opened the gates.

"What do you mean 'a new king'?

"Best talk to the Major"

Alex climbed back in the Landy and drove through. She leaned out of the window. "Good to see you again Nobby, how's the wife?"

"She's gone m'am, ran off a while ago. Never mind I'm happier on my own"

"Was he blind?…the bloke that did the camo?" He said looking at the Defender.

"Cheeky sod…it's called improvisation"

He gave a cheery wave before replacing the hood

"keeps me nice and warm too in this bloody weather"

She laughed. It was good to be back amongst soldiers, particularly those that had served with her, even the wounded ones.

Another wounded veteran came out to meet her at the doorway to the CO's offices. He ran his wheelchair to the edge of the porch way.

"Hello stranger" he said "Nobby called ahead, good to see you again Alex"

"And you too Simon" she said as she walked over from the car.

"Come on in it's bloody freezing out here" He spun round and they both went into a typical army office. Sparse but clean and tidy.

There were some pleasantries then Alex said " I could tell that something big had happened but what the hell has? And Nobby said something about a new king"

"Oh that...you're old mate Edward Gaunt has proclaimed himself King of England, remember how he would say he was last of the Plantagenets, descended from one of John of Gaunt's bastards....who can say, but he's definitely in charge. He's the one calling all the shots, moving the men around to various camps and castles, and putting a large force under the Cheviots, you know, the main underground base"

"Whoa, whoa...General Edward Gaunt you

mean?, you'd better start from the beginning Simon" He poured her some tea, slipped a whisky in it and she sat down next to his desk.

"Gaunt's been pretty active over the last year. Did you know he took over the National Trust and all that lot? No, well he did. Something about bringing back the proper old skills. He must have convinced the MoD as well because he was given carte blanche to move men and machinery around the country. Anyone objected then they'd get silenced somehow. He's been buying up horses left right and centre, and taken over a lot of farms, or at least put men there to keep them secure."

"He's been here too, keeps popping back now and then. Had everyone falling over themselves to please him. Quite a few Ruperts, and the top brass seemed to go along with it all."

"Just before the New Year he moved a lot of the men north, and the rest to the western shelters. Nothing down south. He left the cripples to man the fort which is why Nobby, me, and the like are the only ones left here."

He poured more tea.

"Then on New Year the mains power was cut. As you know we have a separate system anyway so we weren't really affected. You know, it's the first thing to go in an enemy strike. Absolute panic of course. We were turning people away from the gates. Fortunately we're not that near a town or city here .God knows what it must be like in those places. Then a couple of days ago we had the order to take cover. London and surrounding counties were hit with a massive nuclear strike. Everything and everyone in it is gone. Just a big hole in the ground being filled by the Thames I guess. Ditto Portsmouth, Cardiff, Birmingham, Leeds, Manchester, Newcastle, Edinburgh, Glasgow, Belfast and Dublin. I'm not sure how many of those were actually nuclear, or whether they were big conventionals. Either way, it triggered a massive global response. As I understand things, the US, The Russians, the French, Chinese, Israelis, Pakistanis, Indians and the South Africans all launched their weapons. As far as I know we did too."

"So it's global Armageddon . We get a message on the secure comms to stay put. Then yesterday we get another signal to announce that the King is dead, long live King Edward the Ninth. Sit tight."

"Christ" Alex couldn't think of anything better to say for a few minutes while she processed this information. Simon Phillips sat quietly staring at his tea cup.

"The Yanks got hit very hard, as did the Ruski's and the Chinese, probably to be expected I suppose given the size of their arsenals. I understand most of the US is a smoking ruin. I guess we've been a bit luckier. No one bothers about us much these days, probably just as well in the circumstances"

Finally she said "How come the rad levels aren't off the scale?

"Well that's why I think that not all of them were nukes. And we have a south westerly blowing so much of the fallout will be blowing over mainland Europe. I'm guessing the US dust hasn't made it across the Atlantic. Yet. Maybe never. You know the modern nukes and the air detonation make much less crap. Perhaps it's that. Either way there's been no spike in levels, and we've been monitoring it since."

"We've also been checking the light levels during the day but we haven't seen any major dust clouds or light blocking which could trigger a deep winter. Not yet anyway. The Met office is gone, but so far temperatures here are only a bit lower than you'd expect for this time of year."

"Since then we've had a stream of secure comms. Apparently Gaunt has appointed a whole raft of new County Lords Lieutenant, and we are to take their orders as legitimate. Quite a few are officers who you would know. Mainly though the message is to sit tight, do nothing, await further commands."

"My guess is he's waiting for the chaos to subside, you know, there's going to be famine and disease spreading everywhere. The rat population has exploded too which will act as a major vector for more disease, as you know, but I also know that several units are recruiting like mad. Food and shelter in return for service I guess. We'll soon have the place filled up here is my thinking, just a matter of time"

"What about the wives?"

"Well you know the married quarters are now off base but we pulled in most of the women and children onto the base for protection. A few didn't come though so we're sending over food and portable heaters and generally trying to keep them inside their houses. Safest that way until we get firm orders."

"Is Stephanie Bryant still here?"

Phillips looked across at Alex. A curious question given the background. "Yes she is. The daughters have long gone but she's still doing her work with the local cats, that's about all she has left since…" His voice trailed off.

"Still in the same house?"

"Yes, she's one that didn't come into the base. Probably wise I guess given that the other women wouldn't want her here."

"And did Gaunt visit the Special Ops secure room?"

Again a slightly odd question.

"I believe so" said Phillips, "but as you know, even in my lofty position as Quartermaster, I don't get to see what you guys have stashed away in there"

Alex looked at him. Any self respecting

quartermaster would know exactly what was where, especially if they'd be told to leave it alone.

"I'll pay it a visit while I'm here" she said.

The day was wearing on and she became aware that she was getting hungry.

"I could do with some food Simon. Is the kitchen up and running?"

"Come on, I'll treat you to a nice steak and eggs" He said and they headed over to the base canteen which was largely empty. A few men nodded to her. She was still recognised by many in the army as a good officer, as well as known for being a tough bitch who would have your balls if you stepped out of line.

"Thank God we've got our own small nuclear power station here. If there's no electrical power out there then nothing works. No light, or heat, no phones or TV, no water being pumped, the supermarkets in darkness with no refrigeration. All these modern utilities rely on electricity. No petrol, no gas. Food going rotten, sewage piling up. I hear there have been riots and deaths as people are starving and freezing to death. Typhoid and worse will be next, if the famine or hypothermia doesn't get you first. What's that saying 'we're only ever nine meals away from anarchy'? It's been 12 days since the power went so...." He tailed off and looked into his tea again.

"What's happened with the Navy?" She asked

"As I said Portsmouth took a hit, but it turns out that Gaunt was also into the Navy chiefs. Told them to put to sea, so I guess they're still there waiting. Same for the Trident sub fleet. Sit tight and wait. That's the order of the moment. Come to think of it that's always the order" Phillips smiled. He's also tucked away some of the Air force in the Cheviots. Transport aircraft and choppers I believe plus a couple of VTOL's. I think the Navy have a few more at sea. Meanwhile all the satellites are dead so we're using the high altitude comms balloons as relays."

"You're remarkably well informed Simon?"

"It's the wounded brigade. We cripples stick together you know. Lots of us in signals. I have a man who keeps me posted. You know you can't keep a secret for long in the forces."

Alex stood up and walked to the window. She stared out at the base and what she could see of the Pennines in the distance. She was silent for a long while.

"I'm going to need to take some supplies if you don't mind" Alex looked at Phillips.

"I'll do what I can. Give me a list and I'll have what you need loaded into your Landy"

"Also I need a room for the night. It'll be too late to go back over the Pennines tonight, can you accommodate me"

"Of course you can. Joyce will be more than happy to see you and sort you out" Joyce was the legendary facilities manager on the base.

"I'll go and see her, thanks Simon"

Alex had a cup of tea with Joyce who gave her a very nice officer's room along with a 'service pack' including a change of clothes and a set of fatigues so she could get out of the uniform. Joyce took it away to have it cleaned and pressed.

It was getting near dark when Alex slipped out for a stroll. She made her way to one of the buildings marked SO3. Access Privileged. No trespassers.

This had been her home base several years earlier when she and Gaunt were on active operations in Afghanistan.

The access codes had not changed and she entered the building. The lights were on automatic. She found the strong room that she was looking for, marked H.x., and keyed in the key-code. The door swung open and the lights came on. The shelves were completely empty. She closed the door and returned to her room.

Simon Phillips came by later to invite her to dinner with a few of the other remaining officers. Joyce returned with her uniform so she dressed for dinner and had a thoroughly enjoyable evening with some old friends. She retired to her room around midnight and slept until 6.30 when one of the NCO's brought in a pot of tea , with ham, eggs and toast.

Major Phillips was attending to her supply

request, loading the Defender with sacks of coffee beans, tea, sugar, rice and salt. There were also a couple of crates containing amongst other things a couple of automatic weapons, some plastic explosive, detonators and cases of ammunition. Torches, batteries, and a fine crate of citrus fruit of varying types. A couple of side by side shotguns, and a crate of cartridges. A Geiger counter. A couple of female service packs with spare fatigues.

"Simon, mind if I borrow your Landy for an hour or so, I need to see someone off base"

"You can, but she'll bite your head off you know"

He smiled and she smiled back. No secrets in the Army.

She drove out of the base, not far, to the rows of depressing 1950's married quarters. Soldiers have never been paid much so at least it was a home while their man was serving. In theory the army wives and children would keep each other company, and when a man didn't return, a support group. It was also a bed of malicious gossip, fractious relations and downright hostility between some females.

Many of the houses were empty as several of the wives and children had been shuffled into the barracks for protection. The snow gave it a rare hint of glamour where it was possible to believe these were nice little streets of houses.

The streets were deserted. She pulled up in front of the house she recognised from earlier times. The half repaired car in the drive under a loose tarpaulin, the rusting children's swing. The grim brickwork, the peeling paint. Smoke was rising from the chimney.

She walked up the path and knocked on the door.

A woman in her early 40's opened the door. She had short cropped brown hair with patches of grey, her eyes were dim and dark, and her skin a fine sallow, like candle wax.

Her eyes narrowed slightly "You! What the hell do you want? Come to gloat?"

"Hello Stephanie" Alex expected the hostility "I need to talk to you"

For a moment the woman hesitated as if she was deciding whether to slam shut the door, or fire a curse. But there was no fire here anymore. She was a beaten woman. Her shoulders sagged and her eyes dimmed.

"Come in" She backed off up the hallway leaving Alex to step inside and follow her into the sparsely furnished living room. A meagre coal fire was burning in the grate, otherwise the house was cold and slightly damp. Stephanie Bryant was wrapped in an old wool coat on top of her cheap jeans and jumper. Several cats eyed Alex from sedentary positions around the room.

Stephanie slumped down into an armchair beside the fire and gazed at the flames.

"What do you want?"

"I need to know where Henry has gone"

"Huh, everybody wants to know that. I've told them all I've no idea. After being let out of prison he disappeared. No-one knows. He sent me the postcard and that was it"

"What postcard?"

"It's in the kitchen, a picture of Devon, it just says 'gone to stay with the Moores' I don't know anyone called Moore, and even Gaunt's men haven't found him"

"Gaunt came here?"

"Nooo, 'course not. He sent some snotty over to see me last year, but as I said he's in the wind, as the Americans would say. Probably changed his name, grown a beard and shacked up with some hippy. Probably working as a respectable chemist in some high street or other. He was always too clever for his own good"

Alex went into the kitchen. The card was stuck to the side of the fridge with a magnet. It was a collage of things from Devon including Dartmoor. On the back it said 'Steph, sorry for all you've been through, gone to stay with the Moors. Love Henry x'

Alex came back into the living room.

"Where are your daughters?"

"Don't you dare bother them again" she flared up like fat on a fire "They're gone thank God, settled with nice men. No army. I don't see them anymore, it's just too painful, and they don't want to know anyway"

"I'm not going to see them, I was just asking if they're alright"

"Well they are, no thanks to Henry, or you for that matter. I thought you were all mates, You, Gaunt, Henry, how you could end up prosecuting him?, and all the shit that came out about him and young girls… who should have known better" her voice tailed off and she resumed her stare into the fire.

" It was a court martial, and I didn't volunteer, it was classified, it would have had to be me or Gaunt, but someone had to do it. They were under-age girls,… including your daughters…."

"Get out bitch!…" Stephanie had risen from her chair "I'm sick of it, sick of you all, I wish I hadn't been born, you come here, raking up the old coals, all over again" Tears were streaming down her face.

"I'm going Steph, and for what it's worth I'm sorry."

"I don't need or want your sympathy. Not from the other vicious bitches here either, whispering behind my back, …Get out…out"

Alex stepped out of the house. The door slammed behind her. She was still holding the postcard. She noticed there was no postmark on it. She slipped it into a pocket, climbed back in the

Landy and drove back to the base.

Morning was wearing away and she would need to get on the road soon to make it back to Rawston while it was still light.

A military helicopter flew overhead.

Major Phillips had finished having her Defender loaded with supplies.

"A quick cup of tea before you leave? "He said, anticipating her need to get going.

"Thanks Simon, and thank you for the stuff, it's very good of you"

"Oh, all part of the service M'am" he grinned, "Plus, we may not see each other again for all I know. Things are changing fast, Martial Law in force and everyone locked down tighter than a gnat's arse"

She smiled.

"One more thing Simon." When they were back in his office. "The strong room, Hx, it's empty. Don't suppose you could lay your hands on one of the kits?"

"Not sure what you're talking about...but as it happens I've got one of these"

He pulled out a dark green tin, like a small biscuit tin with the letter H 435 in white stencil on the top.

"Thank God for Quartermasters" she said "Devious sods but clever...too clever" she smiled at him and took the proffered tin from him"

"There's always a spare or two lying about you know"

"Even top security stuff that was supposed to have been destroyed"

They both smiled. She dropped the tin into a wide pocket on the fatigues.

"Gotta go"

"I know, take care of yourself, and if anyone asks tell them it fell off the back of a tank in the snow."

She slipped out of the back entrance as she had come in. The guard came out of the hut but she didn't recognise him.

She hit the A1 and then the A66 at scotch corner. The place was deserted.

It was still snowing lightly as she reached the crown of the Pennine road.

Up ahead was a truck standing at the side of the road with snow on it. Thin smoke was rising from somewhere behind. There was a distinct smell of petrol in the air. As she passed she saw a man sitting on an upturned bucket holding something over a flame in another bucket.

Her curiosity got the better of her, and in any case this was the first living soul she had seen outside of an army base anywhere on the journey so far.

She pulled up and stepped out of the Land Rover. The man looked up then stood up and saluted. Another bloody soldier, she thought.

“At ease soldier, just curious” She knew the old army trick for making a jury-rig stove from a bucket of sand and petrol.

The man spotted the insignia, the two pips below the crown, which the ever resourceful Joyce had stitched to the fatigues.

“Welcome to join me Colonel, I’ve got a brew on”

“Thanks, I will”

The man was perhaps in his late thirties, stocky and well built, but short. He looked like someone who could hold his own anywhere. There was a certain air of menace about him despite the woolly hat and long overcoat that he was wearing.

“Army?”

“Ex Army, Royal Marines, ex-Sergeant Jerry Bradman at your service M’am”

“No M’am, just a retired Colonel, I’m Alex Rheinhart, I’m headed to Westmoreland where I have a small farm”

She squatted down to warm her hands near the bucket of flames. Land Rover heaters are shit.

“I saw the bucket and guessed you were Army. Is that ‘burgoo tea’? “ she said pointing at the can of light brown liquid that was beginning to steam.

“It is indeed, just got to add a couple of biscuits, but the tea, sugar and ‘evap’ are already in.

He produced an extra cup, crumbled a couple of digestive biscuits into the gloop, gave it a stir with a stick then poured out two cupfuls, one of which he handed to her.

She smiled and took a sip.

"God it's a bit sweet for my tastes, but I guess it's very good for this weather" she waved her free hand across the snowy wastes of the high Pennines.

She looked at the truck. It was a relatively new cab, but it was attached to a familiar army style fuel tanker.

"So what are you doing here?"

"I do deliveries for a firm in Middlesborough. Marshall's. Fuels and Oils. I go around assorted farms all over the North. I live in the cab. Got stuck here Monday. I woke up to find the engine was dead. The electrics are fucked. Can't bypass the CPU in these modern trucks. The phone has been dead for days before that. I've been waiting for a rescue but you're the first person who's come past in four days. Actually I saw you go past the other way two days ago but couldn't flag you down in time."

"Sorry, I didn't see you. Probably the snow. This looks like a military tanker?"

"It is. Old man Marshall bought six of them when they were selling them off. Very handy bit of kit for this work. Four tanks in one. Petrol, Red Diesel, Heating Oil, and Aviation paraffin."

"A very handy bit of kit, actually it's just what I need too"

"Well unless you've got a spare circuit board for it in that Landy I'm stuck here until Marshall's decide I'm AWOL and start looking for me"

"I don't think they'll be coming." She told him what she knew."That's why I went to Catterick. Just found out myself but I had a guess we'd been attacked."

"What about your family?"

"Oh I haven't got one. The wife left after my second tour in the 'Stan', ran off with a car salesman. Better prospects I guess. Thankfully no kids. No, I'm on my own. What you see is my home." He said pointing his thumb at the cab." It suits me. No bills, no responsibilities, and when the fucking engine's working it's nice and warm in there. Got all my food and stuff in there. It's a good bed in the back. And the army training means I can live off the land if needs be. The shotgun and the fishing rod come in handy. "

"Do you think the Landy could tow this thing?" she said.

"Can't see why not if you can get it rolling. I've got a ten ton strap in the cab which should be strong enough."

"Well ex-sergeant Bradman, would you like a tow? You'd have to come back to my farm and we'll take it from there"

"That would be good M'am"

He stood up, the flames were dying back. He flipped a steel plate over the sand to extinguish the flames and hung the two buckets back in their hold on the tanker. He 'washed' the cups and the tins in the snow which also went in the hold.

With the strap attached to the tanker, Alex put the other end onto the Landy's tow bar.

Jerry climbed into the cab and released the pneumatic brakes. Alex climbed into the Land Rover and slipped it into the low ratio gearbox. Very carefully she pulled away, taking up the slack on the strap. The wheels slipped a couple of times but the four-wheel drive began to move the truck forwards. Once on the road surface the Land Rover had no difficulty pulling the heavy truck.

It took several hours before they pulled in to the farmyard.

Colette and Cedric came out to meet them and Alex introduced Jerry.

Colette, with a smile, said to Jerry "She's very good at collecting up waifs and strays you know, welcome to the farm" and she gave Alex what could be termed a knowing smile. Alex ignored her.

They sat down at the kitchen table while Colette prepared some food. Alex told them all she had learned at Catterick. Not really what anyone wanted to hear. There was silence followed by question after question. For the most part the answer was always 'I don't know'. Four people in a world that had changed overnight. Civilisation that had seemed permanent and robust turned upside down in a matter of days. Misery, hunger, pain, and death for a human society that never thought this would be possible in a modern world.

“We have our Lord Jesus. He cannot be taken away” Cedric said “Whatever happens He will be with us”

Cedric was keen to provide news.

“While you were away I thanked our Lord for you’re generosity Alex, I don’t know how either of us could have coped, or survived, without us staying here in your home. Anyway I’m very pleased that you’re back safely.....Oh, and we’ve had a visit”

He stopped for a moment for dramatic effect.

“What visit?”

“Four men on horseback turned up yesterday, rough looking sorts, but they called themselves ‘The Kings Own Horse Regiment’ or something like that. Apparently they’re camped up on one of the big national trust estates to the north of here. A whole settlement of men, women, and children. They said that they would call each week to collect food and that they were moving around all the farms in the area. The fellow called himself Captain Spears. He said that in return for this they would provide protection if required, and they would make available health facilities if we needed them. I told them that you were not here at the moment and that they should speak to you Alex as we're only guests here at present. I didn't tell them your name but they must have known as they said they would speak to Colonel Rheinhart on her return."

"The sheriff's men" Jerry commented "come to collect the taxes"

"I suppose that's right" said Cedric "what do they mean when they said 'protection' it all sounds a bit sinister"

Alex spoke "Most likely it means that there are gangs of starving people on the hunt for food and shelter, probably armed. Martial law has been declared so these men have been charged with keeping the peace, but we can defend ourselves if it comes to that."

"I hope not, after all we must give succour to those in need Alex, er...as you have already shown"

"Yes Vicar." they all smiled at Cedric.

It was dark and cold by the time Alex and Jerry had decanted the supplies from the Land Rover into the house. They managed to manoeuvre the tanker into the tractor shed after re-filling the farm's diesel tank. Alex threw large tarpaulins over the cab and the tanker to keep it from possible prying eyes.

Despite Alex's protestations Jerry said he would be happy to sleep in the cab. He said it was his 'home' anyway. He said he wasn't bothered by the cold.

Alex had expected to live quietly on her own on her little smallholding, but it was good to have a younger man around on the farm, as well as the visits from Colette and Cedric.

Everything had changed in the world, but in Rawston you could have been forgiven for not noticing that much was amiss. The livestock trundled on, largely oblivious to the world around them, the coal seam, and the tanker of fuel kept the lights on and the house warm, the crops continued to grow.

Alex used the Geiger counter each morning to check the radiation levels, but they remained normal. She also began keeping a sidearm in the pocket of her Barbour. Jerry kept a semi-automatic gun in the cab of the truck.

Jerry was a practical man who added a fish pond to the farm which he stocked with a few trout fished from the Lune a few miles away. The gill kept it supplied with fresh running water and the fish bred well. There's never a shortage of water in Westmoreland.

Alex was up early as always when she heard the horses and riders approaching. She stood in the farmyard as they came trotting in. Four armed men.

Jerry heard them also and dropped down out of his cab, the semi down by his side.

The lead man swung off his horse and approached Alex holding out his hand with a smile. He glanced across at Jerry then back to Alex.

"Good to meet you Colonel" he said

Alex didn't offer her hand but replied "Captain Spears I assume?"

"Yes, your Vicar friend mentioned our earlier visit no doubt."

"He did, and how can I help you Captain?"

"Your farm here" Spears looked around waving his hand "Our men will be coming to help you run it" He smiled again but it wasn't in any way sincere.

"Thank you Captain but I don't need any help from you or your men"

"There'll be many new people moving into Rawston in the next few weeks. We're re-stocking all these small villages and towns. Mainly women and children, and some older people. The men have joined our English Army, but they'll come to help restore the houses and facilities in the village. Of course they'll all need to eat and your farm will feed many people I think."

"It's my farm Captain and I'll choose who or who doesn't come here"

"I'm afraid that's not an option Colonel. The King has ordered us to reclaim all the country's facilities. Your village and your farm are one of many which have been, or will be made available."

"And if I don't comply?"

"I have orders to use whatever means necessary..." he let the sentence tail away.

"In any case Colonel," his tone softened for a moment "you may still live here and do what you need to do...it's just that there will be more people in the village. And the men will take instructions from you, just as they did before you retired"

"You seem to know a lot about me Captain"

"The King is aware of you,... and has instructed me to behave accordingly..."

"Gaunt"

"My Lord King Edward ninth, but yes his family name is Gaunt. I believe you served with him several years ago...old comrades in arms?"

Jerry moved closer. Spears looked up at him. "Tell your sergeant to back off Colonel, we don't want any...unpleasantness."

"I'm retired Captain, as is my guest, and you have made yourself clear. I will make food available as well as I can, and you will stay off my farm unless I give you, or your men, permission to be here"

"Very well Colonel, until the next time..."

Spears turned and mounted his horse. He gave a salute which Alex did not return, turned his horse and rode back down the farm track, followed by his men.

"Pretty sure of himself eh?, how many men do you think they have?" said Jerry

"Yes, too many if you're thinking of a fight, I guess it was inevitable that it would come to this, and once these people start arriving then I suppose I won't be able to just sit here guarding my farm. It'll be share and share alike. I don't like it but he's right...no choice. Another farm taken from me...yet again."

"What does that mean?"

"Never mind, long story, another world"

Two carts pulled by shire horses trundled into the village a day later carrying a few women and children and one or two older men.

Cedric met them outside the church.

"Welcome to Rawston" he said but there was little enthusiasm from his potential new flock.

Armed men arrived on horseback carrying assorted tools and began to order the people about into the various tumbledown cottages and terrace houses still standing.

Spears wasn't with them but a large burly man with a permanent scowl seemed to be in charge.

The older men seem to have been selected because they had a trade and were set to work on the roofs and assorted rebuilding tasks.

Alex and Jerry brought down a wheelbarrow

full of food, mainly bread, bacon and eggs, some milk, butter and cheese along with some vegetables.

One of the older women came over to Alex "Oh thank you, thank you, we're all starving"

Alex said "Can I suggest that two of you take charge of the cooking. There's an old Aga in the school house which will run on anything that burns. I'll bring some coal to get it going and you can get the others to collect firewood. Then they can all come together to eat and keep warm while these men get working on making some of these habitable."

The large man noticed Alex and strode over looking furious.

"Here! I'm in charge of this lot, don't start interfering in other peoples business" and he grabbed Alex's arm to pull her out of the way. Big mistake.

Alex swung round and launched the upturned heel of her palm underneath the man's jaw. He staggered back and as he did so she kicked him hard in the balls. He doubled over and as he did she brought her knee into his face. He fell over, threw up and passed out.

The other men were looking at her.

"Anyone got a problem take it up with Spears"

The other men decided to steer clear of her but from that moment she had won the rest of the crowd. Suddenly everyone jumped into action.

The food was taken into the school cookhouse. The other men and women began tidying up the room. Someone found old tables and chairs and things began to get done that hadn't been done for decades in Rawston.

"You men get some bread and cheese then get on with working on the houses. There's good water in the streams so don't piss in them.

She walked over to the prostrate man on the ground and threw some water over his face. He groaned.

She grabbed his hand and pulled. "Come on, up you get." He looked at her and noticed Jerry standing beside her.

"If you're going to be in charge then you need to take advantage of what's around you and not get all arsy with everyone. Use what talent you've got available...."

The man grunted something. Alex whispered in his ear "and if you ever get the urge to hit me or any other woman again I'll find you and cut your balls off"

The man rose, scowled at Alex, and climbed back on his horse before riding off.

One of the men came up to Alex, "That was good to see, I'm glad he's gone, he was an arsehole"

"Where will he go?"

"Back to the camp maybe though he wasn't popular there either. Maybe he'll go and cause some misery elsewhere. But you should watch your back"

The following day more people arrived but the large man was nowhere to be seen. Another soldier was in charge who was clearly more intelligent. The result was that order was managed and different people put in charge of different jobs.

Two of the men came over to the farm and asked to see the steam boiler and generator. They took measurements and notes. One of them was a blacksmith who said he could make something similar. He and his mate would go off to find a suitable container for the pressure vessel. He was sure the rest was easily constructed from salvaged parts of an old washing machine they had found in one of the derelict houses, and some plumbing fittings.

Sunday came around and Cedric was delighted to see his church fill up with a new congregation. It was early spring. Easter would be soon and with it the beginnings of a whole new year much more promising than he could have dared to hope.

Plans were afoot to find a couple of teachers for the old school house, which remained the community centre for the moment. At least it could be heated and there was warm water.

In short, Rawston village returned to life. Much the same was happening across the country. The major cities and towns were devastated and lost, but the smaller towns and villages began to get better at managing a growing number of people returning to the countryside. Food could be grown and harvested. Shelter built or improved, people began to get used to life without electricity, without phones or TV. They returned to churches and made their own entertainment. Pubs that had been long closed began brewing their own beer and cider and making assorted fruit wines. Stills were made from scavenged items and soon bootleg gin began to provide it's unique problems all over again.

Alex however began to have mixed feelings. She had got very used to the quiet life and the pleasure gained from the changing seasons by herself. As spring turned to summer, and her herds and crops began to increase to feed more and more people life became different. Men and women from the village came to help on a daily basis.

One of her older cows had been taken into the barn as it was heavily pregnant with a late pregnancy. Alex saw that the cow kept lying down then getting up again to feed and she knew that this meant trouble with the birth. She didn't want to call Colette as it was getting late so she took a lamp into the large barn where she'd led the heifer. She'd put down straw and a big pile of hay for feed. The hours ticked by until she saw that the amniotic bag and a pair of legs were poking out from the cows rear. The heifer was lying down and she was talking very softly to it.

By 2am the water bag had burst and it looked like the calf was coming out backwards. She smoothed down the cow's flank with her hand, talking softly as she grabbed hold of the calf's legs and began to pull alternate legs to try to 'walk' it out. The heifer was getting distressed. Alex heard someone approaching behind her and turned expecting Jerry or one of the villagers who might have heard and come to help. Instead it was the large man who she had kicked in the balls a few months ago. He did not look good.

A giant hand punched her in the side of the head sending her reeling into the straw away from the cow.

"I'm going to fuck you bloody you bitch! Then I'm going to wring your fucking neck!" in a deadly whisper his teeth clenched in red anger.

She was dizzy and disoriented by the blow. He hit her again knocking her back again. She began to get her wits about her and lashed out with her feet but he caught he Wellington boot and ripped it off. He was too big and too strong. He grabbed her jeans and she felt the material rip under the strain. She swung up and tried to get her thumb in his eye socket but she was still too disoriented to strike properly. He landed his whole weight on top of her as he began to pull off her sweater.

Just at that moment when she felt she would be overpowered again a strange thing happened.

She turned her head and saw that the heifer had managed to give birth and the calf was lying in the straw. At the same moment the man on top of her was hurled bodily in the air as the cow head butted him, jumped carefully over Alex and trampled the man's prone form into the mud just outside the barn entrance.

The cow turned and walked back to her calf and began to lick it as the little calf came to life.

The man was lying face down in the muck but was starting to move. Alex leapt to her feet and ran across to him and sat on his head, pushing his face into the wet mud. He tried to push up with an arm but the cow must have broken it for there was a muffled scream of pain. Alex sat on his head for what seemed like many minutes but was perhaps no more than thirty seconds.

She heard the cab door of the truck open and saw Jerry coming towards them, finally woken with the noise. His feet were bare but he had an axe in his hand.

There was no need for the axe though as the large man died in the mud, suffocated in shit.

Such was his first, and last, introduction to the farming life.

XV

A Trip to York

In early summer a loud noise descended over the village. People came out of their houses to see what was happening as a large Chinook helicopter landed in the hay field, terrifying the cattle as it did so.

Three smartly uniformed men climbed out and walked over to Alex as she was standing in the yard.

"Colonel Rheinhart I hope?" said the lead man cheerily.

She nodded to them as they made a short salute.

"Retired Colonel Rheinhart you mean"

"Yes of course " the man continued " I'm Captain Davidson, Kings Own. Here on my lord King's business. He has asked to see you, and as you can see he's sent transport"

There was something about the man's cheeriness that grated with Alex.

"I'm busy, you'll have to come back another day"

The Captain smiled. "Yes he said you would be, however the King does wish to speak to you and I must ask you to come with me now."

" Well you'd better tell King Gaunt that he'll have to wait until I'm ready. Best to come back in the winter when it's quieter on the farm."

"I'm afraid that won't be possible, and I see you have plenty of help available, and I will leave a couple of my men here to look after things until you're back. He looked around at the small gathering of farm workers before noticing Jerry carrying a small automatic sub machine gun at his side"

"There'll be no need for that Sergeant Bradman" He said quietly to Jerry who stood stock still and stared back at him with a small grin on his face.

"In any case Colonel, it's a relatively short hop to York in this" he pointed his thumb back to the Chinook. "I'll bring you back tomorrow if that is your wish, but I must insist that you come with me now."

Alex looked at Jerry "I will come but my friend Sgt Bradman will join me, and you will give me some time to get changed". Jerry nodded.

"Very good, I'll wait here and have a chat with your people but please be quick."

Alex turned towards the farm house. "Jerry with me"

As they entered the house she said " Jerry do you trust me?"

"I do Alex, what have you in mind?"

"A precaution, follow me"

They went to her bedroom. She opened the wardrobe and pulled out her trunk. Lying on the top of her uniform was the small green tin she had obtained from Catterick, which she opened. In it was a gas cylinder and some tubing, together with a series of small hypodermic syringes, and some sterile wipes. She pulled out one of the syringes, rolled up her sleeve, wiped a patch on her arm then injected the clear liquid in the syringe into a vein in her arm.

"I haven't got time to explain right now but you need one of these as well. "

Jerry rolled up his sleeve and offered his arm.

"As soon as I get the chance I'll fill you in, but for now..."

She wiped the sterile patch then she stuck in the needle and injected into Jerry's arm.

"Is that it?"

"Yes, you might feel a little dizzy for a moment but it'll pass quickly, now I need to get in my uniform. Better to see Gaunt as a Colonel. Good, you've already got your fatigues on."

She quickly undressed from her jeans and jumper. Jerry turned away. When he turned back she was buttoning up her shirt and pulling up her tie before slipping on the trousers and coat. Finally her brightly polished black shoes, then her hat.

She put the tin back in the trunk and closed the wardrobe.

"Showtime..." she said as they walked out of the farmhouse and towards Captain Davidson.

Alex turned to her helpers and asked them to look after things for a day, but said she and Jerry would be back tomorrow, or Friday at the latest.

She turned to the two soldiers who would be staying.

"You lads can stay in the farm house but you will respect my friends here...and don't nick anything, I'll know...."

Then she and Jerry climbed aboard the Chinook and it rose into the air with a great blast of air and noise from the rotors before sloping away, up and East towards the Pennines.

The aircraft flew in a direct line, about 80 miles, across the upland moors and forests.

They were flying low so Alex could see the farms and occasional camps established across the countryside similar to the ones now based in Westmoreland.

Refugee armies of men, women and children who had found their way, or been found, to swell the new armies of the new King. A few looked up, one or two waved as the Chinook passed overhead, desperate people engaged in totally new lives.

But at least they had food and shelter, and, she supposed, a new purpose.

She had learned from the men and women who came to Rawston that a selection process was in operation. Anyone with a useful trade was taken in. Builders, carpenters, plumbers, metalworkers, blacksmiths, stonemasons, a few electricians. Farmers were especially in high demand which made great sense to Alex. Also a whole raft of supplementary skills, tailors, dressmakers, weavers, tanners, cooks, teachers, doctors, nurses, dentists, as well as all the military requirements for a horse mounted army. Indeed a horse led everything. Younger, stronger men were taken for the armed services. The Royal Navy also had a direct hand in recruitment as new ships were commissioned and built in the old shipyards around the country as they were themselves being restored. The Air force fell under the joint control of the Army and the Navy.

She had also heard that children were being tested for intellect and ability along with university academics in the sciences and the natural world. Oxford and Cambridge along with some of the lesser colleges and famous schools were being protected to train a new generation of scholars.

Most surprising of all was that she understood that many of the derelict monasteries were being rebuilt and a new generation of monks recruited. These would act as hospitals and care for the sick and the dying as well as for liturgy and devotion.

The helicopter touched down in the road outside the main entrance of the Cathedral Church of St Peter, better known as York Minster. Alex noticed that the Bar Walls which surround the ancient city, built originally by the Romans, and which had fallen into some disrepair, had been rebuilt and re-connected. The gateways once open to traffic had been restored with new oak gates. Soldiers patrolled the walls all round the city, Military boats were patrolling the rivers Ouse and Foss that acted as the primary defence of the original old city.

The rotors stopped and the engines were switched off. The small party stepped out into the grey haze that often covers the Vale of York at this time of year.

Captain Davidson and two of his men accompanied them to their lodgings in the old Mayors House in St Helens Square.

"I hope these will be sufficient for you and your adjutant while I inform the King of your arrival. I'm sure he's looking forward to seeing you again."

"Thank you Captain Davidson, they'll be fine, though I hope I'm not staying long enough to find anything wrong with them"

Davidson laughed "Quite so M'am, I will be back to take you to my lord King as soon possible. Meanwhile I will leave my men here as your guard."

"Are we under guard Captain?"

"No no, not at all, you are free to wander the city though I will be back shortly I'm sure. Here are two passes for you both to confirm you are honoured guests of the King"

"A question for you Captain…I notice you and

others refer to him as 'my lord king' not 'his majesty'...is there a reason for that...I'm just curious"

"My lord King is a Plantagenet ma'm, he does not wish to use those grandiose titles invented by the French in later years...'Majesty', 'his Royal Highness'...all that sort of thing. He prefers the old titles of My Lord, and My Lord King as sufficient for his purposes. He believes the only majesty is the Majesty of God to whom he finds himself accountable."

Davidson left. Jerry helped himself to a large scotch. It was a preposterously grand room.

"Want one?"

"Yes...thanks."

"What's going on Alex?, ...I mean apart from the fact that the King of England sends a helicopter for you to have ...a cosy chat? ...Injections of something? .. Honoured guests of the King?... Etcetera...."

"Sit down Jerry"

Alex frowned, as if she was pondering the question and how to answer...which was exactly what she was doing.

She seemed to make up her mind and sat down in the armchair alongside Jerry.

She looked down at her feet. " Once I tell you your life will be in serious danger"

"My life has been in serious danger before, that's

what happens in the Army"

She hesitated a moment then began.

" Are you familiar with the name Rohypnol? Sometimes called 'roofies, or GHB anther drug with similar effects?"

"The date rape drug..yes , not familiar,.. but I've heard of it"

"One of the chemists at Porton Down, a man called Henry Bryant, supposedly a brilliant scientist, developed a weaponised version. Not Rohypnol, but something far more powerful, and in a vapour, or gas form. Spray it into a room and you only have to breathe in a few molecules, or a few land on your skin, and you are almost immediately put in some kind of altered state. He called them Hypnoids. It makes the victims open to commands, they can still function, but in a zombie like fashion."

She paused, still not looking at Jerry, but as if she were talking to herself.

"Gaunt and I were chosen to create a special operation, Psych Ops, along with Bryant and one of the MOD men. Gaunt and I were chosen because we are both fluent in Arabic languages, North African, Persian mainly. They needed a man and a woman. He was a Colonel and I a Captain in those days. So we were deployed east, Afghanistan and others. He would dress as a Muslim cleric, I as his Muslim woman. The full kit.

The Jihadi's were causing big casualties in our ranks, using remote villages to cache their arms. We, and the Americans would strike them with conventional weapons only for them to spring up somewhere else. There was little appetite for bombing mainly civilian targets, dirt-poor villagers, women and children.

Along came Bryant and his Hypnoids. Gaunt and I would walk into a village where there might be an arms cache. Prayer times. He would go into whatever building housed the Mosque, I would go into the women's section nearby. Spray the hypnoid. Ask them where the weapons were hidden. They'd tell us. We'd tell them to pray, that God wanted them to live in peace and not assist the violent, return to your God and your families and your fields. That sort of thing, while we found the dumps, drop a couple of charges, and leave as we came."

She paused again. Jerry stayed silent.

She looked up at the ceiling and smiled. "It was a huge success. It drove the Jihadi's mad, and no bloodshed. Like Rohypnol the victims recovered after about 24 hours but couldn't remember a thing, except they felt that God had spoken to them and they should live in peace, and without a whole bunch of weapons hidden in their ground. We must have hit about 50 villages in a month. IED's slowed to a standstill, RPG's, sniping, all became far less. No casualties on either side."

"The Americans were as bemused as the other side. How did we do it? For obvious reasons it was a closely guarded secret. After all, if anyone knew about the 'weapon' then precautions would be taken. Our advantage lost. Worse still if the other side got hold of it and one of their boffins figured out how to make their own version...."

"The Yanks put pressure on the UK Government, who told the MOD wallah that we had to share this with a select unit of the US Army, they wanted in"

"We did, and then a bunch of GI's decided it would be a good idea to use it for R&R purposes with a bunch of Afghan women. Had them in a tent stripping and dancing and fucking. They 'fried' them as they called it, from the joke 'Hypno-fried' which in typical US slang became ' we fryed 'em'. Somehow this got back to the US top brass in the Pentagon, and a few of their politicians. A giant shit-storm erupted. It must be stopped. It was Abu Ghraib all over again."

Alex looked back at her feet.

"So Gaunt and I were sent home, him to NATO liaison, me to Military Intelligence with instructions never to speak of it to anyone. Bryant was told to destroy all the stocks of hypnoid, and to keep quiet like us. The MOD wallah was given a cushy posting to wherever and told to keep his mouth shut. I guess the GI's were split up, sent home, and crapped on from a great height, deservedly so."

"The Jihadi's went back to blowing us up and we went back to shooting and bombing them with the US Hi-tech stuff."

"Meanwhile Bryant, who it turned out had developed the H for his own use with young girls, and then thought it a bright idea to offer it to the Army, was caught in a paedophile sting. He hadn't destroyed the stockpile, he continued using it, which led to a secret court-martial. They couldn't use just anyone as the stuff was still top-secret so I got drafted to act as Bryant's prosecutor in a very quiet court-martial. He was found guilty. I mean he was a serial paedophile with underage girls,...raped them, and this a man with young daughters of his own."

She paused and her mouth worked for a moment, then she mastered her feelings and carried on. Jerry remained silent.

"He was sentenced to life in a military prison. Solitary confinement."

" A few years later I found out that he'd been released...quietly. Disappeared. As far as I knew no-one knew where he'd gone."

Jerry frowned, "so the injections?"

"Well you can see the flaw in 'frying' a room full of people. You're standing in the middle of them and you'll get fried with everyone else, unless you have an antidote. The injection. It's a kind of neural inhibitor. Stops the chemicals from breaching the blood/brain barrier. Lasts for about 36 hours. "

" ..and you think we may at risk of being fried? ... here?"

"That tin you saw in my room, the one which had the syringes and the gas canister, I got it from Catterick on the visit I made, just before I met you. Catterick was our operations base for the Psych Ops program. The OC there told me that Gaunt had been there, that he'd taken the whole lot of the packs which were supposed to have been destroyed. Hundreds of them if I'm right."

" My guess is that Gaunt has used the hypnoids to make himself king, he's always been serious about him being a descendent of John of Gaunt, son of King Edward III, father of King Henry IV, no-one took him seriously. The H fell into his lap and I believe he's used it without anyone being aware of it's existence...except me, Henry Bryant, possibly an MOD wallah if he's still alive...and now I've told you ...you can see that he must keep this thing absolutely secret or he'll be found out. Simplest way would be to... remove... anyone who's aware of it., or 'fry them until they forget their own mother'...another Americanism of the time."

“Christ..so you think he’s brought you here to get rid of you...and now me?”

“I don’t know but unlikely. After all if he’d wanted me dead he could have had me shot at the farm, dumped in the slurry pond and no-one the wiser. No I don’t think he’s brought me here for that... unless I fuck up when I meet him...”

She smiled, “ but you know me....”

Footsteps at the door. The cheery Captain Davidson re-appeared.

“M’am, the King will see you now, please follow me, he’s holding court in the old Minster school, it’s a very fine house, used to be the headmasters residence before the war”

“The war?”

“Yes, the war, when we were attacked, you know the power cut, the nuclear strikes, three years ago next January, that war”

Jerry got up to join them “Not you I’m afraid, just the Colonel” Davidson smiled at Jerry then looked back to Alex.

“Have a wander about Jerry, I’ll catch up later “ said Alex.

Davidson led the way down the stairs and out into St Helens square, into Stonegate and across to the Minster. They walked around past the main entrance and then through the newly built gatehouse which was guarded by several soldiers.

The school building, a fine old Georgian house which had been added to over the years was hidden behind a gate. They passed through and then across the courtyard and up the steps into the reception hall.

“If you could just wait here a moment M’am I’ll tell the King that you’re here” Davidson smiled and disappeared through a set of doors.

Rheinhart stared out of the window that looked onto the west wall of the great cathedral. She became aware that someone had opened a door behind her.

“So pleased to meet you Colonel Rheinhart” the voice was soft but well mannered. She turned to face the man standing across the hall. He was dressed in a naval uniform but it was black or an extremely deep shade of blue. He had Commander’s stripes on his sleeves. His hair and beard were grey. He wore a black skull cap, a yarmulke, on the back of his head. He stood with a slight lopsided stoop and leant on a stick. He wore a silver ring on his right hand. His right leg was not straight.

“Uganda....car bomb...long time ago.....still got bits of shrapnel in there” he tapped his leg. “aches a lot but I manage....William Levine...I’m the King’s lawyer”

“Pleased to meet you...Commander Levine “ Alex held out her hand. They shook hands.

"The King has graciously bestowed on me the title of Lord High Chancellor, but 'Commander Levine', or Chancellor Levine' ...' or 'Bloody Levine'...I answer to them all."

"What does a Chancellor do?"

"Oh ...I'm all over the shop....I administer the realm on behalf of the King, keep the Dukes and the assorted aristocracy in line, ...and a bit of intelligence work"

"You must be exhausted..."

"Ha.." he laughed "I can almost see what the King sees in you"

"Almost?"

"Well, I do wonder sometimes why he holds you in such high esteem."

It was said without apparent malice. A genuine question. Something she had wondered herself.

"Forgive the straight talking Colonel..."

"Retired Colonel"

"Of course....I'm ex-naval intelligence...sort of thing we old spooks ponder from time to time... you yourself were in military intelligence?...I wonder that we never met?"

"Not that I recall"

"I served the King in his Nato days, had quite a few dealings with your spooks...came across your name of course but ...ah well...one of those things I suppose. How did you meet him?"

"We're old comrades in arms...." She didn't finish

her sentence as Captain Davidson re-appeared.

"This way M'am"

Rheinhart nodded to Levine who smiled and nodded back then turned away to where he had come from.

Davidson held open the door to a large oak panelled room containing a long oak table and chairs beyond which was a large mahogany desk where sat Edward Gaunt, Edward IX, King of England. His back to the two large bow fronted windows and the red and white flag of St George draped from an upright stand in front of one of the windows. Next to it was another flag, a prowling black lion on a yellow background. From the window some sunlight filtering through from above.

There was a brooding menace that emanated from the large bulk of his figure even while he sat. His head was down. He was dressed in the uniform of a Fleet Admiral, navy blue coat with the gold 'scrambled egg' on his sleeves and collar. His shirt was white and he had on a dark maroon tie. His hair was long, past his ears, not quite on the collar, a dark mane of hair like the malignant lion on the flag. His dark brown beard was neatly trimmed with a handful of grey mixed in. His skin was as tanned as if it were only yesterday that he had left the deserts of Afghanistan, his large tanned hands had a large gold signet ring on his middle finger. He held a Mont Blanc fountain pen .

It was maybe fifteen years ago that she had last seen him. Neither of them had aged much in that time.

A secretary stood at his side, slightly behind the king.

Alex walked past the oak table and stood in front of the desk.

“Hello Edward”

Gaunt was writing, scratching away with the fountain pen,

“It’s usual in these circumstances to start with ‘my Lord King’ and then ‘my Lord’, or ‘Sire’ thereafter”, Gaunt continued scratching words with his pen without looking up at Alex.

“But as we are old comrades in arms I suppose you can use my Christian name.”

He signed something and handed the paper to his secretary “Get that off to Northumberland and Normandy at once will you”

The secretary bowed, “My lord”.

Gaunt looked up.

Alex looked him in the eye “ It’s good to see you again Ed….”

“What were you doing at Catterick?” Gaunt cut across Alex’s sentence.

He sat forward looking at her with a steely blue grey eye. The secretary shuffled past and closed the door as he left.

"Supplies"

"I thought you were all self sufficient on your little.... smallholding?"

"Difficult to grow coffee, tea, sugar, rice, in Cumberland"

"Sub machine guns and assorted weaponry no doubt too?"

"Why have you brought me h....". He cut across her again

"Where is Henry Bryant?"

"I have no idea"

"His wife told you nothing?"

"She doesn't know either, she says she hasn't heard from him since he escaped from jail"

"I..." but again he cut her off.

"Roll up your sleeve Colonel"

Gaunt got up. His size had not diminished since they had last met and the air of menace that he exuded remained. He blocked out the light from one of the windows as he came round the desk to stand in front of Alex. He walked stiffly as if his great tree trunk legs would not bend properly.

She held his eye but then looked down at her sleeve, unbuttoned the cuff and pulled her sleeve back.

Gaunt bent slightly and looked at her arm. The small bruise where the needle had been.

He turned and went back around the desk to sit. "Bloody quartermasters."

"They always keep something back. How many did he give you?"

"Just the one pack, I imagine your men have found it by now"

"There was no need for it you know, if I'd wanted to harm you I would have done it at your farm, ... but you've worked that out already."

"That is why I have invited you here.....because you're smart...and you understand what's at stake...and because of your history."

"My history?"

"I want you to be my Queen."

"Have you lost your fucking mind Edward !"

"Not at all" he smiled at her, "My Queen ...of Africa....All of it.

...Accountable solely to me.....Headquartered in Rhodesia.

...I need someone I can trust down there. ...sit down Alex.

Already I have the South African army marching north. Establishing camps. General Voebeck... you know him. Clearing up. You would have a whole army to manage as well as appointing civilian governors to run the territories day to day.... and of course you would have.... the weapon.

...You could reclaim your family's farm and lands.... Stolen from you.

...Vengeance on those who killed your father,

raped and killed your mother, raped you and killed your sister and all your friends and staff. All those men who gang raped you on the boat to England."

Alex stood up "How the fuck do you know all that?!" her eyes bright, her nostrils flared in anger.

"Because you told me" he said softly with a smile for the first time.

"I've never told anyone!" her voice still sharp and loud with anger.

"You were very drunk at the time, and the tattoo of course.....you told me once."

"I...I.."

Alex sat back down. Punctured. She looked down at her hands and held them. Then she mastered herself and looked up at his face. He was looking at her kindly. He knew that he had shocked her. But that was his way, and it was the truth. And she knew it.

"Of course you will need time to consider it...."

There was a knock on the door. One of the officers stepped in. Gaunt looked up.

"Excuse me Sire....the Archbishop, The Dukes, and the Chancellor of the Exchequer are here sir."

" Take them into the drawing room, get Levine in there, and let them know I'll join them in a moment,"

He turned back to Alex.

“Think about it....meanwhile join me tonight at the service in the Cathedral, eight-o-clock. You can meet a few of the senior members of the Court afterwards. They know who you are.”

Alex said nothing as Gaunt stood up.

She stood up without looking at him.

“Why did you do it Edward.....”

“That too if we must... though I’m sure you’ve already worked that one out ....eight o clock tonight....oh and one more small thing ... Bryant’s wife is dead...hanged herself....perhaps you knew?”

Gaunt held out his hand, not as a handshake but to point her to the door. She walked out ahead of him where Captain Davidson was waiting. “I’ll take you back to your quarters Colonel.”

Alex felt sick.

Not because she'd just been interrogated by the self appointed 'King of England', not because she had been asked by the King to become his 'Queen of Africa', not because she had just been told that Stephanie Bryant had hanged herself, or that she had been invited to meet the king's men who were now running the country.

No.

Because Gaunt had known about her defining moment as a person. Way back across the years. She had never been that drunk, and even if she had been this incident was so buried in her conscience. What made her who she is. What had been her driving force. How she saw herself. It was no-one's business but her own. It was buried deep, never to be revealed. Never mind the psychologists…'talk about it' they would say. But she would never talk about it. It was still, and always would be something raw. What she was before had been utterly shattered like a glass vase. Now she was made of steel. Rebuilt from the ground up. There was no glass in the construction, and in that steel vault, a windowless room which could be entered only by her own ghost. Locked and put away in her mind.

Yet somehow this had been verbalised by the man in front of her. Something no-one else had ever done...or known. Except her. Now some sort of public knowledge.

What else did he know?

She was clutching her hands and staring down at the floor when Jerry returned.

“Just been to one of the Inns with a few of the lads, brothels all over the pla....blimey Alex you look as white as a sheet...what happened?”

She looked up, ignored the question “We’re going to church at eight, you’ll get to meet the king.”

The Cathedral was full of people when Alex and Jerry arrived.

She slipped into one of the rows of chairs at the back to watch proceedings. There were many monks in dark brown habits standing or sitting towards the front along with men who Alex surmised were soldiers. There were one or two women but they were far outnumbered by the men. In the nave there was a choir made up of men and young boys who were singing. She recognised Palestrina's Nunc Dimittis quarti which echoed beautifully around the great walls and ceiling arches of the mighty cathedral. A prayer for compline at the end of the day. This was followed by a Marenzio Magnificat toni, and then a Stanford magnificat.

Gaunt was kneeling at the foot of the nave. She recognised his great size even when he knelt. In front of him a monk dressed as the others except his robe was white and he had a red and gold stole around his neck which hung down at the front. His head was bare but Alex guessed that this was the Archbishop.

As Gaunt lifted his head in response to something said to him by the archbishop she noticed he was wearing a small simple gold crown on his head.

He was dressed in a dark navy uniform accompanied by gold braid.

Gaunt rose to stand then moved to the side as

several equally finely dressed men rose from the front row seats and knelt in a line in front of the archbishop.

"Those are the Dukes" a voice said quietly from behind her. She turned her head sideways and was met with a pleasant looking man with sparkling eyes and fine teeth.

"I'm Major Sykes, good to meet you Colonel" his accent Edinburgh Scottish.

The major slid round the row and came to sit beside her. Jerry looked round but didn't move.

"Top chain of command" he continued "the Duke of Northumbria who also has control of Scotland and the Isles, on the left; then the Duke of Mercia who covers everything from Yorkshire down to Hertfordshire, and Wales to Anglia; The Duke of Wessex who controls the south; the Duke of Ireland for all of Ireland, and the First Sea Lord, who controls all the waters around Britain. The fellow on the right hand side is the Lord Chancellor of the Exchequer. The tax man. ...and bloody Chancellor Levine his spymaster... All Gaunt's men from earlier service. Like you."

"....and you major? What's your role in all this?"

" Oh I'm just one of many...passed over for promotion...just when I had joined the old Queen's regiment...now I'm just a major in the King's Own Highlanders."

Alex looked at the kilt, "Black Watch ?"

"Aye " his accent becoming more Scots " you

know your tartans then...but we're all now part of one regiment. Loyal to the Crown...whichever one it might be..." he let his voice trail away.

"And you Colonel, are you one of this fellow's women?" Sykes waved his hand vaguely towards the nave, " Or are you still with the old Queen's family?"

"Neither Major, I'm a retired Colonel, now a small farmer in Westmoreland, and as I understand it the old Queen's family are all dead."

"Well now, not all of them.." He stopped and looked at Alex.

" There are a couple of young heirs that would be very pleased if the renowned Colonel Rheinhart was to help them..."

" You mean a challenge to all this? "she waved her hand forwards.

"No challenge...not as yet anyway, they're way too young, but in time who knows?"

This conversation was becoming dangerous. Was this some sort of test laid on by Gaunt?. Levine?

The service had now reached the rest of the congregation who began to move forward to take communion.

Alex decided it was time to leave.

"Well Major I must be going" she said and quickly stood up and walked away. Jerry followed and they left via the side door and out into the dark evening air.

“What was that all about? “ Jerry asked Alex

“Not sure, but I think I’ve made my decision and tomorrow we’re heading back to the farm.”

Jerry remained silent.

They set off in the dark to return to their lodgings. As they turned into Stonegate two men came out of the shadows. There was a flash of a steel blade. Her training kicked in immediately as she swept her left arm outward to block the knife arm. At the same time she swept the heel of her palm up to connect with the man’s chin, knocking him backwards. The knife clattered to the ground. She saw Jerry head butt the other man. Both men were silent but began to get up, and to recover the knife.

Assassins.

Alex chopped the lead man in the side of his neck, temporarily disabling him again then grabbed the knife from the street and ran it straight through his throat. The man stared for a second before blood poured out of his mouth and he went down dead.

She turned to see Jerry breaking the neck of the accomplice with a quick twist of the man’s head from behind.

It had all happened within 20 seconds.

There was a side alley with some rubbish piled up. Alex grabbed one of the men’s collar and dragged his body into the alley. Jerry did the same with the other and then they covered them with some of the rubbish.

They both stood in the doorway in the alley to get their breath back.

“What the fuck?” Jerry was the first to speak. “Who wants us dead?”

“Gaunt. We’re getting out of here now”

“I had a scout about this afternoon.” Said Jerry “Quickest way out is by the river, and there’s a jetty behind our lodgings with a fast boat moored there…hopefully still there.”

They set off down Stonegate keeping to the shadows.

Two soldiers were guarding the entrance to the house. Alex sauntered over to them with a smile. The two men watched her but didn’t make any sharp movements.

“Hello lads, just getting some….” And at that moment she launched her bent elbow into the side of one of the guard’s head. He went down without a sound and before the other could react she swung a straight chop to the side of his neck and he followed the other to the floor.

They quickly dragged the men through the open door to the lodgings and kicked the door shut. Alex grabbed a curtain from the window and tied it round the man’s head before whacking him again, this time on the top of his skull. Knocked out but not dead. Jerry rolled the other prone form into the loose carpet in the hall. Tied it with a cord from one of the curtains, and shoved a screwed up handkerchief into the man's mouth before tying a scarf round his head to hold it in place.

Jerry picked up both semi automatics and threw one to Alex. "This way"

They slipped out of the rear door of the house that backed onto the river, onto a wooden jetty. A motorboat was moored at the end. Both jumped into it. Alex, found the starter switch and turned it. Clearly there was no need for a key as the engine fired up at once. Jerry unhooked the stern and bow sheets and Alex backed the boat into the river.

A patrol boat was coming under Lendal bridge as Alex pushed the throttle forward and the boat took off fast downstream.

The crew of the patrol boat , not quite knowing what was going on set off after them but the motorboat was fast and they were quickly away under the bridges and out of the town waters with the patrol boat lagging behind, but now gaining speed.

About a mile ahead they rounded the bend in the river where the Archbishop's palace lay. A further patrol boat was moored there and when the crew saw the motor boat race past, and then the patrol boat coming up fast behind it they realised this must be a chase so set off after them along with the first patrol boat.

There was no moon and the banks were dark but Alex's eyes had adjusted quickly to the low light.

They rounded another bend at full throttle. Jerry was grabbing some tools from a locker and stuffing them into his trouser pockets.

"What are you doing?" Alex shouted over the roar of the engine.

"When we get to the next bend I'm going to roll off the side, you keep going."

"What?"

"Just keep going and then when I've cleared them behind us come back for me.... Here around this bend."

With that Jerry lay down on the starboard edge of the boat, feet facing forward, and as they rounded the bend, for a moment out of sight of the pursuit boats, Jerry rolled into the water and disappeared under.

The weight of the tools pulled him down, but upright and he raised the semi automatic upwards. In the dark water of the river, above his head, he could clearly see the keel and wake of the pursuit boat coming towards him as he sank lower.

As the boat passed over him he hit the trigger and bullets sprayed upwards and out of the water straight through the patrol boat's hull, rupturing the fuel tank which exploded in a ball of flame. As the second boat came into view and with his lungs fit to burst he fired again this time at an angle as the second boat tried to avoid the flames spread out on the water from the petrol fire.

It was enough to hole the boat which began to take on water.

Jerry dropped the gun which sank to the bottom, he pulled out as many of the tools as fast as he could and swam upwards. He broke the surface and gulped in wonderful air.

There were other men in the water, along with small pools of fire from the petrol tank of the first boat. He dived underwater again and swam a short way down stream.

When he re-surfaced the other men were scrambling towards the bank with much shouting.

He looked downstream and began to swim again. Alex had turned the motorboat around and was heading back to Jerry. She saw him in the water at the last moment and swung the boat to a stop. Jerry grabbed the side and Alex heaved him over the port gunwale. He flopped down into the base of the cockpit soaking the wooden boards as his clothes drained out.

"Let's go Alex" he said at which she swung the boat back downstream and pushed the throttle forward.

It was a black night and Alex was trying to give them some distance before the inevitable pursuit by other boats so she continued at full throttle before she could find somewhere to get off the river and disappear into the landscape.

What she didn't know was that ahead of her was Naburn lock, a large stonebuilt weir with a couple of locks on the port side, where the Ouse met the tidal Ouse which then flowed into the Humber estuary many miles ahead.

The rain fed river at Naburn flowed over the weir. Warning signs were on the banks but unlit and unnoticed. As a final step there was a steel chain stretched across the river a few yards back from the edge of the weir but this was invisible in the dark.

They hit the chain at full speed. The chain ripped through the hull of the boat which flipped up and over, throwing Alex and Jerry high in the air before crashing down onto the sloping stones over which the river cascaded.

The remains of the boat came down on top of Jerry, and part of it hit Alex on the head knocking her out. The tide was out so she ended up at the bottom of the slope in loose mud from the river bed. Jerry managed to get out from under the smashed boat but his arm was broken and he was dizzy with the pain. He managed to slide down the slope and pulled Alex onto her back before she suffocated. Then everything went black.

XVI
Life is Changed

Alex woke up in a bed, in the lodgings, in York.

She couldn't focus her eyes for a moment. Someone was in the room, a figure standing at the window. A large shadow. She tried to open her eyes more but was rewarded with a piercing pain in her head. She groaned. The figure turned to look at her.

"Back in the land of the living I see"

Gaunt.

Alex tried to focus again, the pain was strong but her focus became more clear.

"My men fished you out of the river, at least the ones your sergeant hadn't killed or wounded. He's a clever man, brave too, and seemingly dedicated to protect you from evil King Edward." There was no humour in his voice.

"Where is he?"

"He's alive and well. Just a broken arm and some nasty bruises. He's already up and about. But you took a nasty cut to the head. But you were lucky otherwise. Just a few bruises and minor cuts."

"Why am I not dead?"

Gaunt considered the question.

"Because you've got it wrong Alex....You come to the cathedral, but then Major Sykes stops by for a chat. Probably tried to recruit you to 'the cause', so you leave and then two men come to kill you, unsuccessfully as it turns out. We found their bodies. So you think I gave the order and it's time to leave. But you're wrong. As I said to you before if I'd wanted you dead you'd be rotting somewhere in.....Westmoreland. I didn't invite you here to kill you. You know what I want from you."

"You know about Sykes?"

Gaunt shrugged "He's on the radar. I've let him run about to see what happens. Unfortunate that you got tangled up in his nets. I know all about Major Sykes, he's got a couple of the old German royal babies stashed away somewhere up north. Trying to recruit a loyal army for them. Strange that it should be a Scot"

Alex sat up in bed. She felt dizzy. She felt the bandage round her head.

"So Colonel Rheinhart, my offer still stands for now, what do you say?"

She looked straight at Gaunt.

"Why did you do it Edward?"

Gaunt was silent for a moment.

"Because I could,...because I have an appetite for war....because I wished to reclaim my ancestral homelands...because I looked into the Abyss.....and saw the monster"

"But why Edward?

Gaunt paused, his head lowered in thought.

"We have taken so much for granted. We flick a switch and there is light, or heat, or power. We turn a tap and there is clean, cold and hot water. We go to a supermarket and we can buy every possible type of food.
No-one wonders what would happen if this were to stop.

We merrily continue to grow our population despite knowing that we cannot produce enough food for ourselves to feed even half the population, nor the type of food, nor any consideration there might be a bad harvest...or an outbreak of disease in feed animals....or that the land may simply collapse from overuse.

And yet history, in every civilisation, is littered with starvation and death, caused by these factors. Populations that grow too large who cannot produce enough food to feed them. Corruption becomes rife. "

"But the enormous murder you have committed, how can you justify that?"

Gaunt studied the question.

"Who will miss them?"

"You've poisoned the cities across the globe, and you've murdered millions of people"

"There's no shortage of shit-holes around the world. Nothing short of a thermo-nuclear clean will do."

He looked down, his voice taking on a lower, more thoughtful tone.

"There is only death, I take what is mine to take. I have simply changed the time that they die. Their time has stopped. I ask again, 'who will miss them?"

He paused .

"The human population has hardly been dented so far. ...fifteen billion...down to perhaps twelve billion? ...If that....

....still far too many to be sustainable. One billion humans are quite enough ...and I'll continue to remove all the 'do-gooders'...they've done more damage than anyone."

"There is more to come.... War, radiation, starvation, disease, pestilence, cold, lack of sanitation, decaying corpses, rats, packs of wild dogs, and little or no food. ...

" The West...western culture was dying fast, law and order all but gone save for the very powerful, or the very wealthy. Civilisation itself was eating itself alive along with everything on the planet. I have the means and the opportunity to bring it to an end relatively quickly...from which a new realm can be built....a new Plantagenet realm."

"But all these lords...the aristocracy...you're just replacing one rotten system for another?"

"Inequality of wealth and power is an unavoidable aspect of human life. It is right that individuals to do what they could to help themselves and their families to succeed, and to help others in need. But the great fortunes of aristocrats are among the fundamental guarantees of the social order itself. Their capital is landed, permanent and embedded in particular communities, not temporary or moveable.

But all power brings with it responsibility and obligations .so I expect them to be virtuous in their public mindedness and independent minded in their decisions. A high public expectation of virtue is on people of property and influence which arises from their wealth and station. Sloppiness, laziness, selfishness and lack of responsibility will be made accountable. They have a duty of service to the people and to the realm. I defend aristocratic power and duty as an anchor of the social order. They are the ancient oaks that shelter and shade to support the growth of new men and new fortunes some of which may put down roots of their own.

This is our constitution which binds the King, the aristocracy and the common peoples together. I expect courtesy and public responsibility, especially towards women, and the literacy, learning and charitable ethos of the church. To be observed in both the spirit and the reality."

"I'm going back to my farm Edward, I'm retired. I shouldn't have come here."

"There is no 'nice' way to depopulate the planet... death is the only tool for it...The offer remains on the table for now. I'll wait to hear from you, just don't take too long, I won't wait forever. Goodbye Alex"

Gaunt left. A nurse came straight in to start fussing with the dressing.

Two days later she was up and about. Jerry was standing outside. He looked a little sheepish.

"I'm staying here Alex" he said. "It's been good being back with the lads. They've suggested a Captaincy for me. My own company. Hope you understand."

"I do Jerry, and I want to thank you for everything you've done. I hope our paths cross again sometime"

She took one of the Army Land Rovers. She didn't fancy the Chinook, might be thrown out of it on the way over the Pennines.

They let her through the main gates of the fortified city and she headed out towards the A1. There was probably a tracker somewhere on the vehicle but it didn't matter.

She headed up towards Scotch Corner to take the A66 back west, but as she drove past the

Catterick turn-off she stopped. Something was nagging her at the back of her mind. Where was Henry Bryant? If Gaunt was reliant on the hypnoid?. Unless he had other chemists who had reverse engineered it?

She turned off towards the base, but headed for the old married quarters. She pulled up in front of the Bryant house. It was boarded up. Someone had scrawled SCUM on the boards.

She found a screwdriver and levered off the boarding that covered the kitchen door at the back of the house. The boards had not been put on the upstairs windows, which allowed some light into the gloom.

The place smelled of cat piss and mould. All the furniture and belongings of the Bryant's remained in situ.

A frayed rope dangled down from the stairwell. A sad reminder of Stephanie Bryant.

She found what she was looking for in one of the wardrobes upstairs in one of the bedrooms. A box of old family photographs. Pictures from happier times. Holidays with the girls at a young age. She flicked through the pages of several of the albums when she found the link.

There were a series of photos of a past holiday in Algeria. Someone had written 'Our Holiday Home' underneath a picture of the family sitting in the garden of a small villa. Another was a picture of Henry and Stephanie with an old man dressed in traditional Algerian robes outside the villa. Underneath was written ' Our Friend, The Moor'.

Alex inhaled sharply. She whispered to herself 'Gone to stay with the Moors'.

"So she knew all along….."

She searched more of the pictures until she found a name 'Angouri', the name of the village .

There were several pictures of the same villa, and a lake with beaches over a number of years as the girls grew up.

She got back in the Land Rover and drove back to the A1 then across the moors towards Westmoreland, to her piece of England, and her home. Away from the madness.

But there was bad news.

Cedric had died. He was old and had taken on too much with his new flock.

Alex stood by his grave in the old churchyard. The rain beat down on the freshly dug earth. She laid a single flower on his grave.

Nor was Colette well. She'd been attacked by a pack of feral dogs which had followed the people from the camp. Old domestic pets that had returned to the wild, led by a large German Shepherd which had badly mauled her before the villagers managed to beat it off.

Alex sat by her bed.

"Poor Cedric….he wanted the village to come

back to life but really, at over eighty, he tried too hard to make these people welcome. He was quite confused in the end, particularly when some monks arrived to stay with him and run the church. He just dropped down dead as he was conducting an evening service for the new arrivals. It was all too much for an old man."

"You need antibiotics"

"I know, but they're all gone, only morphine for the pain now. Plenty of that I understand. New regime. No more medical interventions for people of my age. Just a shot of morphine to ease the pain ....and the passing."

"You're tough Colette, you'll pull through."

But she didn't.

Alex buried her in the churchyard near Cedric and his wife.

The monks took up residence in the Church.

More people arrived in Rawston. The pub re-opened. The village sprang back to life as Cedric had once hoped it would. But it wasn't hers anymore. The farming became a chore rather than a pleasure. She thought about the sea again. Recover the boat and sail away, but to where? The world had been wholly changed.

She was annoyed with Gaunt, but on the other hand he had offered her something that no-one else could. She could go home. But it came at a huge price.

She found Spears and told him to arrange for her

to meet the King.

"He's in Alnick Castle at the moment. Tours round you know. I'll send a message and they'll come for you"

"Tell him I'll make my own way thanks"

She had become good friends with the two women who had set up school and the cookhouse.

"I'd like you to take over the farm, and the farmhouse. Bring your families. Take no shit from anyone."

They laughed, and gladly accepted. She joined them, their family and children, and a few of the new farm hands for a final dinner in the old farmhouse. She didn't know if, or when she'd be back.

She packed her travelling trunk. She noticed that the green tin H435 had gone. She loaded the trunk into the Landy along with a several supplies she thought she would need then drove out of the farm and out of Rawston. She didn't look back.

She took the long road over to Northumberland. She didn't want to pass too close to Newcastle, heaven knows what the cities are like now, she thought. Cholera and typhoid had established itself in all the cities. Piles of unclaimed bodies rotted where they lay.

Gaunt was staying at the traditional seat of the Duke of Northumberland. Not the old Norman family who had moved out. No doubt 'fried' for the purposes.

She met the others. Those that had been pointed out by Sykes back at York Minster. The Court of King Edward IX. She knew a few of them. Men who had served, mainly Captains and Lieutenant Colonels. Gaunt's men. By his side, leaning heavily on his stick, William Levine. He nodded courteously at Alex with a thin smile

Gaunt was holding court with several of them, and a surprise for Alex.

"Alex, I think you remember Lieutenant Colonel Simon Brevard...?"

A tall black American with a southern accent came over to where Gaunt and Rheinhart stood.

"Hello again Alex, Simon Brevard, long time"

"Hello Simon, yes, a long time, how could I forget, what became of all your GI's?"

"Well Alex, too long a story for here" he said , his eyes narrowing slightly, "suffice to say the King and I have remained in regular contact over the years since then.."

Gaunt interrupted " Simon is our new First Senator of the CCSA, the Colonial Confederate States of the Americas."

Brevard bowed slightly. "Happy to be of service my Lord King"

Gaunt continued " I've taken back control with the help of First Senator Brevard, all of it...North and South America, and now Simon, Alex has agreed to become Colonial Governor and Lord Lieutenant of all Africa."

"Well, congratulations Alex, you've got a shit-hole to sort out. Corruption, disease, the lot..."

"She's appointed to clean it up" Said Gaunt "..and she will."

"Let me introduce you to the Duke of Northumbria..."

Later that evening...

"Let me be clear" Said Gaunt

"I am appointing you as my Queen of Africa. Lord Lieutenant of the continent of Africa. Just as I have appointed these Dukes to manage affairs in Britain, or the Princes in Europe, or the Czars in Eurasia, the Sultans and Emperors in the East, and the Senators in the Americas....you are my representative. The title doesn't matter. Call yourself Prime Minister if you wish. You can appoint as many tribal Chiefs as you need, and they can appoint their officials.

You have complete discretion to organise things as you see fit and in accordance with local customs. My only command is that you are loyal to me and to the Crown of England, and all that that represents. Here are your letters of Royal Warrant. Your delegated authority from the Crown."

Gaunt pointed out of the window of the castle.

"There's your transport, the Captain will organise your support when you get to the port"

She looked out and saw a Royal Navy frigate standing off the coast about a mile out to sea.

"No, I'll be going under my own steam Edward, sail actually, I'll take my own boat."

Gaunt looked at her for a moment.

"It's not safe"

"Safe? Nowhere's safe anymore, I'll be just fine"

She stood square on to him and looked him in the eye.

"If you want me in Africa, I'll make my own way, I've done it before"

Gaunt remained silent but in the end he waved his hand and sighed

"Very well"

"I'd like to borrow Sergeant Bradman to help crew the boat"

"Very well I'll make him available"

Alex walked past one of the lower castle rooms where she saw Levine talking to a large man with a savage face. Levine noticed Alex and nodded to her. The large man turned to look. He looked like the gamekeeper....probably was. She nodded back at Levine and walked on.

Levine spoke quietly to the 'gamekeeper'.

"Scarman, I want you to have a dig around Porton Down, see what you can find out about any connection between our wonderful King...

either the place or someone who worked there, and also if there's any mention of the Rheinhart woman?"

"Porton's a hole in the ground..."

Levine paused and smiled as if addressing a child.
"The trouble with you Scarman is you think too much ...for a soldier...I know Porton's a hole in the ground....have a sniff around the camps, the gossip in the taverns..."

"Why don't you just ask some of the scientists that went off to the Cheviots...before the war"

Levine looked up, why was he surprised that Scarman knew about the Cheviots....of course... he's a local boy...the gossip...exactly why I need him to do some digging...people will know him, talk to him...

"Because...that would be too obvious...I don't want this to get back to his lordship...he doesn't like people asking awkward questions..."

"Here's your purse" Levine leaned across his desk and handed him a small cloth bag containing some gold and silver coins..."Go.."

Scarman looked in the bag, smiled, rose from his chair, grinned and nodded to Levine before leaving the room.

Davidson entered....

“Mr Foxton here for you sir...”

“Show him in.”

“Ah Foxton...what news?”

XVII
Boat Tales

Alex took the Land Rover back down to York and picked up Jerry from the city before heading west.

She drove straight over to the coast, to old Tom's boatyard.

They climbed out of the car and were met by Tom's daughter June. The one who had met Alex a few years ago when she bought the farm.

"Hello Alex, good to see you again"

Alex introduced Jerry.

Her boat was the only one in the water.

"Dad's out fishing at the moment, waiting for the tide before he can get back."

Alex saw that the lock gates were shut.

"You got my message then"

"Yes, a Captain Spears turned up with some men and a drum of diesel. So we were able to re-fuel her and what was spare went in the boat-lift to crane it in. As you can see all the others are out of the water. The owners haven't been back so I guess they're gone."

June looked sad but then forced a smile.

"Come on in and have a cup of tea while we wait for the tide. Its acorn tea I'm afraid, but you get used to the taste eventually."

"Does he go out fishing quite a lot? " said Jerry

"Well we've survived on it really. We swap some

of it for a bit of lamb, or some potatoes and veggies. The kids hate it but that's all there is these days and its food so...oh we also do a bit of shrimp from the bay, and some cockles, you know, its enough to get by. We've adapted some of the wind turbines and the solar panels off the boats to get a bit of electricity. Dad has a few big old submarine batteries that we can charge up and that gives us some electric light. We're not in too bad a position really compared to some I suppose...."

She tailed off.

Two children, aged about nine or ten came out of one of the huts.

"We've all moved here together. Our house in town was stripped bare by looters early on. People desperate for anything, either to eat or to burn. So we all came here and my husband and Dad keep a watch out for any trouble. But since the camp was set up a few miles away things have quietened down a lot. We trade a bit of fish for their taxes, and some of them come down and help out with the boat, or bring some diesel when it's available."

"Where are you headed?"

Jerry looked at Alex.

"We're going south to Africa"

"Wow, it'll be so much warmer there"

"Well not always, the winters are pretty cold actually but I have some connection with the place so that's where we're going."

"And the two of you...are you...?"

Alex kept a straight face. "Jerry and I are good friends" and she smiled at Jerry who returned the courtesy.

"Sorry, none of my business really...Ah I think the tide's coming in...it comes in pretty fast as you know...I'll get to the lock gates"

They all stepped out into the boatyard and June went down the quay to operate the gates by hand.

Out to sea they could see a small wooden fishing boat with a mast and a red sail which was heading into the Lune estuary.

After a time it sailed in through the open lock gates and Jerry and Alex helped secure it to the dock.

Tom came up and out of the boat pretty nimbly for a man who must be over seventy.

"Hello Colo...er Alex, nice to see you again...just about the only one who's come back for their boat...you remember June? "

"Hello Tom, nice to see you too, caught some fish?"

"Aye, a few good mackerel and some bream and some bass, here have a couple to take with you"

"That's good of you Tom, I don't want you or your family going hungry."

"We're alright ...Colonel..er Alex...so you're off

to Africa eh?...that captain said you were going down there is that right?"

"Yes that's right, and it'll be good to get back on the water"

"Well, weather's good at the moment but watch out for that Bay of Biscay, very tricky water... but then what am I saying, you've been all over haven't you, an old hand eh?"

Tom gave then a smile with his increasingly toothless mouth.

"...and someone to keep you company too I see"

Alex introduced Jerry as Sergeant Bradman.

"Well that's good to know, anyways tide's in so you'll want to be away I'm sure...come back when you're done though, we'll still be here. Come on June get the boys and help me unload this fish, get it in the smoker eh?"

"And we need to get our stuff out of the Landy" said Alex. She and Jerry transferred their bags and a load of salted hams, beef, wheels of cheese, tea, coffee beans, bottles of whisky and rum, and assorted food into the boat along with the shotguns, a couple of fishing rods, some odd looking green tins. She checked the lockers and found the long life tins of food untouched. Tom must have known they were there but not one was missing. She checked the fuel and water tanks, all full.

She spent an hour or more checking all the boat's equipment. Once you're at sea if anything goes wrong it's too late. The batteries were self-charging from the wind turbine and solar panel and were full. The desalination plant was working fine. In fact the boat had never been in better shape. She fired up the engine to test it. It started first time. The generator lit up all the lights. She switched off everything and killed the engine once she was sure it was working fine and the cooling system was ok.

The satnav had no satellite, nor were there any radio signals to triangulate which meant she would be navigating with the sextant, the compass, the sun and stars, and the boat's clock.

"I'm leaving the Landy here Tom. If you want to use it that's fine, but you'll need to put some diesel in it."

They left Tom and his family, Jerry pulled up the sail, Alex swung the boat round and they headed out of the gates, into the tidal Lune, headed west, out into the Irish Sea, then south into the Atlantic.

"So we're good friends are we?" Jerry grinned at Alex

"That we are ..Sergeant," she emphasised the 'sergeant'

"Aye, aye Captain" Jerry grinned again and Alex let slip a small smile.

The weather turned nasty after three days. The swell grew and the waves crashed onto the deck. The wind came up from the south-west making them tack and gybe, reefing the head sail which was on a roller, and slab reefing the mainsail. It was proper sailing but hard work.

The Bay of Biscay lived up to its reputation and so Alex took the boat into one of the small ports along the French coast after a week so they could rest for a while. They were making good progress and there was no need to rush. Alex checked the Geiger counter every so often but the readings remained normal.

They ate well and found the locals were happy to trade some ham for a few bottles of good red wine.

Her French was good so she chatted to the locals and discovered that 'le Roi Eduard' had already made his presence felt. He had appointed a Duke of Aquitaine and assorted Mayors to oversee the west coast. The locals didn't seem to mind. Apart from the lack of electricity, life continued as it always did in the French coastal countryside. Plenty of good farming across the region and a reduction in population meant there was plenty of food and wine. In fact many preferred the arrangements as they now stood, without 'les politiques'.

In fact they didn't consider Edward to be an English king at all. He was an Angevin king and they had the planta genista to prove it.

After a good meal and a few drinks with the locals the pair staggered back to the boat for the evening. The weather had cleared and it was moderately warm.

Jerry leant down and swept some of Alex's hair that had fallen across her face. They looked at each other. Jerry attempted a kiss.

Alex pulled away.

"No…I can't, I'm sorry, it's not you, it's me, …"

Jerry smiled at her. "I know you have a thing about men Alex, I'm guessing there was some trouble a long time ago?…but that was then and you're a fine looking woman,....at least with the wine and all that…" he grinned and approached again.

"It's …I can explain,"

"You don't have to, I just thought you might like to fuck, but it's okay, I'm not upset or anything… it's just we're very good friends…" he grinned again.

"I'm sorry Jerry, I just can't.." She turned away.

"I was gang raped when I was fourteen by the men who killed my family and friends. I escaped and found a boat out of Angola that was heading for England. But they had me too, paying for my passage they said.

By the time I got to Portsmouth I was pregnant but bleeding badly. They dumped me on the quayside. Someone put me in an ambulance to take me to hospital. The baby didn't survive and I had to have a full hysterectomy because of the damage that had been done. I would never be a proper woman from that day on. It took a year for me to recover. A very nice 'navy' family took me in and gave me the strength to get back on my feet. I could have gone into the Navy but I chose the Army instead.

They made me what I am today. Even as a girl I managed to pass all the fitness training, and the many courses. Better than most of the boys actually.

I was a bit of an anomaly then but it made me fight even harder. Eventually gaining a commission and getting into Sandhurst, one of only two women at the time.

Any way... I don't hate men, at least the nice ones."

"Like me you mean"

"Yes like you" she laughed "I'm very sorry, but I can never be a..... proper woman."

"In fact I've always felt myself 'one of the boys' even if I'm not...."

The following morning they headed out of port and back to sea. The wind was coming from the North-east which made sailing south a joy. The swell was largely moderate and they were soon passing the Atlantic coast of Spain and on to the Portugese coast.

"So what are your plans ? ..straight down the African coast to Angola or what?"

"Actually Jerry ...no. I have to find someone first. We'll be going through the Gibraltar straits into the Med. Then to the Algerian coast."

"Who?"

"Henry Bryant…I think he's there"

"Why?…I thought he'd be the last person you want to see again."

"Several reasons, but I'll know when I get there."

They sailed fast as the wind was good, and the boat seemed to cut through the water like a knife. It was almost perfect sailing conditions. The days were warm and sunny, and the nights quiet and calm.

Soon they were off Cadiz, then off the Cape of Trafalgar where they dropped sail and had a very decent lunch in honour of Admiral Nelson. Jerry had caught a large fish. They weren't sure what it was but it grilled well, tasted great, and not too bony. Alex had run the Geiger counter over it just in case, but things were normal.

They turned East and kept the sails high. The boat lay back from the wind and shot along.

Normally the strait was one of the busiest lanes in the world. But there were no container ships or tankers to be seen. Only the occasional small fishing vessel.

They must now be on the lookout for pirate vessels and Alex had retrieved her guns from the bilges. Jerry had kept his semi automatic stowed but now brought it out.

However they weren't approached by any other

vessel so they were soon through the gap and heading past the Moroccan coast towards Oran in Algeria.

The wind turned back to a south-westerly which suited them fine. The Med had an above average swell but the boat handled it well, though going became slower.

After a few more days they stood off the Algerian coast, about 15 miles out, heading slowly east. The Algerians are very protective of their coastline at the best of times so there would be long range radar sweeps by the military, and offshore patrols at regular intervals.

They stayed out from the coast for two days and watched, through binoculars, for the timing and position of the patrols.

"We go in tonight" said Alex. "There's a small fishing port at a place called Cavallo on the charts. Seems to have a small breakwater and a jetty. Not too busy, and about sixty kilometres from where I think Bryant is hiding. There's a small island just off the coast from it. We can come in behind it and we won't be seen. "

"How will we get from there inland?"

"Not we, just me. You drop me off at the jetty then pull out and stand off. If I'm not back in three days then head back to England without me. If I return I'll light a fire on the El Aouana beach next to the port about 10pm on the third evening and you come in and get me."

"I don't like it Alex, surely it'd be better if I go with you...to watch your back"

"You don't have the Arabic Jerry...and the two of us would attract suspicion. No... on my own. You know me, I can take care of myself. Don't get all protective all of a sudden" but she smiled when she said it.

"Whatever you say M'am"

XVIII

Algeria, and Revelations

Night fell, the sky turning a rich deep purple to black velvet.

There were a few lights on along the coast, so they had some power here from somewhere.

Jerry brought the boat round and guided her into port. Alex trained her binoculars on the shoreline but there was no noticeable movement and the port appeared to be dark.

An hour later they were through the breakwater. Jerry dropped the mainsail and the boat coasted into the jetty, nudging up to the fenders.

Alex jumped off and quickly disappeared into the dark. Jerry partially raised the sail and swung the boat out into the pool then out through the breakwater and within an hour was back out well clear of any patrols or radar. If anyone was watching it would look like a fishing boat bringing in the catch and leaving again.

Alex walked a few hundred yards to the main road and found a tree and some posts. She tied a length of strong fishing twine to the tree then walked across the road and looped the other end over one of the concrete posts. She let the line go slack so that it lay on the road then she sat down and waited.

She waited several hours in the bitter cold of the Algerian night, until it was nearly dawn when she heard the sound she was waiting for. A motorbike was approaching.

The man on the bike was hunched forward to keep his face out of the cold wind. He was wearing an old style crash helmet and black gloves, and he had a light grey anorak zipped up tightly to keep out the cold.

As he was about to go past Alex raised the fishing line, pulling it tight around the post in a loop much like she would do with a winch on the boat.

The rider drove straight into it at head height, jerking him backwards as he fell off. The bike slid on its side and into the dip at the side of the road.

He tried to get up as Alex walked over to him from behind, pulled off his helmet and hit him hard with the side of her hand in the carotid artery and vagus nerve. He went down in a heap. Alive, but out cold. She dragged him over to the side of the road, then recovered and stowed the fishing line.

She put on his anorak over her own jacket, took the gloves, his scarf, and the helmet, wrapped the scarf around her mouth and nose then donned the helmet and the gloves.

The bike engine had stopped, She pulled it upright and waited for a moment to clear the carburettor. The bike was a trusty Honda 50, the type you see all over the world. Cheap, old, easily maintained and attracts absolutely zero attention.

She kicked the starter and it fired up. She jumped on it and rode away.

The W137 road runs away from the coast, winding and twisting its way up and through the mountains. The little bike had plenty of petrol but struggled up the hills. She had thought she could get to Angouri within a couple of hours but in the end it took her nearly four. However the road was quiet with little traffic, mainly bullock carts, and as the sun came up the scenery was particularly beautiful. It began to get very warm so she stopped and took off her own jacket , stowing it in the box at the back of the bike. She left the grey anorak open to catch the breeze, but left on the gloves as she did not want to be recognised as female which in these parts would look highly suspicious.

As she rounded a bend in the road the lake came into view. A beautiful spot. Across the centre of the lake she could see the barrage which provided the hydro electric power which was key to the area. Some sort of large estate, hidden by trees, was on the far side of the lake, and there seemed to be some houses spread up the side of the mountains behind it.

The village was on this side of the lake, no more than a hamlet. She had memorised the Bryant villa she had seen in the photographs. She recognised it as soon as she drove past.

A poor place, somewhat overgrown with weeds

in the gravel around the outside. It was in need of some care and attention. An old man was digging in the garden.

She parked the bike and walked to the gate of the house. The old man looked up. He spoke French with the distinct Berber accent of these parts. "Can I help you?"

She replied in french, "I'm looking for Henri, Henri Bryant, I am a friend of Henri"

"Henri? Henri and Stephanie?" the old man said and smiled " That was a long time ago. Henri is a big man now, he doesn't come here anymore, he's at the Emir's palace now."

"Is that near here?"

"It's there" and he pointed across the lake to the large estate surrounded by fir trees and gardens. In the distance she could just make out some structures.

"You can take the road round the lake but it's quite far ...er madame."

She was right then. He was here, her hunch paid off.

"Thank you I will find my way there" and she walked back to the bike.

"How is Stephanie and the girls? "said the old man with an expectant look "I liked them, they enjoyed their time here"

"They're well, I shall tell them that you asked after them when I see them again"

The old man's face lit up. "Yes say hello from an old moor. She will know" he said.

Alex got back on the bike. The sun was now high in the sky. She rode a little further on then noticed a rowing boat tied up on the shingle beach. No one was about.

She pulled the bike into some bushes. Removed the helmet and flipped the hood of the anorak over her head.

Moving quietly she walked down to the boat which was half in and half out of the water. Two oars were laid out in it. She undid the rope that was tied round a rusty hook embedded in a small concrete block. Checked to see if there was anyone around. Then pushed it into the water and climbed in.

She slotted the oars into the rowlocks and pushed out into the lake. The palace lay alongside an inlet that fed off the side of the lake. It was cooler on the water and it was perhaps only 400 meters across at this point so she was under the trees on the far side in a few minutes.

She pulled the boat up onto the shallow bank and a moment later a jeep appeared with two uniformed guards.

They came round to the side of the jeep. Each was wearing dark blue trousers with a light blue shirt and a peaked cap. Each had a white leather Sam Brown belt with a white leather holster and a sidearm. They also had light sub machine guns,

Ouzi's, hanging from a strap round their necks.

"You can't land here, get back in your boat and piss off."

"I'm Colonel Rheinhart, tell Henry Bryant I'm here to see him."

A look of slight confusion crossed their faces. A woman Colonel? And dressed like a tramp. But she said Bryant's name. One of them shrugged and went back to the jeep, to radio it in. The other stayed watching her. She stood casually waiting. There was no point stirring things up.

The second man came back.

"Better come with us" he looked her up and down, she opened the anorak and raised her arms to show she wasn't armed.

She climbed into the back of the jeep and they set off round a very finely laid gravel road. The grounds were beautifully laid out. There were several stands of Royal Palms. Big old trees, towering overhead. Bougainvillea of assorted shades grew everywhere. Amaryllis flowers were everywhere, big waxy red blooms with large yellow stamens and box hedges, neatly trimmed.

As they came back up to higher ground the extent of the palace became clear. It was huge, and typically Islamic with sweeping arches, and tiled or mosaic features. There were many different buildings across the estate including some very modern looking ones.

The jeep pulled up at the grand entrance and she

was escorted inside.

“Down there” one of the men pointed down a cool shaded corridor.

She set off but half way along came over with an extremely strange feeling before blacking out and falling to the floor, unconscious.

She woke slowly. Her limbs wouldn’t quite respond properly. She was sitting on a soft sofa, in a large room with open sides looking out across a courtyard at one side and gardens at the other. Islamic arches abounded at each end of the room.

She brought her eyes slowly into focus.

There, standing in front of her dressed in a light cream djellaba with a red turban wrapped round his head was the man she had come to see. Henry Bryant.

“Hello…bitch”

“What the hell have you done to me Henry?”

“Don’t worry, it’ll pass soon, just one of my little inventions to catch unwanted guests”

She stayed silent for a moment while she tried to marshall her thoughts and her limbs.

“What are you doing here, how did you find me?”

“Gone to stay with the Moors”

“How very clever you are Alex, but then you always were”

Alex looked around. Her vision was clearing.

“Not bad for a holiday rental”

“Oh this” Bryant stretched out his arms theatrically looking around as if he hadn’t seen it before “This isn’t mine, this is Edward’s, its his home....you didn’t know?”

“What do you mean ‘his home’?

“He was born here, he’s the Emir, or should I say His Majesty the Sultan of the Ottoman’s Algerie, Eduard Abdel Al Jazair.

He doesn’t use his title of course, and since the republic he’s not in an official capacity, but his mother was an Ottoman Princess, descended from very old Algerian Berber Royalty. This was hers, now it’s his.”

“I never know when to believe you Henry, you’re such a bullshitter. He’s been Edward Gaunt for as long as anyone has known him”

“That’s true of course. His father was French, descended from the old Castilian, or was it Capetian?, never quite sure which is which, old royalty, via the famous John of Gaunt. As I understand it, from one of the bastard lines. Old John was a bit of a ladies man. Died of syphilis I believe.... The Black Lion..... I believe that’s what the British soldiers in Portugal called it during the Peninsular Wars with the French.

So his father’s name was Gaunt and that’s the one he uses. But he was born here and lived here until he was sent off to boarding school in France, then the Sorbonne, then Oxford, then Sandhurst. So now he’s so very English, but that’s only on the surface.

Meanwhile the Algerians, who do things the old fashioned way, like to keep their royalty on, even if it's unofficial. This place was very run down, but Edward has paid to have the place renovated and extended so it's now fit for purpose."

Bryant stopped and clapped his hands. Two half naked young women appeared, dressed only in chiffon harem pants and assorted jewellery, bearing plates of food and drink.

"I do like my pearl breasted houri's as you know....would you like something to eat?"

Alex's limbs were slowly responding. she pulled herself more upright on the sofa. She felt enormously tired, but at least she could move a little.

The young women placed their trays on a couple of small wooden tables inlaid with mother of pearl.

She was starving after her long journey, and there's an old soldiers rule 'eat when you can, you don't know when you might get another chance'.

She helped herself to a flatbread and some hummus, together with some fresh dates. The girl poured her some mint tea.

"Why have you come here?

Bryant was still standing but had moved over to look out at the garden where some more young women were sitting. Some of them were pregnant.

A warm and pleasant breeze blew through the room, scented by the flowers, or by some perfume.

“I’m not entirely sure Henry. At first I believed you were in some danger”

“Danger?...from who?”

“From Gaunt....in the same way that I was and still am. If the existence of the hypnoids becomes widely known then he has lost his only advantage”

Bryant smiled. “Well it won’t come to that”

“But I also came to tell you about Stephanie”

“That she’s dead?...yes I already know that. Poor Stephanie..she didn’t deserve me really...and my daughters too. They have disowned me anyway”

“ ...so I ended up without a specific reason... maybe to kill you?... except that I must know where you are and what you were doing...were you still supplying Gaunt with the weapon?....a case of pure curiosity got the better of me. How did you escape from prison?”

“Escape?...I didn’t escape. Gaunt had me released. Sent me here...to carry on my work. ..and it’s the perfect place. Do you know they consider girls to become women as soon as they have...flowered. Suits me just fine.”

“They’re still underage Henry”

“I was never interested in pre-pubescent girls, in fact 14 or 15 seemed to me to be a good age...I still do. Here they consider that quite normal for a man to marry these girls. I have four, and that's not including the slave girls, and the surrogates. I'm very much at home here as you can tell. Edward funds the research. I have everything I need."

"Surrogates?...What research?"

"I call it Quantum Chemistry. You've just experienced some of it. When you came down that corridor you passed under a device, a quantum magnetic resonance screen, similar, but not the same as the MRI scanners used in hospitals, but much more sophisticated. Haven't I always said to you Alex, 'it's all chemistry'. And so it is. But this is chemistry at a sub atomic level. Do you know the term Quantum Entanglement?"

Alex knew that he could talk for hours on his favourite subject so she would let him ramble on while she gradually got back the use of her legs.

"No I don't"

"No, not many people do. But it's a fundamental part of nature, of our very existence. It means that every element, every atom, is made up of a host of specific sub atomic particles, at varying levels of order. And these particles can be manipulated as it turns out by the phenomena of certain high, or very high, frequencies of magnetic resonance. I can scan your mind, identify the very structure of the particles that make up your mind, your very personality. We know so much about the brain and neurological tissue but up until now, virtually nothing about your mind, which by the way sits not just in your brain but in all your neurological tissue. Your spinal column, around your stomach, in all your nervous system. All over.

This is what I used in its crudest form with the neural inhibitor injections that you are aware of. The thing that stops the hypnoids from getting to your mind. But this is far more subtle...and clever. I can actually change your mind using these resonances. In a crude way the device you walked under simply scrambled your mind temporarily causing you to lose consciousness, and altering the way your brain sends instructions to your muscles.

Something moved in the corner of the room. Alex had thought it was a fur rug. It slowly stood up and yawned. An enormous jet black panther.

"Oh don't worry about him." Bryant caught the movement. "He's been altered, quite tame, I removed his fight or flight response. He was a present for Edward. He's not afraid of humans so he just pads around. Sleeps with the girls. They love him. They call him Cacahuete.

The panther looked up on hearing his name and padded over quietly to nuzzle Bryant's leg. He turned his yellow green eyes and large head towards Alex, sniffed her then wandered off into the garden where the women and children were playing.

“Edward will be mighty pissed off that you’re here”

“Why?...if he wants me for Africa....this is Africa...”

“Southern Africa, not here. He’s given all this to the Ottoman’s on the understanding they support the crown...which they do....North Africa is not the same as sub-Saharan, nor Southern Africa.

I suppose he hasn’t told you all. Just wants you out of the way in Rhodesia while he gets on with ruling the world. You’re his useful fool...”

“..and yet here I am...his suppos’ed ‘Queen of Africa, why would he do that?”

“Because you’re a thorn in his mind.. Ever since the first operation in Afghanistan he’s had a sweet spot for you...damned if I know why...but he has”

“You mean sexually? He’s got a hard-on for me?”

“I doubt it, he’s got plenty of attractive females when he wants to scratch that itch. No, it’s guilt...”

“Guilt?...for what?”

Bryant paused, turned back to face Alex though he seemed to be talking to himself.

“I suppose it’s testament to my genius with the hypnoids that you don’t remember a thing....”

He looked at her.

"You really have no idea do you? Let me explain it to you, at least as far as you're concerned. ...The psych ops team...me, you, Edward, was a huge success and it drove the Yanks crazy. They didn't know how we were doing it...wanted in..."

"I know all this Henry...its old news"

"No you don't Alex, you see Edward realized that the hypnoids gave him real power, but he wasn't in control anymore. It was Edward who met me long ago, we were here on holiday, he was back from Sandhurst for his mother's funeral. We met by accident. I told him I was a chemist at Porton Down. Well he was already a Captain, I'd seen him on various official visits to Wiltshire. We got chatting, got drunk, I told him I could get any woman I wanted. Had this special drug, way better than any date rape thing. Edward....sensible, decent, clever, gentlemanly Edward thought this would be a useful field weapon. So he persuaded the MOD to put our team together. You came along because he needed a woman, one who could speak the language. So off we trot to the 'Stan. I create the packs for you to use..and ...well you know all that. But then Edward sees the immense possibilities for his own purposes. To reset the world. Get rid of all the PC crap, all the politicians, all the stupidity and damage, ... and to fulfil what he sees as his destiny, the

Plantagenet thing. So he has a plan. Get the Americans in. He knew they would fuck up with it. ...You remember Simon Brevard?"

"I just met him at Alnick, Edward has appointed him First Senator of the America's."

"Yes exactly, he was CO of a group of GI's , so Edward gets the call from the MOD. They've been leant on by the Pentagon to share the secret about our operation. Edward agrees to share and gets hold of Simon. Brevard, who has his wits about him, says he doesn't believe that it'll work. He wants a demonstration...and not with some raghead that he doesn't trust. I give Edward and Brevard a shot of the inhibitor. You are called in to the room... and fried."

"I don't believe you.....this is more of your bullshit Henry"

Bryant ignored her and continued.

"Here is a British Army Captain, one of the special females, and, of course I couldn't help myself..." Bryant gave an evil grin.."I had you stripping to some Arabic belly dance music, stark naked, dancing around the room. Gaunt put a stop to it. Unlike me, he's a very decent man, suitably embarrassed by what I had done to you. Brevard wanted to be sure you wouldn't remember any of it so I told him to come back the following evening for drinks where he would see for himself that you had no idea or recollection that you'd been fried, or the dancing, or any of it."

"Gaunt told you to get dressed, and he sat with you while you poured out your heart to him. It was positively cringe worthy. The gang rapes, your mother and father and your sisters...how they died...your attempt to get out of Zimbabwe...the ship, more rapes...the still birth...the hysterectomy..all of it."

Alex sat very still. So she hadn't been drunk...and here was Bryant finding it all so very amusing... but she could do nothing...she tried to get up... her legs were still unable to take her weight..she fell back into the chair. Bryant continued.

"So the next evening Brevard returns. You're invited in for drinks unaware that everyone is watching you to see if you have any recollection of the previous evening. But there's nothing. You are oblivious to it all. So Brevard is given the kits for him and two of his team, a man and a woman, and told how to use it. Meanwhile Gaunt eggs on the men to get a few Afghan women in for the lads for a bit of R&R. Then he tips off one of the Pentagon wonks that they're compromising the mission, as predicted, all hell breaks loose and the whole operation is disbanded and put into 'highly classified, black ops', to be covered up and forgotten.

She sat there blinking...it all fitted...how could she have been so stupid not to think they would do this...

Bryant continued.

"So now Edward has what he wants. He sets me up with a full laboratory and a private plane to take me back and forth to England...there's a landing strip in the mountains at the back of the palace. I continue to make the weapons for him, and to pursue other avenues, other ideas. Money's no problem...Edward has always been loaded, as you may or may not know. I convert to Islam, which I quite enjoy actually. He gets in to NATO which gives him access to military chiefs all over the world. He keeps Simon Brevard close and the two of them hatch the plan to restore order to the world."

"Then someone at Porton starts bleating about my extra curricular activities with girls. 'Oh my god, the reputation of the army is at stake'. The MOD can't find any information about the hypnoids, but Edward worries that all his careful planning will be undone if I get to speak, so he arranges for a secret court martial, and who better to act as prosecutor than his favourite fool.....then he selects the three generals as the judges who he can fry at a later date for further use."

"I get dropped in the shit, but it turns to Gaunt's advantage as he can now plausibly have me disappear after a brief spell in solitary...and a promise of a life of ease in Algeria."

"And yet after all this he still has a soft spot for you....still guilty about what we did to you, still has respect for you as a soldier, and as a woman. So he's kept an eye on you ever since. He knew you would take the secret of the hypnoids to the grave...but he forgot about the 'nosey female' characteristic in all women. So now you've come here, ...and now you know it all."

" ...and you've fallen into the spider's web my dear Alex..."

She stared at Bryant for a long time, processing, or trying to process all that she had heard. Her legs were still not responding.

"It'll be dark soon, my girls will help you into a wheelchair and get you all cleaned up, then you can join us for dinner"

It was as if he had not just told her that her whole life since Afghanistan had been carefully managed by Gaunt and this man Bryant, ...as if she was an honoured guest who would join them all for dinner and talk about old times...yes, a fly caught in a huge spider's web,...the analogy was correct...and she'd walked right into it.

There must have been something in the tea because she felt faint and drowsy. She fell asleep. On waking she found herself being bathed and dressed by several of Bryant's harem girls. Then wheeled into a plush room filled with cushions and carpets, and elegant little oil lights as if she were in some version of the Arabian Nights.

Music, dancing girls, warm starry nights and a desert breeze.

Cacahuete came over to lay his head in her lap as if he knew she had suffered the same fate as him. No longer a wild animal to roam the South American rain forests at will. Just an emasculated and pampered pet, for the entertainment of others.

She slept a drugged and uneasy sleep.

The following morning she found herself back in the garden room, dressed in a fine green silk gown and matching Algerian slippers. Her hair had been washed and styled. She felt rather than saw that make-up had been applied, and some powerful Oud scent wafted from her at every movement. She was in a wheelchair, propped up by colourful cushions. Something itched in the back of her neck.

Henry Bryant came in and held her hand.

"My my, how glamorous you look Alex, my girls have done a fine job with you.....I'm afraid I had to run you through my UGT again... my unwanted guest trap. .....your motivation for coming here...well, not sure you know....but, now you're here you may as well have the full tour..."

Alex stared at him but said nothing.

"Come, let me show you something..."

He took control of the wheelchair and pushed her along a covered walkway at the edge of the garden and into an elevator which began it's descent underground.

"We can thank the nazi's for this actually. They came here towards the end of the war because of the continuous bombing of all their facilities in Europe. They expanded the old cave system that sits below the palace. Ancient water courses I believe that come down from the mountains behind us which in some cases still feed the lake and drive the hydro power. They dug it out further. Expanded beyond all recognition. There was a huge underground manufacturing and assembly plant inside the mountains with a ramp up to launch the aircraft and rockets they were building onto a disguised runway running along the top of the nearest mountain. We use it today for our own air facilities.

Of course they couldn't keep it going and it all fell into ruin and forgotten after the end of the war. Edward has upgraded most of it to hold what you're about to see.

The elevator doors swished apart. Two uniformed and armed guards were standing beside a set of glass doors leading on into a short corridor. The guards nodded at Bryant, looked at Alex then waived them on.

He pushed her through into an airlock. Once the doors behind had closed another set of glass doors opened and she was pushed into a white corridor with similar sliding glass doors along the sides. He pushed her in through one of them."

"These are our special laboratories....things have come on quite a lot since the hypnoids...well we still make them of course ...they have their place in the armoury but we've got much more advanced since then...as I mentioned to you yesterday we have been able to learn a lot about the quantum field effects in chemistry, and applied those to new systems...so here is one of my magnificent quantum magnetic resonance machines"

They were in a large white room. The temperature was quite cold. In the centre of the room was a machine which looked like a huge gyro-scope, except the flat bed at the centre was made from clear Perspex with raised edges and filled with a clear gel. The flat bed was supported at the top and bottom by two metal rods which went into a giant circular ring, and the ring was again supported by two axles at the top and bottom so that the ring could revolve 360 degrees around the flat bed at the centre.

"Sorry about the cold in here but the machines and the electronics have to be kept at low temperatures. The ring here has to have liquid hydrogen fed through it so that it works at very low temperatures. About minus 200 degrees Kelvin actually. Super cold.

The gel in the bed is warmed so that when you're in it, it holds you still while stopping you from shivering. We have to keep the movement down to a minimum. Once you're in, the top section of the ring fires sub-atomic particles at you which 'read' your mind chemistry. The bottom half of the ring 'collects' the data, from underneath. The whole thing swings over you several times to get an exact copy of your neural mind chemistry which then copies it into a quantum memory and a 64Qbit quantum computer."

He pushed her past the ring and another set of doors slid open. The room had a set of control desks and a window into another room which contained two large tubes, one coming out of the ceiling, one from the floor, with a gap between each tube with thin glass tubes connecting the two.

"I'm afraid we can't go in there. That's the quantum computer. It sits in a vacuum room at about absolute zero..well just above it....and in this room..."

Bryant pushed her through another set of doors into another control room.

"Is the quantum memory where we store the minds..."

Through another glass panel, in another cold vacuum room were a series of vertical racks containing millions of tiny strands of silicon gel tubes, transparent, but slightly off-yellow in colour.

"You keep saying 'we' ...but I see no-one else here" said Alex

"Oh there's no reason for them to be here if we're not working.

"There's a whole town of them built into the hillside up the sides of the mountains . Edward has been collecting the most brilliant minds in all sorts of fields. Sciences mainly, physicists, geneticists, mathematicians, engineers, computer boffins...even chemists. All sorts collected up from the ruins of their respective countries along with their families and brought here to safety. They do most of their research from their own homes but come in here when we're ready to do the actual tests."

A second elevator opened at the end of the corridor past two more armed guards.

Bryant pushed Alex into the lift and they began to rise, coming out into a large lounge area with a boardroom table and several TV monitors around the walls. One wall was entirely glass, outside of which was a beautiful stone patio surrounded by a low wall. They stepped through one of the open panels into bright sunshine. The patio faced the mountains in front of them.

"There...you can see the small town and it's collection of houses set into the hills. ..and at the top look..."

A small jet was about to land on the runway. It wasn't visible from below and the aircraft quickly disappeared from view.

"More science refugees arriving..."

Between gaps in the wall that surrounded the patio Alex could see more formal gardens laid out with quadrangles and lawns. Children were playing in two of the gardens. Bryant looked over ..."Ah come along let me show you our beautiful children"

He pushed her back into the elevator and they descended back to ground level. He pushed her along an outside covered walkway resplendent in greenery and fine flowers. The air was sweet and warm. From around a bend she could hear children's voices rising and falling as they do the world over.

Seated on a bench along one shaded wall were four young women dressed in Islamic black. They were talking quietly but stopped when Bryant and Rheinhart appeared from the side of the walkway.

"Hello ladies! " Bryant announced to the four women. "Stay where you are we'll not be long, we've come to have a look at your charges."

Bryant wheeled round the chair to face the garden. The children carried on playing, impervious to adult presence as always.

Alex, not being a particularly child friendly person at the best of times, looked on casually until she noticed that several of the children looked very similar.

"What do you see Alex? Does anything strike you about these children?"

Alex was not interested in playing Bryant's games.

"I'm sure you're going to tell me anyway so get on with it."

Bryant smiled a thin smile. "Children!" they all turned at once to the sound of his voice. "Come over here for a moment and say hello to Aunty Alex here"

The children came over obediently and stood in a huddle around Alex.

"They're all boys, mixed ages but all probably under 10 years old." She said in a level tone. "..and some of them are brothers , or twins."

"All right children go back to playing" Bryant smiled at them and they ran back to whatever they were doing with a few shouts and laughter.

"Not just brothers, or twins. They are identical children, three of each. They're clones."

"Do you recognise the three eldest ones at all?" he looked into Alex's face from above.

"Not really" Alex lied, awaiting the inevitable reveal from Bryant.

"They're Edward's clones!, and the next ones down are me!. We've found the best geneticists from the world and re-created our own children. Science and chemistry are such marvels don't you think..."

Alex stared up at Bryant and saw the glint of madness in his eyes but said nothing.

"And these ladies here.." he said pointing to the four seated women "are the surrogates…even I can't produce a child from a test tube, well not yet anyway, but women have all the equipment needed to grow and deliver a healthy child, even if the DNA is artificially implanted into one of their eggs, it's the perfect combination…."

"Oh sorry Alex, for a moment I forgot. You haven't got the equipment anymore… sorry….but on a brighter note you could still have children…let me have some of your DNA and one of these ladies will pop one out for you!"

Alex had to remind herself that she'd fallen into this camp of her own free will. She had needed to find Bryant, to find out what had become of him. Now she knew. It was information …intelligence gathering to her. Now it had become much more dangerous than even she had thought.

" I'm not sure what you want me to say Henry. Do you want a medal? Are you planning to be the saviour of all the infertile people in the world?"

Bryant took the bait.

"It's succession Alex, that's what I'm doing here. Having helped Edward conquer the world with my chemistry I'm now engaged in preserving what he's done. He has no formal children. Though I believe there are a few by-blows around from his youthful passions. But this… this is something else. He's not going to live forever, and as we've seen over countless years the handing-on of the baton to new generations is most usually a disaster. The child, however pleasant and co-operative of the parent inevitably can't wait for them to die so they can plant their own imprimatur on the world. Weakness creeps in and suddenly they're usurped, killed, or corrupted by others and the whole mess unravels."

The four women looked on, flicking between keeping an eye on their children and half listening to Bryant's monologue. Alex was unsure if they knew English at all or whether they just knew from instinct what was being discussed.

"Who's the third set of boys? " she said

"Can't you see? They look just like him....Simon, your old friend Simon Brevard, now First Senator Brevard, Colonial Governor and Lord Lieutenant of all the Americas."

"You see we're all going to go immortal, and once I've discussed you with Edward, and assuming you're still on our side, then we'll have three little girls running about. They'll be ready in time when you become an old maid"

"You're missing one thing Henry"

"What's that?"

"These are independent children...yes they'll no doubt grow up to look like the original, but they're running around here, speaking Arabic or Berber as far as I can hear, with totally different life experience from you, or Edward. Different mothers, different environments, probably life is very easy for them compared to the originals."

"You're not getting it Alex, you haven't been paying attention have you. The machinery you saw that copies people's minds can be downloaded into another person. It's better that the copy is physically the same as the original… though it seems to work ok when its not….."

"Once these children reach adulthood their minds can be wiped…replaced with the original mind from the computer's memory, and we now know that it works…the original is re-born into a new, younger body."

"Anyway, enough for now. I have to greet some of my new guests. You saw the plane arrive. Making sure they're settling in, then we'll be having a little soiree this evening so I'll get my girls to brush you up and we'll meet for dinner…say seven?" and he laughed. A clap of the hands and a harem girl came over to take her to her room.

Alex was washed, brushed, perfumed and clothed by a couple of Bryant's girls then wheeled out into the corridor past the guard at her room and into the open-sided salon.

The air was sweet from the garden. A couple of Berber musicians were playing some Moorish music, squatting next to a tiny fountain at the corner of the room. Carpets and cushions were spread about the place. An ornate, carved table had been laid with dishes of food. Cachouete lay on one of the carpets next to a lounging Henry Bryant who was eating some sort of meat in little cakes. The panther kept glancing up towards the garden. There was a smell of almonds. Algerian wine was being served in delicate crystal glasses. Some of the girls were already drunk. One or two were swaying and dancing to the music. Two guards were standing, out of direct sight in the garden and at the end of another corridor.

There was no sign of the new arrivals.

"Well don't you look nice again Alex!....well done my little beautiful girls" He clapped. They smiled but carried on. "Such a shame I'm going to have to sell you on."

"I wish you'd just get on with it Henry, you're boring me with your Arabian fantasy. What happened to your other guests, can they not stand the company either?"

"Now now Alex, no need to get bitchy, girls bring her some food and wine."

The girls dutifully obeyed, and Alex ate. As before she was starving, which would be no good if she could got her legs back.

"No they're just tired. Chinese you know. Long flight etcetera. None of that lot in the mountain town are social types anyway so it's just you and me."

Alex waited for the follow-up that she knew Bryant was cooking up but as he seemed lost in watching his dancing girls and puffing on a hookah pipe she decided to force the pace.

"Time to let me go Henry. By now Edward will be wondering why I'm not in Rhodesia doing his bidding as his Governor"

"He's no idea you're here." Bryant spoke without turning his head but Alex felt his attention snap back.

"Just about now, if the wind has been good, my sergeant will have made contact with England to say that I'm in Algeria...word will get back to Edward and you can expect a call."

Bryant laughed. It was an unpleasant laugh. Had Edward already been in contact? Was he annoyed, and if so had he said to leave matters with Bryant?, he'd get someone else for Africa?

All this shot through her brain in a second.

Bryant turned and looked at her. He clapped his

hands and jerked his head towards the gardens. One of the slave-girls got up and sashayed out into the garden. Cacouhette suddenly rose up with her and padded after her, the great sleek black fur shining a satin black amongst the carpets, plants and draperies.

"You mean him?"

The girl was leading a man in from the garden. Alex could only turn her head so far but she knew it was Jerry. Not the Jerry she knew however. His face was blank. Quite peaceful. He neither looked left or right. He didn't acknowledge her or indeed anyone else. The girl stopped and so did he. He just stood there.

"The marine patrols were curious about this little sailing boat hovering about just offshore. Nice boat by the way. I might have it brought to the lake. I could keep it as a souvenir."

"What have you done to him?"

"Can't you tell? You, queen of the hypnoids?... Actually I've had his mind wiped. I didn't bother keeping a copy. He's a walking zombie now. ....Doesn't know his name ...nothing." He turned to the girl who was standing at Jerry's side. "Take him back to the garden. Tell him to lie down and die."

Alex tried to sit up but her body wouldn't respond. "Put him back Henry, he's not part of this"

"Sorry, can't do it. He's gone. Only the core bits of

his limbic system remains to keep him upright. I told you he's been wiped. I didn't take a copy first. Actually he's been quite a useful demonstration of an idea we've been developing. A quantum field magnetic resonance bomb. Just on a small scale with him, but I'm actually very pleased with the result."

The girl led him away.

"He'll just lie there until he dehydrates, probably in a day or two, his organs will fail. Or I might sell him at the slave market in Algiers though he's a bit far gone even for them. There's a thriving slave trade. Back to where it was before the British stopped it all in the early 1800's you know. Big markets all across the middle east. Just as it has been for thousands of years. That's what will happen to you."

"Edward is a long way a way and by the time he's aware that you came here you'll be some Arab's concubine, ...though you're a bit old for that now aren't you....most likely a kitchen maid or suitable for field work perhaps...yes a big strong girl like you..."

"I'll tell him you both came in as part of a boatload of European captives and before I was aware, the staff had 'processed' you and you were gone to the market."

"Tomorrow I'm going to mess with your mind in that machine I showed you. Then off to market. A fat little piggy, sold for a few gold coins."

He called one of his harem girls. "Run her through the UGT then take her back to her room."

The girl pushed the wheelchair out of the salon and along the corridor towards the arch. She didn't notice one of the guards coming up behind her. She paused, and at that moment the guard grabbed her quickly and pushed the girl through the arch. She dropped down in a heap on the floor.

"Look as if you've been fried" he hissed very quietly in Alex's ear. He bent down and grabbed the girl's ankles, pulling her back through the arch without getting his head in the way of the beam. Then he pulled her limp form up and threw her over his shoulder like a sack, grabbed the wheelchair and spun round.

"Who are you?"

"Quiet" he hissed. He had an accent she didn't recognise at first. He pushed her out of the main corridor and round to a side entrance leading back to her room. "Look as though you're out of it."

The guard on the door saw them and smiled at the man.

"Pissed again" he said as they came to the door, jerking his head slightly at the unconscious form resting on his shoulder. The other guard smiled and opened the door for them.

The door closed. She opened her eyes. The

mystery guard stood in front of her. He dropped the prostrate form of the girl on the bed.

“Lieutenant Jens Lanscki Ma’m, ex Polish Army, we met in Lansdorf on a joint exercise when you were with British Military Intelligence. You won’t remember me but you came to brief us at a conference and made quite a mark.”

“Well Lieutenant Lanscki,...thank you...I think... but what are you doing here?”

“I’d left the army some time ago but after the attack I re-joined under the Gaunt’s German Governorship. I have some Arabic...long story... and they were looking for guards for this place. Me, and one of my mates applied and came over here. Been here maybe a year, took a while to make out what was going on but now... I don’t like it. I recognised you, Colonel, the other day and tonight I realised if I didn’t act then you’d be gone like those other poor souls that have come through here.”

“What’s your plan Lieutenant Lanscki?”

“First I have to remove the nerve implant they’ve injected in your neck. It’ll hurt.

Lanscki turned her round and examined the back of her neck. “it’s there, I’m going to cut it out so ... sorry...but you’re going to have to hold still and keep quiet. Grit your teeth...”

He pulled a knife from his belt. “Here we go” He made a small sharp slice into her skin at the back of her neck. She tensed her mouth as best she could and closed her eyes. He pushed the very tip of the blade under a small plastic capsule and pulled it out. He held out the bloody object. A tiny micro-capsule.

"It's a time release nerve agent. The UGT only knocks you out for a short while, but enough time to stick one of these under your skin....."

She took hold of the slippery capsule. So, not so much the quantum magnetic resonance bullshit, more the tried and tested drugging and clinical chicanery.

She was bleeding. "You're bleeding,"

"It's fine, I heal quick."

Lanscki tore off a strip of her dress and made a field dressing, wrapping it round her neck over the wound.

"You need to get the blood moving now, takes about an hour to get this shit out of your system enough to get you walking."

He came round to her front, grabbed both her arms, turned round and put them over his shoulders then stood her up on his back. They walked round the room like this and she began to get some small movement in her legs.

The girl on the bed moved.

"She's coming round" Lanscki tapped her hard on the left side of her neck hitting both the carotid artery and the vagus nerve. The girl slipped back into unconsciousness.

"So what's you're plan Lieutenant?" Reminding him of her earlier question.

"My mate Januscz is down in the car pool. He's got a jeep. We'll get out of here as quietly as we can, head east to the Morocco border, hopefully get us across and then sort out the rest. The Moroccans and the Algerians don't cooperate with each other much so we should be ok once we're out of the country."

"I have a better plan" she said looking at him..."do you mind?"

"Go ahead Colonel"

"You knock out that guard outside the room, bring him in and I'll get his clothes and his gun. I can't be charging about in the desert in this." She flicked the flimsy chiffon dress and slippers. "Then we grab Bryant and my old Sergeant, the one lying on the grass and head for the airport in the mountain. We dig out the pilot for one of the jets and we fly out of here, heading south to Rhodesia where I'm expected"

"Do you know where Bryant sleeps?"

"Yep"

"Are there jets and crew on standby up there all the time?"

"Yep"

"You and your mate gonna be ok with that?"

"Yep"

" I'll need some time to get my legs back so we'll

wait until it's after midnight....get that guard will you."

Lanscki left the room, as he closed the door behind him he smiled at the guard on duty and began to walk past him...but the guard never saw him pass as Lanscki's elbow struck him hard in the side of the head and he went down in a heap. Alex heard the thump on the ground and managed to wheel the chair over to the door to open it as Lanscki came back in dragging the unconscious guard behind him."

They stripped him off then tied him and the girl together on the bed, facing each other. Lanscki looked around..."where did you put that capsule? ...might as well make the most of it"

He pulled out his knife, made a small incision into the unconscious guard's neck in the same position as Alex's incision and pushed in the capsule. He tore off another strip from the dress and secured it over the wound.

"She's gonna freak when she wakes up and comes face to face with him"

So they tore off another strip and made a makeshift gag to stop her sounding off. They covered both with a sheet and messed up the bed so it looked as natural as it could.

For the next hour Alex, by stages, got her motor reflexes back. Lanscki went off to find his mate to tell him what was planned and to check for any trouble. All was quiet. He reported back.

Alex had changed into the trousers and shirt of the guard. She'd got his weapons belt wrapped round her. The boots were too small for her big feet so she'd cut off the tips of the boots and put on the guards socks. It was good enough for now. She could walk.

She checked the gun. It was a typical small South African nine millimetre used by civil and military forces the world over. She checked the chamber and the safety then holstered it. There was a decent quality sheaf knife in the belt too, and spare ammo clips.

She ran her fingers through her hair, pulled it back and tied it with a strip of cloth from the dress. Then she tore off another set of strips and pushed them into her pocket.

"I need coffee" she said

Lanscki disappeared and came back 15 minutes later with a pot of disgustingly strong Algerian coffee. She drank it all.

Lanscki slipped out just before midnight to patrol round his part of the complex. When he came back it was time to move. Bryant had retired for the night. His guard was sent off on an errand.

The two left the bedroom and she followed him down the corridor and across a large courtyard to Bryant's private quarters.

"I'll deal with him myself"she'd told Lanscki, "you get Bradman off the grass and bring him back here."

Bryant was asleep on his side on top of his bed. A sleeping girl was next to him.

He woke to a hand clamped tight round his mouth and Rheinhart breathing in his ear "Make one sound or one move Henry and I'll push this knife through your spine."

She pushed the point of the knife against the skin of his spine. He shuddered but didn't speak.

"I'm going to take my hand away but not the knife so verrrry carefully get up, nice and slow... that's it, nice and easy. She still had her arm braced round his neck.

"Outside now" she hissed.

He walked slowly to the door and Alex followed.

She quickly pulled the gun out with her other hand and pushed the barrel into his arse crack, pointing to the back of his genitals.

"Now Henry, same rules, but this time if you say anything or do anything stupid I'm going to pull the trigger and your favourite toys will be shredded. Come with me" and she pushed him forward out and back across the courtyard towards the main palace"

At that moment, from under the shrubbery appeared a great shiny black fur head with startling yellow eyes. The big cat took in the scene then came forward and sniffed Henry then Alex. His tail was up. Perhaps he hadn't lost all his hunting skills after all. Maybe he remembered something about the night.

Then Lanscki appeared with the blank Jerry Bradman. The panther looked at them both, sniffed the air. Lanscki touched the panther's head and it lay down.

"It's just a pet" he whispered. "Come on, this way."

The four of them got in the lift leaving the big cat behind.

As the lift doors opened a great bear of a man , bursting out of an ill fitting uniform, was standing there. He seemed to be covered in short wiry hair, even the backs of his hands.

"Januscz…this is my good friend Corporal Januscz…very handy in a fight as you can see."

Januscz grinned a big toothy smile except several teeth were missing.

Alex nodded. Bryant kept his head down.

Januscz had secured an electric jeep. One of the jeeps to be used in the tunnels where exhaust fumes would be a problem.

Moments later the Jaguar re-appeared. He'd got down there so fast, but it seemed he was aware that this was his chance to escape also. Lanscki and Januscz took no notice. They put Bryant in the middle of the back seat. Januscz pushed Jerry into the right hand seat and Alex got in on the left keeping Bryant in the centre. She held the gun into his crotch. "Do as you're told and you won't come to any harm Henry" she said.

The two Poles got in the front and with a leap the cat jumped on the back of the jeep and flopped a large paw on Jerry's shoulders. They set off.

Five people and a large cat make a lot of weight for an electric jeep so top speed was no more than about thirty KPH. Nevertheless they made good time. No-one stopped them. The place was deserted until they rounded the last bend and drove into the huge underground hangar.

It was a huge cavernous place carved out of a mid-brown stone. The ceiling was high up and contained sets of flood lights which weren't on, only a few bulkhead lights around the walls lit the place. Enough to see by at night, inside, but not enough to give it away from above via a huge ramp, via a 180 degree turn, that led up and out onto the runway at the top of the mountain.

Three aircraft were lined up against one of the walls. In one corner was the control building and several huts for sleeping quarters and barracks. A machine shop and several tankers were lined up on the opposite wall, screened slightly by a stone arch. The place smelled of kerosene and oil. A guard unit was there. They looked at Bryant.

"Tell them to find the duty pilot and co-pilot, and get a long range plane ready to leave straight away"

Bryant repeated the instruction and the guard unit veered off towards the control centre.

Januscz pulled up next to a Beechcraft Super

King Air Turboprop painted in SAAF colours. The military variant of the civil aircraft. The aircraft had additional fuel tanks suspended under each wing.

Two pilots came out of the control centre and ran across the vast cavernous space to the aircraft.

"Tell them to take their orders from me, ... Colonel Rheinhart." Alex told Bryant which he did.

"Is the aircraft ready for flight Captain? She said to one of the pilots who looked somewhat taken aback.

"It's ready to go M'a.m...Colonel."

"Good, then we're getting aboard. We're heading for Makhado, do you know it?"

"Yes Ma'm"

"Does it carry enough fuel, it's a long way?"

"Yah Colonel, easy, we got here ok so no worries getting back. Got plenty of juice, this bird can go a lot further...if the weathers right."

Alex took it they were from the very place they were heading, not to mention the strong South African clipped tones.

It struck her at that moment that she was going home. This was the land of her birth. She used to speak like that. Rhodesia, South Africa, the same clipped tones. Yet she'd lost it save for a few words that would occasionally surface. Life in the British Army had changed her forever. But now she wondered if it would all come back. Probably. She shrugged a silent shrug.

The party went aboard and the pilot began firing up the plane.

A ground crew scurried about attaching the tug to the front wheel and the plane spun round towards the huge ramp at the end of the cavern. The plane was pulled up the slope, then round a 180 degree turn and up into the black night. The runway lights were switched on.

Alex pushed Bryant into one of the chairs, tied his hands behind him with one of the strips of dress then fastened his seatbelt. “Be a good boy, keep your mouth shut, stay put, and you’ll be going home asap” she said. Bryant looked up at her. If looks could kill.

Jerry was fastened in to another seat along with Januscz, who, it turned out, didn’t like flying. The Jaguar came and curled round his feet.

Lanscki and Rheinhart sat together and the plane shot down the runway and into the air.

Alex breathed a sigh of relief. It had all gone so smoothly.

“I want to thank you Jens” she said. “I thought I’d had it, but you saved me”

“I wanted out of there anyway” he said. “It was too creepy for words and all those weird scientists and the like… Januscz and me had already decided to get out via our earlier plan. “He smiled “but yours is a better plan.”

Januscz had stopped sweating and holding on to the arms of the chair. He sank back into the seat.

The Jaguar came over and sat with Jerry. Perhaps their sixth sense can figure out things.

Alex got up and went forward to the pilots.

"Thanks Guys, I'd like you to radio ahead to Makhado. Ask them to get a message to General Voebeck. Tell him we're heading their way and I'd like to meet him when we arrive. Tell him it's Colonel Alex Rheinhart, Prime Minister, and emissary of the King. Tell them I don't want any fuss, just a guard squad, and some transport, plus somewhere to stay for a few days before we head north to Rhodesia."

"Ok Colonel, will do"

"Do you have any paper and pens onboard?"

"Yah, in that cabinet behind you" and he nodded sideways without taking his hands off the yoke. The aircraft was still climbing but the pressurised cabin was doing it's business. Soon they were in clear air heading south under a star filled African velvet night.

"Jens, can you try to get Jerry to take some water, I don't know when he last had a drink and I doubt if our friend here knows either" she looked briefly at Bryant.

She sat back in her chair and pulled the armchair table top out of its pocket and unfolded it in front of her. She wrote a message, very briefly, then added the addressee to the envelope. Before she sealed it she leant across to Bryant and showed him the note. It read: ' I have Bryant. If you want him back in one piece you will need to travel here personally, by return flight, to collect him. If not then I'll assume you have no further need for him and I'll let him bleed out.'

"A nice sense of urgency don't you think Henry, ...still if he doesn't come.." She left it hanging.

Bryant gave her a sarcastic smile then resumed his annoyed face.

She sealed the letter and went forward to the cockpit. She gave the co-pilot the letter.

"When we get to Makhado I want you to get the plane refuelled immediately, and fly back to England. Whichever one of you is awake by that time needs to hand this letter personally to the King. Not another soul, capisce...from me, Colonel Rheinhart, I expect him to return immediately, so get ready for a long set of flights boys."

"Got it.. yah, Colonel"

"What's our ETA?"

"We've got about another 9 hours, so around 10 in the morning yah?"

"Ok, time to sleep. Wake me an hour before we land"

"Yah Colonel, no worries"

She sat back down. The others were already drifting off.

“Januscz,... actually what is your name?”

“You wouldn’t be able to pronounce it ” replied Lanscki without opening his eyes. “Just call him Corporal Januscz”

Januscz grinned at Alex in that child like way when he heard his name.

“Corporal Januscz, I guess you’re unlikely to sleep so please be good enough to watch our prisoner here. Make sure he doesn’t do anything stupid while we’re asleep.”

Lanscki said something to him in Polish to which he got a “Ja, Ja” in reply.

XVIIII

Reports, and Further Revelations

Lord High Chancellor William Levine leant heavily on his stick. He was standing outside the Kings chamber in York. The Chancellor of the Exchequer was in with the King.

Finally the doors opened and the Exchequer stepped out. He nodded curtly to Levine. "Listening at the door William?"

Levine simply smiled back and watched him leave.

He stepped through the King's door and gave a small bow of his head before approaching the desk. The doors closed silently behind him.

"I want you to keep and eye on him." Gaunt didn't look up as he studied a set of papers on the desk.

"Already doing it Sire, as you know, I keep an eye on all of them . I have good people in the various offices who keep me appraised of the....comings and goings. As far as the Chancellor of the Exchequer is concerned he's doing well. His men have been successful in retrieving much of the gold and silver bullion from the rubble of the Bank of England. Each day more of it is transported to the Cheviots stronghold. There's no evidence yet that he's siphoning off anything, but I keep a very close eye on it all Sire. He's also got men digging through the remains of the Tower of London. So far he's recovered substantial amounts of England's heritage items which are also going North, including the Crown jewels collection."

"That's the thing William. The ones in the Tower are copies. Extremely good copies, but copies nevertheless."

Levine looked up at him in surprise.

"Yes, that's right. Which is why I want you to take charge of a more delicate operation. The real ones are located in a nondescript tunnel that runs under St James's palace just off the Mall. They're in simple lead lined oak cases. No markings save for a very small 'crown ' cut into the wood."

"Are you sure Sire?...how do you know?"

"Quite sure William" Gaunt smiled briefly, as if addressing a child.

"I want you to find a team of your most trusted men. Get them down there to locate the tunnels. Here's a map of the tunnels, though I don't know exactly where the relics are located within them. Your men need to enter the tunnels which may or may not still be standing, and pull out whatever they find. Bring them here to me....and whatever else they find down there. I'm particularly interested in the Plantagenet crown of King John, presumed lost but possibly recovered and kept in secret."

Gaunt handed the map to Levine who eyed it suspiciously.

"It will be done my Lord King. I have a good team of men who are to be trusted. I'm advised that radiation levels are relatively low as long as the dust remains undisturbed, but tunnelling and digging bring additional risks of course."

"They will be well paid…in gold, and there are precautions they can take."

"Indeed Lord, I will make arrangements"

Levine looked up at the King who had risen and was standing by the window. He looked strained and he seemed stiffer in his legs.

"What reports from abroad?.."

"It seems that the Germans and the Russians are slaughtering each other in their millions sire, as you predicted. Meanwhile the Balkans have joined in… when they're not killing each other they're slaughtering the Italians…. the Sicilians are killing them as fast as they come over the border. Meanwhile most of the water supplies across that continent are now heavily contaminated …so cholera and typhoid are mopping up those that have avoided the fighting…so far….as for further east…the same story..I don't have numbers but with the removal of the pharmaceuticals they're dying in their millions…"

Captain Davidson appeared at the door. "The Royal doctor is here Sire."

Levine swung back from the interruption "Just one more thing my Lord King…."

Gaunt looked up.

“My people tell me the Scots are forming into brigand groups and attacking our camps…the horsemen are fighting them off…same down south…quite a few mobs being organised by local criminal gang masters as far as I can tell…”

“Let them fight” Gaunt sat back down “They’ll murder each other…same as the rest of the world…let them fight and die…the strongest or most capable will survive…keep the horsemen well supplied with weapons and ammunition… drop a few crates into the other side too… Eventually the numbers will fall and I will bring the survivors and their leaders over to my side…”

“As you wish Sire…” Levine

Gaunt turned to Davidson “Thank you Captain….William I will leave you to make your usual arrangements and no doubt you will keep me advised”

“Sire” Levine rose and left the room. He nodded to the Doctor who did not return his gesture. Levine made a mental note to find out for himself about the King’s condition.

He called for one of his staff, Foxton, a tall heavy set man in his forties…one of Levine’s trusted men.

“Foxton, have we got a man in the doctors office?”

“No Lord Chancellor, we do not”

"Well get someone in there...I want a report on the King's health as soon as possible....meanwhile please send for Scarman. I have a nice little job for him and his diggers."

"Yes Lord."

XX
Makhado

The co-pilot woke her about an hour out. He brought coffee and some sort of baklava for breakfast.

The others were in various states of waking.

She looked across at Bryant who was still sitting tight lipped. Januscz gave her another big grin and she smiled back. Jerry just sat there. Lanscki had patiently fed him with some coffee and some pieces of baklava but there was no sign of life beyond the zombie stage.

She wondered if Bryant could put someone back in there, even if it wasn't the original. For another day perhaps she told herself.

Air currents were getting bumpy, buffeting the small aircraft as they descended down into the morning heat of the southern hemisphere. They all got strapped in.

Military pilots don't have to worry about passenger feedback so they land the plane as they want to. As pilots. So it's swoops and tight turns, however it wasn't too long before the wheels hit the tarmac.

Januscz looked as if he was about to throw up.

The plane taxied off the main runway and headed for the main building.

It's a military air base known as *Castrum Borealis* (Fortress of the North), or more locally; 'Fighter town' on account of its premier size and the SAAF units stationed there. A relatively modern facility, just south of the Rhodesian southern border.

The party stepped out of the aircraft into the bright light. Assorted fighter jets and helicopters and various military kit were lined up in orderly fashion with uniformed men and women stalking about.

A well kept, but vintage Vauxhall, painted in drab olive was waiting for them. A late middle age man was standing by the car wearing a Generals uniform.

Alex strode over and gave a sharp salute which somehow surprised the General.

He gave the reply salute. "I must confess Colonel I'm not sure how to address you?"

"I think Prime Minister is the most accurate now, but let me say General Voebeck, before you ask, you remain in charge of the Army. I would be happy to be consulted but I know you already have the situation under control. I am new here so I will be guided by you."

It was the diplomatic thing to say, she hadn't been made Colonel for nothing, and she could sense the tension that could easily have existed between them melt away a little.

The rest of the aircraft party was approaching.

"Let me introduce you General Voebeck. This is Dr Henry Bryant who is currently my prisoner pending the arrival of the King. This is Captain Lanscki and Corporal Januscz of the Polish Army, now in the King's service, and this fellow is Sergeant Jerry Bradman... who has been wounded in the King's service....and this is ....Cacouhette, the King's Royal Jaguar. She smiled.

Voebeck really didn't know what to make of this somewhat ragbag collection, and Alex knew that the best way was to just go for it and let him catch up later.

"General I will need somewhere for me and my party to stay briefly while we await the King's arrival, which, most probably, won't be for a couple of days. I could also use some new uniforms and a decent liaison officer. As you can see we're not exactly in a good shape to meet the King at the moment."

Bryant was still wearing his djelaba night-shirt and Algerian babouche on his feet.

She looked as if she was wearing someone else's clothes.

Before the General could reply the Jaguar turned rapidly and shot off across the tarmac towards a group of Cheetahs that were staring at the large black cat.

"We use Cheetahs to keep the local wildlife out of the field" he said. "Looks like your animal is about to set the cat amongst the ...er.. cats."

The cheetahs paused for just a second before

moving away at high speed in all directions. Poor Cacouhette had lived too much of a pampered life and whilst he was fast enough for a big cat there was no way he could catch any of them. The other cheetahs realised this quickly enough and ran about, wearing him out. Except for one female that slowed down enough to let him approach.

It was a light moment which completely broke the tension, and they all laughed. People on the base stopped to see.

"Well Colonel, ...Prime Minister, you've brightened my day at least, and we might soon have the first black cheetahs in Africa if I'm not mistaken....let me introduce you to some of my group and we'll sort out you and your party."

Jerry was led away by one of the medical orderlies. Alex told him he'd suffered severe trauma to the head. They would look after him at the main hospital for now.

The pilots scurried about with the ground crew and around an hour later the Beechcraft took to the skies again heading north with a letter for the King.

At the edge of the base was an impressive officers mess, built by the British, and resembling a small French Chateau. The perfect place for the rendezvous. As with many Officers messes it was extremely well equipped. There were several staterooms for VIP guests and these were set aside for the Rheinhart party. There was also an excellent dining room and a temperature controlled pool for relaxation and exercise.

Bryant was put in one of the rooms with Januscz who handcuffed himself to Bryant and promptly fell asleep.

Rhienhart was provided with a state room and a private office as befit her status. One of Voebeck's officers arrived as her liaison officer and dashed about settling in the party. Lanscki settled in with a few of the native officers and had a few drinks at the bar before checking on Januscz and then getting some sleep.

In the evening an SAA tailor arrived and they were all kitted out with new uniforms, then joined Voebeck and his officers for dinner.

As the cigars were passed round by the mess staff Voebeck turned to Alex.

"Come and have a smoke with me outside, I'd like to know a bit more about you"

The two stepped out into the warm African night onto a large balcony overlooking the base and the good Limpopo region.

The general remained silent leaving Alex to decide how much to say.

"I was born on my parent's farm, 'Rheinland', About 3000 acres around Jumbo, about 40 miles north of Salisbury. Tobacco, Cotton, Maize, Citrus, and bit of tea and coffee, the usual stuff."

She found herself slipping into the accent before

she knew it. She pulled on the small cigar and let out a stream of smoke into the night air. She stared at it.

"Mugabe's crazies arrived and killed everyone a few years after independence. I escaped and went to England. Joined the army. Amongst other things, served with Gaunt in Afghanistan before joining MI services as Colonel. That's how we know one another. Retired a few years back, sailed the world, bought a farm in Cumberland. Thought I'd settled down. The attack happened and Gaunt called for me. So here I am back in SA, a full circle, yah"

Voebeck looked at her for a moment.

"I sense there's a lot missing from that story Alex. ...but at least I've now got to meet the famous Alex Rheinhart" He smiled and looked down at his cigar. Despite your name I hadn't quite realised you were from here. No wonder Gaunt thinks you're right for the job."

"I like to think so, Paul, and ditto, good to meet the notorious Paul Voebeck...!"

They both laughed quietly.

A shadow passed under the balcony, darker than the night. She thought she saw a flash of yellow green eyes. Then it was gone.

The following day she visited Jerry in the medical centre on the base. One of the hospital orderlies accompanied her down a corridor to Bradman's room.

"How's he doing?"

"Pretty good actually M'am, ..a tough cookie actually, pretty dehydrated and slight malnourishment but he's ok now. Also we scanned him earlier today and found a nasty little capsule under the skin in his neck. Some kind of neural blocker...slow release. We've taken it out and the lab are having it checked out. Never seen a bio-weapon like that before....interesting...er ...sorry, professional curiosity M'am."

Jerry was sitting up in bed...he wasn't able to speak as yet, but he gave Alex a faint smile. She held his hand for a while but the medics had said it would take several weeks for his system to clear, and they would need to keep him under observation for a while longer in case there was any longer term damage.

She left him and went over to see Paul Voebeck, to get a view on operations.

"We've got most of the south secure, at least as secure as anything ever is in Africa.

All the power stations have been destroyed so all non-military electric power is disabled, I've got military forts and camps spread about the country, as the King has instructed.

We've brought in small semi-portable nuclear plants for the main camps. Pretty good control of the farms and the bush. The towns and cities are deadly now. Completely rat infested.

I've left them to get on with it, let them kill each other, if the disease or starvation doesn't, again as instructed. Lots of self appointed chiefs and trouble makers, assorted militia groups, you know the sort, but we've swept north as far as Zambia so far.

The south was never going to be a real issue anyway. Rhodesia also has the infra-structure, just needs re-building under the no power rules. Martial law everywhere of course…the real problems will come as we get into the centre… the jungle areas, the equatorial coasts.

I'm relying on re-establishing the old
tribal areas, with a suitable Chief as the
headman. It worked here for centuries
and it's well remembered,… before the do-gooders stepped in and fucked it all up."

Voebeck looked at her and she could tell that he was weighing up whether he'd been saddled with another one.

Two days later she and Voebeck were standing on the tarmac again watching the Beechcraft circle down and land on the runway.

The plane taxied round to where the King's reception party was standing to attention.

The door opened and Gaunt stepped out and down the steps. An air of menace preceded him as he stalked towards the reception party.

Voebeck greeted him but he quickly swung his attention to Alex. Their eyes locked. It was impossible to gauge exactly how annoyed he was, but that was the plan.

"I need some time with the Colonel" he said to Voebeck, glancing at Rheinhart.

"Understood my Lord King, there's a car for you."

Back at the mess, and after a brief stop for an honour guard inspection, Gaunt entered the building. Rheinhart directed him to her office overlooking the airbase. She shut the door, Gaunt turned to her, pulling out the letter she had written three days earlier.

He waved it slowly back and forth.

"You have a minute to explain yourself, but be advised your life now hangs by a thread."

Rheinhart was not intimidated by him.

"Is it true?"

"Is what true?"

"That you used me...to bring the Americans on board...that you used the hypnoids on me...had me stripping and dancing for you, Brevard, and Bryant?"

Gaunt was motionless for a moment, then he turned and walked over to the window, staring out at the sky, his great head tilted backwards slightly.

"Yes....and I regretted it from the moment I did it...I have regretted it ever since...even though it was a necessary evil"

"....and you lied to me Edward. When you told me I had been very drunk and filled you in on my earlier life...you couldn't tell me the truth...it had to be bloody Bryant who spilled it out."

"Yes...a white lie perhaps....ever since the day I fried you I decided there was more harm to be done to you if you knew the truth. Better not to know. As is the case in many things....and it's a shame that Henry poked his oar in and told you. Otherwise it would never have come out and we'd all be that bit happier."

"No Edward....if Bryant hadn't told me, then, who knows, Brevard might be telling his story....having a laugh with the boys about Colonel Rheinhart's tits...'she's quite a good dancer you know...with her clothes off..'

"If it's any consolation to you, the moment I knew Brevard was on board I closed it down, made you get dressed and sat with you to make sure there was no abuse...Bryant was always a risk in that regard."

"Talking of whom, what was all that 'where's Henry Bryant?' bullshit when we met at York. You knew where he was all along....no, don't say it, I guess you were testing me...well you did... and I found him anyway."

"Where is he?"

"He's handcuffed to a large Pole at present...and he doesn't like it...but bearing in mind he was going to wipe me and sell me on as some sort of slave before I got rescued, I don't give a shit about him."

"I want him back. You've now seen what I'm doing in the Bou Izem facility. Even though you were uninvited. I don't know what Bryant has told you...."

"Oh I got the full tour before I got out...."

"Then you understand the importance this has for me and for the Kingdom...and for the world."

"Are you sure he's not playing you?"

"About...?"

"All this quantum transfer bullshit....he's a chemist...and a clever one, but 'mind transfers'... really?...turns out he's much more reliant on his old kitbag of nasty drugs and sprays than I think you're aware of."

"We shall see" Gaunt let a rare shadow cross his face.

"...and there's something else...."

Dinner was a strained affair. Bryant had been

released and sat next to Gaunt but there was no social chatter. They ate their meal, said the right things, didn't stray into any difficult questions. Alex could see that Voebeck was keen to get back to his business as soon as possible. No good soldier likes the politics. There were no cigars.

One of the flight crew arrived to advise that the aircraft was ready and they could leave as soon as required. Gaunt thanked Voebeck and his men.

"There's a consignment of H435 kits on its way here. For your personal attention" Gaunt spoke to Rheinhart. "Voebeck will need your skills...."

Bryant sidled past and gave Alex a slight grin, pleased with himself, he was going back to his palace.

Alex, pulled his sleeve towards her and through a smile said "Come near me again Henry and I'll cut off your balls, and your cock...capisce?"

Bryant pulled himself away. " Oh do come and visit us sometime, it was such a pleasure."

He walked after Gaunt. The dinner party filed out into the night through the gardens of the officers mess towards the car that was waiting to take Gaunt and Bryant to the aircraft.

Out of nowhere a huge black shape leapt from the undergrowth onto Bryant's back, it clamped its jaws round the side of his neck and the razor sharp teeth tore a huge chunk of flesh, arteries and veins out of the side of his throat. Blood sprayed everywhere. Bryant went down.

As quickly as it came the Jaguar sprang away and disappeared into the night. It had happened in a matter of seconds.

Alex looked down in horror as Bryant lay on the ground, the huge wound exposed and shiny, blood pulsing out in great fountains, his breathing panting for a moment before his eyes froze over and his dead body lay in an ever expanding pool of blood.

"Who brought that fucking beast here?" Gaunt glared at Rheinhart.

"I did.....and it's your fucking beast"

Gaunt's eyes were fixed on Rheinhart like a snake eying its prey, she could sense the coiled tension as if he were about to strike.

Voebeck had left them after arranging fatigues for them to wear while their uniforms went off to have copious amounts of Bryant's blood removed. The general was sending orders for the beast to be shot but Gaunt had stopped him. "It's a wild animal, let it return to the wild where it belongs" he'd said. Voebeck had the medics remove Bryant's body with instructions to have him frozen as soon as possible.

Gaunt and Rheinhart now stood facing each other in what had been Rheinhart's quarters and office. Rheinhart had taken Bryant's quarters. The Beechcraft had been stood down until morning.

She felt the tension release. The coil unwound. Gaunt let out a sigh and turned to look out of the window at the base, lit up under the night sky.

Rheinhart decided to break the silence. "What will happen to the hypnoids now?"

Gaunt turned back to face Rheinhart. "What do you mean?"

"I mean that without Bryant you're going to lose your weapon advantage."

Gaunt continued to look at her, a faint smile crossed his face.

"Oh its not the hypnoids....Bryant has a team of chemists working for him, he hasn't actually had his hands dirty with those for years. His chemical team produce them, not Bryant himself, so there will be no interruption in supply....but you're forgetting something..."

"Such as..?"

"Bryant's mind still exists..."

Rheinhart paused, her eyes locked on Gaunt, as if processing the information.

"You can't be serious Edward...even if I'm wrong about Bryant and his crazy chemical mind transfer process those clones are just children. It'll be years, at least ten years, before you can even try."

"Yes, the clones, they'll have to wait, but in the meantime I'll re-create him in someone else's body...or rather his team of engineers will. I just need a donor who has the right body chemistry and similar brain capacity. The acid test.."

Alex stood staring at him for a moment.

Gaunt continued "I'll be flying back to Algeria tomorrow morning to meet the engineers and the scientists. Hopefully Bryant will have been frozen by then and I'll take him back with me just in case they need tissue or blood samples. I want you to stay here and work with Voebeck to establish the military, and more importantly civilian control."

The following morning the Beechcraft took to the air once more, heading north with the King, and Bryant's frozen corpse on board.

Voebeck came to outline his plans for his military command centres and more permanent bases into Zambia and Angola, before operations began in the Congo. His army and navy forces were expanding rapidly and he was eager to proceed north.

Alex could see his successes so didn't interfere but told him that it would be best to arrange visits for the various leaders who would be put in place so that she could establish her own position once any fighting was settled and that if he encountered any difficult resistance that he could call on her to assist.

Next she called for Lanscki and Januscz who would act as her personal protection squad.

"Get hold of another company of decent men that you can work with and get some transport organised. I want to head north to Salisbury tomorrow to establish the main headquarters for the country. Also get hold of one of the intelligence officers, Samuels, Voebeck tells me he's our man for Rhodesia, ask him to come and see me"

XXI
Scarman

Levine looked up from his desk where he had been writing his records for his files containing his intelligence information.

Captain Davidson was standing in the doorway "There's a Sergeant Scarman here to see you Lord High Chancellor"

"Show him in"

Davidson swung out backwards and Levine heard him say "Go in"

Through the door came the man who had done several of Levine's more discreet...not to say... more dirty jobs over the past few years.

He was tall, about six feet, with broad muscular shoulders. Lean and fit. He wore a slightly tatty uniform in dark green which made him look like a gamekeeper from a rich estate which was exactly where he had come from prior to the war. He smelled of horse and lived in, and ran, one of the tightest run camps in Devon. A Kings Own Horseman to be reckoned with. Despite his name he bore no scar on his face but had he done so it would have fitted him to the core. His face was his life, hard, pockmarked with a permanent scowl. Short cut dark brown hair and deeply tanned from a life out of doors.

Without being invited he came to sit in front of Levine.

"Lord High Chancellor" he nodded as he sat as if

this was the best 'polite' he could do. His voice had the characteristic Devon burr.

"How was your trip Scarman?" Levine had sent one of the steam locomotive trains south to collect him and his men.

"Very fancy thank you, didn't know you could still do that"

"We've returned to the old 'permanent way', there's a man every mile whose job it is to walk the track every day to make sure its not damaged....we can move troops and all sorts all over the country...now.." Levine paused.

"I've got a nasty little job for you and your men... you'll be well paid...in gold and silver...it's in central London."

"I thought that was one large hole in the ground now....with radioactive rubble everywhere?"

"Rubble yes...radioactive no...there's been a few years of rain and weather, the dust has mostly washed away...into the ground...into the river... I've already got teams down there in the old City...no issues with radiation provided you don't kick up too much dust. I've also got teams of patrols sweeping the area to keep out the inevitable scavengers. I'll let them know not to bother you. In any case I'll issue you with Geiger counters and some iodine pills."

"What's the job?"

"First parachute your men into the Mall...clear it to allow a light aircraft to land and take off...

should be easy with, say, twelve men...perhaps a week maybe ten days...it's mainly trees and rubble. No heavy equipment will be feasible so it'll be men with shovels and wheelbarrows, plus a few chainsaws and all. Grunt work I'm afraid. Clear a strip.

Next to the Mall is St James's palace ...or at least what's left of it. There are tunnels beneath it. I don't know what condition they're in, nor how deep they are but that's what I want you to find. Get in there somehow, find a set of boxes...oak boxes unmarked save for a small crown carved in them, have a look for anything else that's there, get it on the plane and bring it back to me here. Here's a map which I understand shows where they are in relation to the Mall and the palace."

"My men aren't para's..."

"You'll be trained..."

"What's in the boxes?"

"Not your business"

"What if they're flooded?...I'm told the tube lines and all are filled with the Thames?"

"I'll send you pumps...but I doubt they're that deep...and they've been there a long time so it's unlikely."

"What about Sir Oliver?" Sir Oliver Boulton, Lord Lieutenant of Devon.

"Sir Oliver is aware that the King has called for you and that you are at his command temporarily, in other words my command, until

I return you to him, probably no more than a month....anything else?"

"How much...when do we start, and where from?"

"Ah...good" Levine got up slowly from his chair leaning heavily on his stick. He grunted as a piece of Ugandan shrapnel moved in his leg. "You'll get paid well...enough to keep you and your men in a comfortable position for the rest of your lives...a small estate for you to lord it about...and houses and farms for your men and their families.

You start straight away...I've re-comissioned an old airfield here...just outside York at Acaster Malbis...old WW2 runway...you and your men can stay at the local pub...The Ship Inn next door...the pilot and the parachute trainer will meet you there. A few days training for the jump then they'll fly you over the drop site. You'll have your weapons and equipment supplied ... everything you need, including radio to keep in contact....and by the way I'll expect a daily report from you personally....then the plane will come in to take you and the cargo out...if we need more than one run that will be done too...I'm guessing the boxes will be heavy and the plane might not cope with you, your men and the cargo all in one go...we'll see."

Scarman fixed his dark eyes on Levine, he was weighing up the relative dangers but decided it was not that bad and the reward would be

welcome.

"One final thing…just to be absolutely clear….this is top secret…neither you or your men will talk about it…at The Ship or to the people at Acaster. They don't yet know where the drop will be, nor anything about the operation….er… let's give it a name…Operation Ballast. And nothing after it's complete either. You can say you helped the King in a national matter and he rewarded you accordingly."

Scarman was about to rise from the chair but sat down again.

"One more thing Levine…"

"You mean Lord High Chancellor…."

Scarman ignored him. "Some while ago you asked me to have a dig around Porton way…"

"Christ yes!…I'd forgotten…tell me."

"I had a chat with some of the locals…one's who didn't get to go to the Cheviots….some of them knew Gaunt back then…said he was very tight with one of the chemists…you'll have heard of him…Henry Bryant…the one who was screwing around with young girls…including his daughters… if there's any truth in it…..said he had a way to get them into his bed…date rape drug…something like that."

"I have heard of him…rumour and gossip mostly…but surely Gaunt was not up to that sort of thing?"

"Don't know…can't say…but it was Gaunt that

sprung him from the sweat box at Porton....and something about Algeria?."

"Algeria?...what about it?"

"Don't know...just a word someone had heard."

Levine frowned and stared at his hands in thought.

"Anything about Colonel Rheinhart?"

"They'd seen her with Gaunt and Bryant in the early days , yes...some sort of secret unit....transferred to Catterick before heading out to Afghanistan...but it was a long time ago....but one of the wives has a mate up at Catterick...said Rheinhart was there a couple of years ago...poking around and she visited Stephanie Bryant, Bryant's ex-wife....who's now dead by the way"

Levine listened and tried to make some sense of it. But couldn't.

Levine rang a small silver bell on his desk. Moments later Captain Davidson appeared.

"Davidson please show Sergeant Scarman and his men to the truck please and get them set up at Acaster, thank you"

Scarman rose out of his chair, Levine held out his hand and the two men shook hands. The operation was sealed.

XXII

The Farm at Rheinland

The party headed north up the old highway one then onto the old A4 road into Zimbabwe. More or less a straight drive northwards under those strange southern skies where it seems that the light is different from the northern hemisphere. Alex had forgotten how beautiful the light and the country remained with its odd mountains, stones and forests.

But the devastation of more recent times was all too clear. Abandoned cars lay about. The farmland once ordered and highly productive was destroyed by years of neglect. The jungle had returned with abundant weeds and scrub overtaking the once flourishing maize, tobacco and fruit crops. Corruption, fraud and theft had taken a massive toll. Money siphoned off by corrupt officials into exotic European cars, Swiss banks accounts and apartments in the Champs Elysee, Knightsbridge and Lausanne.

No wonder Switzerland had taken a heavy hit. She had wondered what the Swiss had done to deserve it, but of course the targets were the foreign residents. Must have been planned... Gaunt of course...he had planned it all to clean away the corruption and the thievery...from all parts of the world...what better way to clean up with one blow.

They pulled over after a few hours where a group

of men were selling melons, and palm wine. She cut a slice of melon but left the palm wine. Too often the latex drawn from the palms gets infected by bats urine resulting in the nihab virus, one of the many bat diseases present in Africa. None of the men in the convoy touched it either.

Back on the road she had time to think. Now she would re-build the farms, starting with her old farm. Had to start somewhere. Not selfish, this would be her base, build on it to be able to train and replicate across Africa. This would be her job. She would need to establish a police force too. The army were too remote for the people, highly trained, armed, no good for most people. A police force drawn from the local people, and a visible but local understanding of the country. The army would still be there for the big events.

The group bypassed what was left of Harare. A once thriving city now reduced to rubble and gangs. The stench of rotting bodies swept in waves when the wind blew in their direction. No-one shot at them. Maybe they thought better of attacking such an obviously well armed group… or maybe they had just run out of ammunition.

The small town of Jumbo lay about 30 miles ahead, and a few miles further out 'Rheinland'.

As she drew nearer to her place of birth she began to recognise some of the landscape, some of the old landmarks. She began to feel strange.

She found her heart rate was up and she was sweating slightly. Then the flashbacks. She had dealt with many cases of PTSD with others. She had thought that she had been prepared. The events of more than 30 years ago had been pushed away and locked in a small, windowless room in her mind. No one would ever be able to enter there.

She pushed the feelings away. Nothing good could come of it now. It doesn't pay to think too deeply. She brought herself back firmly to the present. That was then. Gone. This is now. She is a different person now, with a totally different history. She looked around her to get her bearings again. Lanscki and Januscz were with her now. Voebeck's men were here with her in the truck. This is the present she told herself, and the future.

"Which way M'am?" the driver shouted. They had slowed down at a junction on a steep hill in the road. Two laterite roads were ahead forking left and right.

"The right one" she yelled back over the straining engine noise.

The driver put the truck into gear and they headed up the road. All too familiar to her. She continued to mentally focus on the present. About two miles later she saw the old gateposts. The 'Rheinland' sign across had gone but this was it. The convoy headed through and up to a wide gravelled area that, somehow was relatively jungle free. Someone was still working the land here. A small field had some crops growing. There was a fruit cage made up from bits of timber and metal with a badly repaired net thrown over.

Then they swung into view of the house. What remained of it. A burnt out shell. The workers cottages along either side also burned out. The stonework still blackened from old fire.

The trucks came to a halt.

The men got out and without needing any orders spread out to secure a small perimeter.

Despite some selective weeding in the courtyard the encroaching jungle was everywhere. A tree had made its way up through the centre of the house and plants grew on most of the walls. In between the shrubs and weeds were traces of blackened timber and slates.

It was late in the day, the sun would be down soon. The heat of the day was slowly dissipating. A quietness was all around except for the footsteps of a few of the men.

Alex stood still for a moment. Her heart rate had evened out. She gazed around her then snapped back into the present.

"Jan, get a camp set up in the courtyard here, near the trucks. Let's set a perimeter for the night. It'll be dark soon. Get a fire going."

"Yes M'am"

There was a sudden crack of rifle fire. She swung round. The men drew their side arms. One of the men shouted.

“M’am ?”

One of the soldiers came out of the bush pulling an old woman alongside.

“It was me who fired M’am... saw a small Impala in the bush back there so I shot it for dinner...and this woman jumped about three feet in the air just at the side...thought I’d hit her by mistake but she’s alright...just a little frightened I think.”

The old woman looked terrified, she was shaking like a leaf.

“It’s alright...we won’t hurt you” Alex spoke directly to the woman.

“Come and join us for dinner if you like....Januscz get her some water will you please, and stick a brew on as we could do with a cup of tea.”

“Ja Ja”. The woman cowered at the sight of the giant pole but he smiled his big tooth challenged grin and turned to get the supplies off one of the trucks.

“I cause no trouble madame...please...” the woman spoke with a strong southern African accent. She was kneeling with her head down repeating ‘please’ and shaking.

Alex went over to her and knelt down with her.

“We won’t harm you...come, you’ve had a nasty

shock but you'll be alright. I'll get you some tea in a minute or two. We didn't mean to frighten you, we just didn't realise you were there…see. These men are with me we've come up from the south to find this farm and to try to rebuild it."

The woman looked up into Alex's face. She stared at Alex. A shadow passed over her expression and she frowned.

"I'm Alex Rheinhart, I used to live here…" but she didn't finish her sentence as the old woman rose up with an expression of awe as she grasped Alex's sleeve.

"Alex??" "Alexandra Elizabeth Rheinhart??"

Now it was Alex's turn to look slightly confused. She hadn't heard her mothers name for a long time. She had her mothers name as her middle name.

"Yeess?… Do I know you?"

"Oh praise the lord" shouted the woman and grabbed hold of Alex as tightly as she could. The woman was crying.

Alex looked down at the small woman clinging to her. Her hair was grey and her brown skin wrinkled from a life in the sun. Her hands were small and calloused from too much manual work. She was dressed in old clothes that were torn and mended. She was barefoot.

"Angel..?…is it you?"

The woman lifted her head and looked up at Alex. She nodded.

"Oh God.." Alex looked away for a moment. Angel Mbane, her nursemaid and early confidente as she and her sister were growing up all those long years ago.

Darkness fell. The men had set a campfire and placed fallen logs around as benches. One of them was roasting pieces of the Impala over the fire and passing round chunks of beautiful roast meat on sticks. Tins of beer were stacked up or passed round as needed. Four men were patrolling a hastily prepared perimeter. Not only possible murderous gangs roaming the bush and seeing the campfire, but also wild animals that would be attracted by the scent and may make a dash for one the group.

Alex and Angel sat talking together. Angel wouldn't touch the meat but she had a beer.

"I've got a vegetable stew at home" she said. "Meat only attracts danger"

Alex wanted to hear her story from the very beginning.

"I saw the soldiers arrive that day and I knew they were bad men. My cousin had told me 'If you see the men in trucks arrive you must leave quickly before they see you' . She'd seen her family attacked and killed by them and she'd seen what they did to the whites, begging your pardon. Now I wish I had shouted or tried to warn you and your family and Alex I'm so sorry..." tears ran down her cheeks and she bowed her head.

“Alex put her arm round her shoulders “There’s nothing you could have done Angel, they were bad men fired up on palm wine and coca, you would have been killed”

Angel pulled up her head and carried on.

“Yes ...bad men. I ran into the cornfield before they could see me, ...but I could see them. They went into all the workers field cottages..” she waived her hands around the edges of the darkened courtyard where the remains of small burnt-out cottages still stood.

“Any of us who wasn’t in the fields they dragged out...cursing and shouting at them...calling them traitors...slaves of the white man...all that terrible rubbish ...and one by one hacked them to death. ...My father, my brother and sister...”She stopped again to control the grief that she still felt. She looked back at Alex. “You know we were all very happy here. Your papa and mama were good and kind people. We enjoyed working here...it was good.... and we were proud to produce all that food for the Rhodesian people.... And they looked after us and gave us a good wage...and homes and electricity....” She sank back down. Alex dropped her head, she could feel the tears but pushed them away again.

“Anything they fancied they took...then poured petrol in and set them all on fire....your papa must have seen the smoke and suddenly he was driving that old tractor back into the courtyard. He must have fired his gun at them, I think he shot two of them but they had guns and they must have shot him because I saw him fall off the tractor....but he wasn't dead...then your mama came out with your sister and her gun and shot two more of them but they overwhelmed her... and...." She stopped and looked down at the ground. "...they were bad, bad men..."

Alex held her tightly. She knew Angel would spare her the details of how her family were killed. She knew Angel would not want to re-live what she saw, in the telling.

"I saw too" said Alex "like you I saw them coming and hid in the near bush. My gun was in the house but I was frozen to the spot with the horror of it all. I couldn't move, could barely breathe. But I saw too....." her voice tailed off into silence and both women sat staring into the edge of the fire without speaking.

After a while Angel looked up at the flames. "They found all the booze in the house and went on a drinking binge until most of them collapsed. Night came, I slipped away through the fields towards the town but when I got near to it there were more of them. Shooting their guns, torching the buildings, raping the women and either killing or capturing the men. ....I crept away and ....oh I can't remember if I slept or where I slept. I stayed out in the bush for days.

I looked for you. I knew I hadn't seen you with them but I didn't know if you were still in the house or if you'd managed to escape. After a few days I crept back nearer to the house. I saw that they'd burnt it to the ground. It was still smoking, but the men had gone. Later on I found out they'd moved from farm to farm…village to village…looting, murdering, burning. I waited for a few days by the big oak tree…you know the one, down in the tobacco fields. I pulled up some of your father's vegetables and ate those but I wasn't ever hungry. I don't know when I stopped shaking"

She paused and stared into the fire which was now burning low.

"So how have you managed to survive here? "

"A few of the people from the town and some of the other farms came here and we banded together. The old church that your grandfather built in the valley down there was hidden away and we moved there. Things quietened down although the town was still a dangerous place for us. But we had everything we needed to survive here and so it has become our new home. We've built small cottages around the church. The land here is good and fertile so we've got crops. Nothing on the scale that you and your family did but quite enough for us to survive. "

"But surely the new government looked after you?"

"Ha!." Here eyes widened and the flames from the fire were reflected in them. "The new government cared only for themselves. Many people have starved to death at their hands, any opposition was brutally crushed ...I have heard that Harare was kept in good condition for those who were supporters, but the other towns were controlled by bad men. Just gangsters dealing in people's misery and getting rich until a rival gang threatened them then back to the bloodshed. No, we have remained here where it has been relatively safe and made our own little world, without electricity or running water, except for the stream. We're hidden from view in the bush."

The fire burned low and the men began to retire to their tents for the night. Lanscki came over.

"Your tent is up M'am and one for the lady too"

"Tomorrow I must show you something" and with that Angel disappeared into the bush and into the night.

Alex slept badly and was up before dawn. The soldiers had coffee on the fire and she helped herself to a biscuit.

Lanscki came over. "We had a quick scout around. Nothing much moving around here. There's a quarry which I guess was used to build all this" he waved his hand around the small settlement. "And there's a small set of bush huts and building around a church over there " He waved again. Alex knew where it was. "I've sent some men into the town but from what I've seen I'm guessing its pretty derelict like everything else round here."

As the sun rose up Angel re-appeared and took some coffee from the stove. "Not as good as ours" was her only comment.

"Come with me..."

Alex followed her down past the ruins of the house and headed south towards a very large oak tree that stood at the edge of a field. The jungle had all but returned, however a few wild tobacco plants still grew and it looked as if some had been harvested.

As she drew nearer to the trunk she could see three light grey stones embedded in the ground. The sparse grass had been cut back from each in a tight circle. Angel stopped to let Alex go forward on her own. The stones were neatly laid and on each one a cross had been carved with a name under each. 'Charles Rheinhart', 'Elizabeth Rheinhart', 'Anne Rheinhart'. Her father, mother and sister.

Alex knelt down in front of them and Angle came up quietly behind her. "I gave them a Christian burial, and I know that they lie here in peace, protected by the big oak tree for as long as time itself...I'll go back to the camp now and leave you here for your prayers" and with that she quietly slipped away leaving Alex bent over on the ground.

She returned to the camp later. The men had cooked more of the antelope for breakfast and she ate well.

She took Lanscki down to the old church which was surrounded by small stone and wood huts where Angel and her settlement lived. Around the base of a giant Jacaranda tree were laid out in concentric circles further sets of stones set in the ground. Each carved with a cross and in most cases a name.

Several people were standing or sitting around a communal cooking pot which contained ground corn meal and assorted fruits and nuts. An African staple. One or two had pipes and were quietly smoking. Lanscki offered his pack of cigarettes which were gratefully accepted. A few of the people remembered her family though most were too young now. It was all in the past.

She and Lanscki returned to the base camp.

"What do you want to do?"

Alex didn't reply but went over to the open edge of the courtyard and stared out into the distance.

"I know what you're thinking..." Lanscki came over to stand with her.

"What am I thinking..."

"You're thinking that if you start to rebuild this farm and the town... you'll end up endangering the people who have survived here... and that maybe it would be better to leave the past behind and start afresh somewhere else....but wherever you start will have the same risks....you don't want to be beaten by the events of the past..." he stopped.

"Something like that..." as she finished speaking a loud shrieking sound came from above and behind and they had just enough time and training to drop to the ground before a missile came flashing overhead and detonating in the old cornfield.

Immediately after a shot was fired from the bush. One of the perimeter patrols. Then the chatter of short burst automatic fire.

Showers of soil and stones flew up.

Alex looked up to see a silver military jet pass over at high speed and low altitude before banking hard to the left and rising up fast in a wide turn to make another run at them.

"What the f..."

There was a flash from the plane and seconds later another missile flew past overhead just missing the trucks and landing in the bush not far from the church settlement. There was a loud explosion. Branches and leaves sprayed up and out.

Another sound, more of an approaching whisper came suddenly from the south. Two grey ghost SAAF F15s came out of nowhere. The whisper changed to a deafening roar as they passed overhead. The silver jet banked up at almost 90 degrees and rose amazingly fast into the sky. But not fast enough for an F15. The lead aircraft banked up straight up into the sky. There was a flash followed by a fireball as the air to air missile from the F15 blew the silver jet into powder.

The two F15s turned wide and were gone over the horizon before anyone dared to move.

"What the fuck...." But Alex was up and sprinting for the church clearing .

Burnt leaves were still falling from the sky but thankfully the settlement was intact. Angel was on her knees outside the church. From out of the bush a large force of men were emerging and Alex had just enough time to drop behind cover as the rain of bullets spewed out over the ground.

She pulled her side arm and shot two of the men approaching, firing what looked like old Kalashnikov's. More men were coming out of the thick bush.

A flash and explosion. Lanscki's men had launched two RPG's into the trees killing the nearest and cutting off men coming in from behind. Several of Alex's group broke away and swept wide whilst keeping up a firing position.

More RPG's went into the tangle of bush and jungle. The men on the wide sweep closed in from both sides in a classic pincer movement and within minutes the shooting stopped.

Lanscki came over "General Voebeck on the radio M'am" and handed her the radio.

"Are you ok?" his first words. "Yes, no damage thankfully...what the hell was that?"

"Some of the better organised rebel bands have got hold of old planes and jury rigged them with whatever they can find. That was an old English Electric Lightning fitted with French rapiers. We didn't pick it up on radar until it was almost upon you. Fortunately we had two F15s in the air and they got there quick. It's par for the course I'm afraid. Mostly out of Mozambique where there's a strong Jihadi presence."

"But how did they know I was here..?"

"Unlikely that they knew it was you....but you're pretty close to the Moz border. My guess is one of their forward scouts saw the convoy yesterday and shot back across the border overnight to fit you up."

"They also had some men on the ground...but they've been dealt with also"

"Well I'm sending you some extra gear....."

The radio went dead as a bullet smashed through the case in a cloud of smoke and burning plastic.

Lanscki came over.

"It's not over yet....

XXII
Parachutes and Tunnels

Scarman and eleven of his men climbed into the truck that Levine had provided. Their rucksacks were piled up in the centre and they sat along two benches facing each other.

"We've got a nice little job lads"

The men grinned. They trusted Scarman with their lives. They knew he wouldn't let them down and that there would be a good reward for them once the job was done, whatever it was.

"Hope none of you are afraid of heights as we've got some parachute training lined up"

A few of them smiled, a few of them groaned.

"Bit of Dutch courage that's all" Scarman pulled a bottle of whisky from his pack and waved it at them, smiling.

The truck trundled off, heading out to Bishopthorpe, past the Archbishop of York's palace on the banks of the Ouse. The road out of Bishopthorpe ran along the river's bank. Soon they arrived at The Ship Inn.

Waiting for them were two men who welcomed them and led them into the pub to sort out the rooms.

"I'm Sergeant Johnson, I'll be training you for the jump, and this is our pilot Fred Saunders who'll be flying the plane. Your kit has arrived at the airfield along with ration packs and tents. I see you've already got your weapons, but I've got some more ammo just in case."

"We start at dawn tomorrow so get some rest now. I understand you've had a long journey. Don't get too pissed. The Landlady here, Liz, will sort you out with food and beer. He pointed to a small fat woman who seemed unfazed by the arrival of a pack of strangers to her previously quiet corner of England. She smiled and said to sit at the tables and she'll bring the food in.

The following day the truck took them over to the airfield. Men had cleared off the topsoil and weeds from the main runway. It was cracked and old but apparently flat enough for the plane to take off and land. An old DC3 stood at one end of the runway painted in the familiar drab olive of the Army.

"We'll be using these ram-air canopies" said Johnson. "Anyone used them before?" no-one nodded.

"Ok good. No bad habits then."

Over the next two days Scarman and his men, he had nicknamed them the 'Ballast Men', were trained to jump from the DC3 and manoeuvre their chutes so they could land in the right place as softly as stepping down from a chair.

At dawn on the third day, after Liz had given them a full cooked breakfast they clambered aboard the DC3 and took off heading south. The forecast had said light rain, which was what they wanted. Levine told them to clear the rubble while it was wet to stop any dust which might have some plutonium dust mixed in. If it didn't rain he would call in a plane to spray water across the surface like a crop sprayer.

An hour later they were circling over the remains of what was once central London. It was unrecognisable except for where there were areas that were greener than others. Hyde Park, and St James' park showed up as a lot greener than the surrounding piles of scorched and tumbled rubble. There was a faint smell of burning in the air but the stench of rotting bodies had finally subsided to a background scent. In any case this was the familiar scent to all men who had approached any of the once big cities and towns now lying in a similar state to what they could see below.

Saunders brought the plane in from the east and Johnson lined them up ready to jump out from about 3000 feet. The jump light went from red to green and they followed each other out in a descending line of drab olive nylon canopies. They touched down onto the rubble and fallen trees that made up the once famous Mall.

The plane swooped round to make a second

pass. This time several traditional chutes came down as bundles of shovels, wheelbarrows and assorted equipment and rations landed with a thump at various intervals along the route.

The men began to look for a suitable place to bivouac. St James' park was a mass of fallen trees and long grass, however behind the remains of the palace was a grassy garden area that seemed relatively unscathed. Scarman ran the Geiger counter over it. Just background noise registered.

"Ok lads, get the gear collected and bring it here. Phillips, get a fire going, Sam take three of you and set up a patrol perimeter. Organise a rota, two hours at a time. The rest of you get the tents up and sort out the kit and the rations. Get a wet and dry pit dug somewhere out of the way. I'm going for a recce to see what's what.

Scarman loped across what was left of the Mall. He went to the far eastern end where the crumbled remains of Admiralty arch once stood. He cast his eye over what was once Trafalgar Square. Unrecognisable. He wondered if the big bronze lions were still there under all the crap.

He looked west towards what was once Buckingham palace and the Victoria memorial. He was working out how much would need to be cleared so that the plane could land , turn round and take off again. Saunders had given him the approximate distances he would need.

He walked in average steps of about one yard, stepping over the charcoaled remains of the big London plane trees that had once lined the Mall on each side. A few stumps remained along the way. There were even some green shoots on a few of them. Nature always finds a way to survive he thought.

He scraped away some of the lighter rubble and found that the tarmac surface remained intact under all the detritus. However, when he reached the end he'd only measured around 3000 feet. Saunders had said the bare minimum would be 4000 feet, and that would be unloaded. He would need at least 5-7000 feet with passengers and cargo even with the SAS variant he was flying with the more powerful engines.

Surely they should have known this...then he realised that Levine had probably only told them to drop them in, not that they would need picking up...bastard.

Back at the camp things were taking shape.

"Corporal Philips, get me the radio will you....the rest of you get the shovels and the barrows and start at the eastern end clearing the crap off the road. Put it in heaps beyond the tree stumps so we have a nice clear level for the plane to come in. Get started while its still raining."

Once the men were gone he fired up the radio to get hold of Levine. He reached Captain Davidson who went to get Levine into the radio room.

"It's not long enough Levine."

"What's not long enough?"

"The damned Mall, its at least 2000 feet short for the plane to land and take off"

"Scarman I know perfectly well how long it is, what you don't know is that the Navy uses rocket boosters to get them off carriers. Same here. Just get on with the job....let me sort out the collection details....I didn't plan this without a means to get you and the cargo out. Do you think I'm stupid?"

"No sir I don't but you could have told me more of the detail"

"I appreciate that you are the kind of man that thinks for himself...very useful in some situations...but here let me do the thinking...you just get on with the operation."

Scarman scowled but just gave a curt "Yes sir", out"

Levine gave Davidson a nod "Bloody soldiers"

"Yes sir"

It took the Ballast men five days to clear the whole road from one end to the other leaving a relatively smooth strip, enough for the plane to land...and hopefully get off the ground when needed. The weather had continued to be wet and cold but the men had made a wide shelter with the nylon canopies and a decent fire pit. There was no shortage of charcoal. Their tents surrounded the shelter and the patrols had not encountered any scavengers. On the third day one of Levine's patrols had made contact but didn't ask any questions, just asked if they needed anything. They brought some more food including a whole side of a pig which provided them with several days of barbecued pork until they were heartily sick of it. They also rolled in a couple of barrels of beer which was accepted with great pleasure.

Scarman pulled out the map that had been given to him by Levine. He had developed a good understanding of the layout of the palace rubble during the last few days and the map began to make sense.

In the evening he gathered the men together having decided to leave the perimeter patrol to Levine's existing team so that he could concentrate all the men on first the clearing of the runway, and now to start digging for the tunnels.

"Well done men" he said "You've all done well to get the runway cleared so now it's time to get to the actual job we came here to do. Here's a map of the place" Scarman laid the now scruffy paper on the ground and his men peered over to look.

"The job is to get into these tunnels that run under here...somewhere. The palace entrance with the steps is no good as it's under too much brick and rubble... probably collapsed anyway.

This arm here...” he pointed to the map “ runs under somewhere below us which I think will be the best place to dig as it looks like it’s mainly soil. I don’t know how far down but we start here....” He pointed to a section on the map “ which is over there..” he pointed over towards one end of the garden “ and we keep digging until we find it”

“What’s in the tunnels sarge?”

“I don’t know much more than you Tennant, “ Scarman looked up at the eager face of private Tennant. “ all I know is that there are some boxes that the King wants us to take back to York....I guess we’ll know them when we see them...”

“Any questions?”

The men shook their heads. Soldiers know when to say something but more likely to not say anything unless it’s life or death.

“Right we start at first light tomorrow. Get some kip”

It took two more days before they found the top of one of the tunnels. They had gone down about 20 feet. No one had thought to bring a ladder but Private Thompson made one out of tree branches lashed together with rope. They cleared the soil over an arch-work of brick and stone. Scarman slid his spade in between the stones and worked one of them loose. They managed to get it out and started knocking the surrounding bricks and stones. A whole section collapsed inwards leaving Private Cauldwell to fall into the hole.

"You alright Cauldwell?"

"Alright Sarge, just a few bruises....pretty dark down here, we'll need some lamps"

"I'll take you three with me, the rest of you can rig up a hoist system to pull up the cargo once we've found it."

Scarman and three others stayed in the hole and slid the ladder down into the tunnel opening before climbing down.

They lit the lamps.

"One of you stay here to keep in contact with the others, the three of us will start at this end under the palace and see how far it goes. If anything collapses....." He let the matter hang. "String out in a line..."

The tunnels were old but very well made. It became clear that there were several branches running off in different directions, one towards St James Street, another towards the North West, presumably Buckingham Palace, and another running south west towards Horseguards. In addition there were several underground rooms with vaulted ceilings held up by pillars of brick and stone. Some had thick oak doors which were locked. One of them was open and empty. The place was remarkably dry. Somewhere there must be air vents as the air was not stale and the circulation of the air kept away the damp.

They passed by several locked doors until

Scarman found a door with a small crown carved into the wood.

“Let’s start with this one, Cauldwell, get that open please…”

Cauldwell brought out a crow bar but the door stood solid and wouldn’t budge.

“This old oak is as hard as iron sarge, better if we can pick the locks….get Grimson down here… he’s done his share of burglary”

So Grimson was called down and sure enough he had his ‘tools’ in his pocket.

“Piece of cake” he said as the lock clicked and the door swung open.

In the light of their torches they saw a room filled with shelves on which were a series of oak boxes, just as Levine had described, each with a small crown carved in them on one side, facing out.

Scarman pulled one out and put it on a table that sat in the middle of the room. It was extraordinarily heavy for a box of its size.

“Grimson, can you open one of these and then lock it again without it looking obvious?”

“Course I can Sarge, let me have a look…”

Grimson looked at the key hole, sighed, then selected a thin bar from his tool roll, drew out another slim bar and within moments heard the lock click open.

He looked at Scarman “There you go Sarge….”

Scarman lifted the lid carefully. It was lined in

sheet lead, but cushioned with padded red velvet as was the rest of the box. An object, covered in a red silk cloth lay inside.

Three of the sides folded down. he pulled away the silk and they all let out a short gasp.

Grimson whistled. Scarman slipped his hands around the sides and pulled out the Imperial Crown of England.

The dazzling jewels caught the light of the torches, the polished gold framework gleamed. Their faces were at once lit up by the brilliance of it, their look one of awe.

"It's a copy of you know what..."said Cauldwell. But Scarman looked carefully at the object in his hands. He spoke slowly as if speaking too loud might do some damage

"No... it's not a copy lads...."

Someone said 'bloody hell'. Scarman put the crown back in its container and pulled up the sides before closing the lid.

"Grimson, lock it up now...Alright you three... no-one mentions this to anyone...we didn't open the box...we don't know or care what's inside... we're just the grunts given the job of heaving this stuff out and onto the plane home...got it?"

"Yes sarge..."

"Let's have a look at what else we've got here.

At one end of the room was an old Victorian trolley with two central wheels and castors at both ends. Along the shelves around the walls were similar boxes in different shapes and sizes though each one had a small crown carved into the front panel.

"We can use that trolley to get them out of here, but first let's have a look at what's behind those other doors we passed. "Grimson get your tools and start opening them up, Cauldwell, start loading these onto the trolley"

"Aye sarge"

Grimson opened a second room and Scarman, Murray and Grimson looked in. In the torch light there were more shelves each containing various boxes and bags, but without a marking on them, including some leather boxes which were badly decayed.

One of the leather boxes had split open and from it spilled a pile of gemstones, gold coins and pearls.

"It's like a pirate's treasure!" Grimson was handling some of the stones." They look very real to me"

"These boxes are very old...look it's got ER printed on the leather…I wonder if this is stuff that Drake and others took from the Spanish way back in the 16th or 17th century?" Scarman was something of a history buff." He came back, kept what he wanted and gave the rest to the Queen? The first Elizabeth? Then there's all the pirates robbing the Spanish and Portuguese around the Caribbean...confiscated by the English authorities and brought back here?"

"Look at this lot sarge" Grimson had opened another box. He was holding what must be Mayan or Aztec gold figures and masks. "Heavy as hell...the real stuff!"

"No wonder it's all been salted away down here... who would ever know...they couldn't show it or reveal it as it would have led to all sorts of trouble."

"It's perfect" said Grimson with an evil grin "No one knows it's here, it's not in anyone's records... we could have a bit of it ourselves."

"Grimson you have no idea who you're dealing with up top. If they find out or if anyone blabbed you'd be shot and shoved in a hole...don't be stupid."

"I know...I know, but still Sarge it's just that... well we're a very tight unit...you...and all the lads. A bag of stones and some gold each, just a pocketful. It would be in all our interests to keep schtum...you know" his face was sweating with excitement.

"Get the other room open Grimson and stop pissing about"

Grimson left on his light feet and soon there was a call "Sarge...come and have a look at this!"

In an adjoining room on the opposite side of the tunnel was another 'Royal' collection, but this one was not English...

"I think these are Russian royalty....look at that crown...I've seen something like it before...the Tsars had them"

"Bloody hell" this time Scarman couldn't keep a straight face "Just suppose Tsar Nicholas...after all, he was related to our lot....got most of his stuff out and sent it over here to his cousin for safe keeping?, Christ it's like a Tiara shop!"

"Some of this is more western European... same thing I guess...after the Frogs revolution a fair bit of their royalty and aristocracy got over here...no doubt with their jewellery and regalia...left it with our lot and it's stayed here. And again...what are they going to do? Send it back once the original owners are dead?"

"..and we're the only ones who know sarge..." Grimson was making a mental inventory, walking up and down the shelves with his torch. Scarman ignored him.

In another room was a hoard of paintings, assorted boxes, and under a sheet, a pallet of solid gold bars marked with a swastika. "Fuck me...you know what this is don't you...! And we had it all along...! Must have been collected up by Tommies in '45/46?"

"And in here Sarge..." Grimson called Scarman over to another room which was stacked full of large flat crates, filling the room."

"Not paintings...they're too heavy" Grimson heaved at one of the crates but it was way too heavy.

"Scarman had a feeling. He took the crowbar and prised one of the crates open and pulled back the soft wool sheet inside. He let out a soft whistle.

"The Amber Room...it's here...after all these years...folks have been searching for this for ever....my god, and it's been here all along..."

"What is it Sarge?"

"The Amber Room...made for Peter the Great and installed in the palace at St Petersburg. They're panels of heated and worked amber stuck to large sheets of wood along with gold leaf and jewels...mirrors too. One of the wonders of the 18th century world....looted by the Nazis when they stormed St Petersburg...Leningrad back in the second world war...took this and may other priceless artefacts."

"While the Yanks and the Ruskies were grabbing up their scientists our lot were pocketing all the loot!"

In another room were boxes filled with assorted china, bric-a-brac and more jewellery and gold items. Valuable stuff but most likely gifts for the Kings and Queens of the time from foreigners, shoved down here as it wasn't wanted in the palace.

In another, a collection of the most beautiful and delicate Chinese porcelain and jade items as well as a variety of jewels. "The Summer Palace..." Scarman said "Lord Elgin...not the Marbles one..the other one…supposed to have destroyed it all but here we are, stashed away from the eyes of the world…no doubt a gift for Vicky…"

"Grimson, Murray, have a recce along some of these other tunnels, see what's there and where they go…don't nick anything…there's only one way out and I'll be searching you …just so you know…he grinned at Grimson who grinned back. I'm going up top to radio Levine to get a suitable hoist and packing cases, and we're gonna need a bigger plane…or more of them."

Cauldwell was pulling the trolley with several of the boxes from the 'crown' room towards the hole in the tunnel roof. Scarman joined him.

"Sarge, that hoist they've jury rigged is not going to be strong enough for this lot. This is only one shelf load and it already weighs a ton"

"One box at a time Cauldwell. Get them up there so we have something to load on the plane. Hopefully they'll bring us some better gear now that we know what we're dealing with"

"Aye sir."

Scarman radioed Levine.

"We've found what you're looking for …and a lot more….I've retrieved the first lot but you'll need to send the plane as we're going to need several trips…you won't believe what's down there…and we'll need more equipment to get it out…"

The following morning the Ballast men watched the DC3 come into land on their newly cleared runway. It came in low from the east and touched down almost immediately beyond the rubble of Admiralty Arch. A drogue chute came out of the tail end and the plane stopped easily before reaching the far end.

Under the tail, mounted on the underside of the fuselage were two sidewinder rocket motors minus any warhead. These would provide the acceleration needed to get the plane aloft before running out of runway. Also the engines had been tuned to maximum efficiency by the RAF mechanics to provide maximum prop thrust.

But the test would be to manage the weight of the cargo.

The pilots stepped down from the plane and came over to Scarman.

“We’ve got the gear you asked for and also a set of heavy duty scales. We know what we can and can’t take weight wise so let’s see the crates and get them weighed in.

The equipment was pulled out of the plane by the men and a loading area created to organise the cargo. Each crate or box was weighed then loaded in onto the plane until they reached just under the maximum load.

“Better stand away now....the engines and the rockets will kick up a fair bit of dust”

The ballast men returned to their camp to watch from a distance.

The main engines coughed into life. They were

still warm from the flight but the pilot let them re-heat for a minute or so before increasing the throttles to bring the aircraft round and up to the end of the runway, into the light wind.

The engines came up to full speed, the noise echoed across the wastes of the capital. Then a shower of sparks flew from the two rocket motors, the brakes were released and the plane began to moved forward. It gathered speed remarkably quickly and began to rise up from the ground. Even so it was a close call with the wheels only inches from the rubble of the Victoria memorial. The plane, still under rocket power rose swiftly up before the rockets spluttered out. It was enough. The aircraft was travelling at speed and the two Rolls Royce engines driving the twin propellers sped forward . The plane turned slowly and passed over the men, dipping its wings port and starboard. The men waved and shouted.

XXIII

A Trip to Mozambique

Lanscki ducked behind one of the cars and Alex dived for cover.

“Men circling round the fields M’am....”

Alex peered out to get her bearings. More men were emerging from the jungle to the north and the west.

“...and we’re low on ammo M’am...”

More bullets flew overhead.

Alex stood up.

“Ok you men,” pointing to some of the soldiers crouching behind the lorries firing at the northern incomers. “Two of you gather up those beer cans...empty them out then drain the petrol from those trucks and fill as many cans and bottles as you can....you two..” she pointed at two of the men who were particularly small and thin..”Get into the chimney over there “She pointed at the ruins of the house and the only wall still standing because of the chimney structure "...take a box of ammo and those rifles, take 'em up the chimney and start sniping ....pick out the officers or anyone giving orders... the chimney will give you cover."

She had climbed up it as a girl. It had a wide flue and there were bricks that acted as steps.

She stepped sideways and down as more bullets flew over her head.

"You two" she pointed towards another group. "Get down to the church, get them to stay low or out of sight and bring back those two bicycles... get the inner tubes out and make a catapult with them and the frame...get me some flares too"

More men began circling the encampment, hiding in the fields of corn and then standing up to shoot inwards or lob a grenade before ducking back down.

She noticed they were throwing the grenades too soon. She crouched and ran to the side of the house where she had seen a couple of tennis rackets.

She ran back and just in time she saw a grenade flying over. In an instant she reached out with one of the rackets and hit it straight back out into the field. It landed somewhere near the original thrower and then ..boom. A scream and a gout of smoke, blood and earth flew up.

The men cheered.

Lanscki called over Januscz. “Get up that tree and take some ammo with you.” Januscz grinned and shot away.

Alex looked at Lanscki.

“He might be big but no-one can climb a tree like him, and he’s a damned good shot”

They both grinned. There was always something comic about the big Pole despite the fact that he was deadly in many ways.

The men had returned from the church and had stripped out the two rubber inner tubes. Two more men held the frames down on the ground upside down and the tubes slid over the upright cross members.

The men filling the cans with petrol ran over with their cargo.

“Don’t light them, just fling them into the fields and the jungle all around” shouted Alex over the noise of the gunfire.

Tins and bottles of petrol began to rain down in the surrounding fields, fired by catapult from the old bike frames. The men swung the frames to rotate the direction of fire.

Alex loaded the flare gun and stood up. She fired a couple of flares south into the ripe and mainly dry cornfield. Seconds later there was a loud ‘pop’ as the petrol vapour exploded. Suddenly there were flames everywhere. The field containing many of the attackers was ablaze. Men on fire were screaming and running in all directions spreading the fire to new areas of the dry vegetation.

She fired north and again the jungle burst into flames. A huge explosion followed as a section of the attackers ammo caught fire and detonated, probably grenades.

She looked up at the chimney. The two snipers were picking off attackers as they ran to escape the flames leaving those on fire to die a horrible death.

Rifle fire also rang out from the big Jacaranda tree in the courtyard as Corporal Januscz picked off the men in the jungle also escaping the flames.

An hour later a group of bedraggled men came out of the jungle holding up a white shirt tied to a stick.

Alex and Lanscki went forward to accept their surrender.

"Get the wounded into the tents and burn the dead"

She used the surrendered men to collect the bodies of their comrades.

Of her own men there were three dead and two badly injured.

She sat down with the man who carried the white flag.

"Who ordered you here, and why?"

"It was Duchesne...a bad man...'The Duke'" he spoke in broken French and Saswati.

"He got big militia in Mozambique…control the country…take what he wants…kill those who don't agree…rape and torture everywhere… Duke is very bad man but powerful….big chief."

"But why come here?…we're 100 miles from the border."

"Not that far when you're starving….no food there….here plenty of food…he says 'kill them…. take their food… bring back slaves'."

"What is your name?"

"I am Saint-Pierre….old Mozambique family… slaves of the French before they left….but proud old family…the Duchesnes' were our neighbours….he gives me these men ….gives me orders….I know what will happen if I say no."

He looked down, and rather sad.

"Take me to him."

San-Pierre looked at her.

"He will kill you…no, worse…you will be his slave…as a woman…." His voice tailed off.

"Take me to him…tell him you have brought a valuable slave….then leave me to kill him"

San-Pierre looked up at Alex. "How will you do this?…he has many men…you will be in great danger."

"Leave that to me"

So a day later the party set off. She rummaged around in her trunk. Alex changed into a bloody and torn shirt , and an ill fitting coat, stained, and with bullet holes that she took from one of the dead soldiers. She wiped her face with dirt and undid her hair which she wiped with some mud.

Lanscki insisted on coming with her but she told him to stay to take charge of securing the base and to wait for the reinforcements sent by Voebeck.

"I'll take Januscz with me and some of the men, but we will look like prisoners, we'll take some of the supplies too, and some of the cattle in one of the trucks.

The road west was in a state of disrepair. As they approached the border it became impossible to use the trucks so they went on foot. It took a whole day but they crossed the border into Mozambique looking exactly as they should look as prisoners. She made San-Pierre lead the party, with some of his men in front and the 'prisoners' and supplies in the middle. The cattle wandered along as cattle do…prodded occasionally to keep them on track.

By late afternoon they came over a ridge to see a large camp spread out before them. Smoke was rising from camp fires but in the centre was a large traditional African round house made of timber and thatch. Surrounding this were several Ferrari's and Lamborghini's together with an old Rolls Royce. Symbols of wealth. Next to this were three naked bodies hanging by their feet, their charred remains hanging over what was left of a set of small fires at the base. Symbols of brutality and a reminder to those who might be tempted to challenge the 'Duke'.

San-Pierre led his party of prisoners into the camp and made straight for the round house. People cheered as he made his way through the rows of small huts and tents. The smell of smoke mingled with the dust and stink of the dunghills....and roasted flesh.

Two of Duchesne's men were sent out to see what was happening.

"I bring the Duke some gifts of food...and slaves!" he announced.

He turned theatrically waving at the seemingly bedraggled group of prisoners and men, and the cattle and supplies.

The man himself appeared in the doorway with a big smile on his face.

He was a large man, dressed in silks and with gold chains around his neck. He wore two large gold Rolex watches on each wrist. Two scantily clad females stood behind him. He had a gold plated pistol in a holster on his belt....a gangster.

"San-Pierre...my old friend! You have achieved a great victory....you will be rewarded well....what have you brought me? "

"I bring many supplies and here...good slaves including this one" he pushed Alex forward who fell down on her knees.

"She be the great one...the one in command of the rebels in her camp of thieves...she is yours great Duke...along with the food and the cattle... there is much more now that we have taken control..."

Duchesne gave an evil grin as his big sweaty hands grabbed Alex's chin and lifted her head.

"A bit old don't you think San-Pierre but never mind she will be good sport...bring her in to my house along with those boxes" he pointed at the ammo boxes.

Alex was pushed into the house. Expensive carpets were laid badly all over the floor. There was a raised dais on which was a leather armchair, beside which, a huge bed. More scantily clad girls. There were armed guards at the door and inside, around the walls.

Duchesne sat down on his 'throne' like one of the old Chieftains, and Alex was pushed into the centre of the room in front of him.

"So great one...not so great eh?" He laughed.

Alex stood up slowly and raised her arms, waving them about slowly.

"What's....?..." but his tongue caught in his throat. The room fell silent. The guards stood still looking blank. The girls stood still.

"You!" she pointed at Duchesne "Will come with me"

She turned to the guards. “Lower your weapons and take them outside, give them to the big man that came with me.”

She took the gold pistol and led Duchesne out of the arched entrance of the house. He walked meekly as a lamb.

San-Pierre, who had been at Alex’s side followed meekly too but she made him stand next to her.

Januscz and her other men were outside looking on with some curiosity.

“Januscz…take the guns from these men and come over to me”

He grinned his big smile “Ja, jam”

Alex hailed the surrounding men and women from the camp who stepped forward slowly, looking frightened.

She made Duchesne kneel down in front of her, she took the pistol and shot him through the forehead. An execution.

“He is gone….there will be no more of this..” She pointed to the hanging corpses. “San-Pierre will be your leader now…”. She turned to San-Pierre who was still standing looking blank next to her. “Raise your hands and wave to the people”

He did so.

“Smile”

He did.

The people started to cheer and clap.

“Take these cattle and the supplies of food and

share them around the camp. You will get more soon and there will be no more death or war... you will return to your farms...you will grow your crops...school your children....build your homes and live a life of peace. Make sure that no-one becomes like him...." She pointed to the corpse of Duchesne. "Choose honest men and women to lead you and to honour your laws"

A man stepped forward.

"These men must also die...they are bad men, Duchesne's gangsters."

The man pointed at Duchesne's Guards.

"Who are you?"

"I am from Malawi, I was a high court judge before I was captured by this man. We are all refugees...or should I say slaves...from the tribal wars in this land"

"Then you will help San-Pierre...to build a new justice....and arrange a trial before you decide your sentence."

"That I will do."

"Who are you?"

"I'm Colonel Rheinhart, from Rhodesia, and we will be friends with the people of Mozambique... and Malawi..."

XXIV

Thieves Gold

The King rode out from York. He sat astride a great Sable stallion. He wore a simple gold crown on his forehead. His cape that hung from his shoulders was a dark bottle green. He wore black and brown leather boots.

Behind him, and on either side were a small troop of Household Cavalry, dressed in their finery, their swords and headgear glinting in the pale watery sun.

Behind them rode the four Dukes. Ireland, Northumbria, Mercia, and Wessex..

Behind them Lord High Chancellor Levine and the Archbishop of York and Canterbury. Both looking uncomfortable on a horse, but the King had insisted.

Levine looked particularly pained. His leg was giving him more trouble...and Foxton had brought the news that the King was dying. ....“..In his letter to the doctor he says that if the people cannot have this medicine then neither can I. It would be an injustice if there was one law for the King and another for the people of my Kingdoms, ...and an abuse of power. So there will be no more medical interventions other than for pain relief. The rest I trust to God, and to let nature run its course....”

Levine wondered what would happen once he

was gone.

Behind them an assorted collection of men on Horseback and following up behind, a battalion of infantry troops.

The procession passed over the Ouse and on towards Bishopthorpe, past smallholdings along the river, and the great Knavesmire to their right. The race course remained. There were many race meetings held for entertainment of the people and the soldiers. But not today.

The party passed the Archbishops palace and onwards to the airfield at Acaster Malbis.

Several aircraft of varying types were on the apron, or in the hangars which had been built.

A large round tent stood outside in regal red and black. Soldiers and airmen were stationed around the perimeter.

Men came forward to hold the horses. The King and his royal party dismounted and went into the tent.

Levine had arranged a 'viewing' of the Royal Treasures that Scarman and his men had dug out of the ruins of the palace. The English Crown Jewels were displayed, still in their cases , but unfolded to show off their contents.

Around the sides of the tent were several tables on which were displayed the opened boxes and cases of jewels and gold from the other rooms of the palace tunnels. The pallet of Nazi gold bullion was also there, along with Crown jewellery from assorted European estates, now long gone. Some of the panels of the Amber room were on display, on top of a huge pile of crates containing the rest.

The hoard glittered and sparkled as the sun filtered through special panels fitted into the roof of the tent.

Gaunt saw the Crown of Richard III, but next to it was the older crown of King John. The original Plantagenet crown. He held it up to the light and the jewels and gold shone out. He smiled. No longer buried in the shifting sands of the Wash. Now back in the hands of a true Plantagenet.

Gaunt removed his own simple gold crown and placed the ancient crown on his head.

Levine had briefed the assorted nobles and clerics on the significance of this so as Gaunt turned round the gathered men all knelt as one... except for Levine...who walked forward holding in two hands an ancient golden sword which he placed in the King's outstretched hands.

"The Sword of Tristram"

Gaunt studied it carefully them pulled the ancient steel from its jewel encrusted scabbard and held it up.

It was certainly a sight. It could have come from the twelfth century itself or earlier. Despite the fact that assorted aircraft and the paraphernalia of the 21st century lay about the airfield.

Levine bowed low. His leg was not kneelable.

He looked up at the King. At his long hair and thick beard, but knowing that underneath were a growing number of black sores that would eventually cover his whole body and take his life.

The assembled men rose and clapped and cheered.

"Sire, the men who recovered this are outside and I would like them to be presented to you."

"Yes, I would like to meet with them also they have done a marvellous job…far better than any of us expected, bring them in."

So Scarman and his men were summoned. They walked in together and all bowed low…as briefed by Levine.

The King spoke to them and thanked them all individually with a handshake…"..and the Lord High Chancellor has given to you the reward that I have agreed?"

The men looked a little uneasy amongst the assembled grandness of the occasion but Scarman spoke for them, in his characteristic south-west burr.

"Yes my Lord King, you have been very generous to us, and we are pleased that we have successfully retrieved such great treasures for the nation."

Levine had done his job well.

"You will all join us for the feast, and after I will present you with a commemorative medal fitting for your achievements." but Gaunt looked in their eyes and especially at Grimson who shuffled a bit and wouldn't look him in the eye."

Inside one of the new aircraft hangars a long table had been set with food and wine. The King and the Archbishop sat at the end. The rest found whatever place was appropriate. Levine had done a good job organising the day. A small group of musicians began to play. The wine flowed, the food was excellent.

As evening approached Gaunt stood and called for the 'Ballast Men' to join him in the jewel tent.

"Join us Lord High Chancellor, and you Sergeant Johnson, and Mr Saunders our worthy parachutists and pilot"

The men stood in the tent as Gaunt strode in waving his arms in welcome, but as he did so the men…and Levine…found themselves slipping into a blank state of mind.

"So men, you have done a great thing for your King, and you have been well rewarded…but what I want to know is what rewards you have also taken for yourselves?"

There was a silence. Levine spoke.

"They have taken nothing"

"That's not true is it Mr Grimson?" He turned and looked Grimson in the eye.

"No, we've all got a bag of jewels from the pirate treasure"

His voice was monotone. There was no emotion

or recognition in it, just the plain truth.

“Where are they?”

“They’re hidden in our quarters here”

“Very good...you will all go now and bring them to me in this tent”...”Go”

The men filed out except Levine who stood there looking blank.

The King turned to him

“Oh I know you haven’t got anything William... but I hear that you have been poking about in my affairs...affairs that are of no concern to you. Tell me what you have learned”

So Levine told him about Scarman’s reports from Porton Down...and about the letter to the Doctor...and the Syphilis....the black lion.”

“ Well I suppose it is to be expected...you are after all my High Chancellor...and my principal spymaster...and head of the Privy Council...Do they know all this?”

“No Sire”

“We will speak again tomorrow when you have recovered from your...tired state William. I will call for you. Now leave.”

Presently the ballast men dutifully returned. Each of them laid out a small cloth bag on one of the tables.

Gaunt walked over and began to empty the contents into a small pile of gold coins, assorted gems and pearls.

"So my generosity was not enough....temptation came your way...not surprising I suppose given your backgrounds....I think a special prize is necessary. Mr Saunders is your airplane in a state to fly?"

"Yes sire"

"What is its range on a full tank?"

"About 1300 nautical miles"

"Is it full?"

"Yes sire"

"Then I suggest that you all get in it now, fly south-west and keep going."

"Yes sire"

So all the men filed out of the tent and walked steadily across the apron to the old DC3 which sat warming itself in the sunshine.

The aircraft taxied out and took off, its tuned Rolls Royce engines throbbing rhythmically as the sound faded away. Gaunt saw the plane turn far out slowly disappear over the horizon.

The king's face was expressionless as he watched it fade into the distance. Then he turned away and called for his horse and his household escort. He left the airfield and returned to his quarters in York before attending evening mass in the great cathedral.

Someone found the High Chancellor standing aimlessly inside one of the hangers and guided him home to his small apartment in the city.

The men from the treasury began their task of securing the treasures for the Exchequer.

The Plantagenet crown remained on Gaunt's head.

Two days later Levine was summoned to the King.

"So William, you have been poking about in my affairs?"

Levine looked at him. Gaunt could see his mind processing the statement.

Gaunt smiled.

"Let me refresh your memory as you've been acting rather strangely since the day at Acaster... your man Scarman poking around Porton Down asking questions....your man Foxton and a copy of my letter to my doctor...your knowledge of my illness?"

Levine decided he had no other option but to lay it all out and hope that he could avoid his apparent fate.

"Sire I am your Lord High Chancellor. It is my job to manage the affairs of your realm in all its manifestations...and to consider the future....in particular your succession. What happens to the realm when you die? What continuity can be achieved? Who will take over? You have no heirs. There are no Princes or Princesses to fall back on. Your medical condition is important not just to you, but to the Nation.

There is also the matter of who is working directly for you. I know much of what goes on...its my job...but there are significant...and I consider important and relevant gaps in my knowledge concerning certain individuals. Henry Bryant is one, Colonel Rhienhart another...and some connection with Algeria? What is the realm's business with them?"

Gaunt's expression changed. A stern expression. The grey eyes seemed to fix Levine. An imaginary portcullis had fallen between the two men.

"I am the King, these matters are my concern, not yours. You are a good High Chancellor William, and I rely on you and your men to keep the realm as straight as it can be. But there are several areas of my sovereignty, including its future that are mine, and mine alone. You are not to make any further enquiries about Henry Bryant, nor Rheinhart, nor Algeria, is that clear? There will come a time when I will reveal the future to you, but now is not the time. "

"I don't understand sire, but I assure you I will comply with your command"

XXV

Anniversaries, Decisions and Farewells

Over the next few months a small armed town was built around what was once the peaceful farm of Rheinland. The town took the name. Men and women were gathered up from the surrounding area and, along with a few of Voebeck's engineers they built a fortified residence and barracks along with workers barns and huts.

Farming machinery was in scarce supply but horses and oxen were brought in along with ploughs made up by the blacksmiths forge. Gradually, many of the fields were tamed and replanted.

Alex buried Angel next to her parent's graves under the old oak. She had been caught in the crossfire of the attack. Alex pondered the question of life and death once again, as all soldiers do. But she had a farm to rebuild, and other people's lives to improve, and churches, farms, and institutions to re-build.

As before she had to move on and be prepared to work exceptionally hard.

People began to look to her lead. She travelled about the country to find other leaders, other farmers, other teachers, and policemen, blacksmiths, carpenters, engineers, doctors and nurses, butchers and bakers, and all the many people that can create the conditions to enable life to be worked and lived.

She learned that Saint-Pierre had met with Voebeck who had made troops available to restore peace to Mozambique, but not before a wave of bubonic plague had killed up to forty percent of the population.

It was much the same story across much of Africa.

Gaunt had been especially keen to restore the central belt as pure natural jungle. The wildlife that had been under constant threat returned in numbers to roam the vast jungles and savannahs as they had done for millions of years.

As the military presence declined they were replaced with a civil police force built around the original lines of Robert Peel. Drawn from local communities, known to the locals, smart uniforms but unarmed, on foot, a reassuring presence to deter crime....keep and eye on things. A simple and effective thing.

The farms were well managed by professional agriculturalists drawn from the new colleges that sprang up from one area to another. Machinery was built locally and red diesel returned for fuelling tractors and fishing boats.

Monasteries were built to care for the elderly, the sick and the dying. Sunday churches were well attended in the South. In the North the mosques fulfilled their traditional role. Some synagogues were built for the relatively small

Jewish populations.

Food was abundant from a continent where everything grew well. The surplus was exported, mainly to the north where tropical items were not able to grow.

Rheinhart and Voebeck worked well together.

At a dinner to commemorate five years since her appointment in Africa she pulled Voebeck to one side and they stepped out into the warm African night as they had done five years ago at Makhado.

"The people respect you Paul..."

"You too Alex..."

She took a puff on her cigar, staring out at the night sky.

"As you well know I took on this role more for personal reasons... some sort of reconciliation with my past...and although there is still much to be done here I wish to leave and return to a quieter life...." She laughed "...again!"

" I will be sorry if that is so..."

"I will be informing the King of my decision soon, then I shall return to Algeria to recover my boat if it has survived"

Voebeck remained silent.

" I will be advising the King that you should take over as ....whatever this is...Prime Minister... Lord Lieutenant...King of Africa. You have the respect of the armed forces, the institutions, the people...and the King, but before I do that I wanted to be sure that you will accept such a burden?"

Voebeck remained silent for a long time.

"In short..yes. I have a number of good officers who could take over the Generalship, and Africa is in my blood...I can never leave."

Alex smiled. "it's in my blood too but mixed with other blood...I can't settle here...I probably can't settle anywhere...but there is a constant nagging...no, pain...to find somewhere quiet... on my own...I'm a retired soldier Paul, not an civil administrator...you'll find someone much better than me for the job."

"I doubt that....he won't be pleased."

"Maybe, though I'll be keeping out of his way nonetheless"

"What will you do?"

"I'd like to borrow one of your aircraft if you don't mind...I'll go back to Algeria, get my boat, and sail away....a long way away. The call of the open sea."

Rheinhart gathered her team together over the course of the next few days to announce her departure and to confirm that she was leaving things in the hands of General Voebeck. She expected them to follow his commands from now on.

Lanscki and his corporal came to see her.

"We'll come with you"

"You can't, I'll be leaving on my boat, and you'll be in danger if you return to Algeria."

"We'll handle it....in any case Januscz says he's sick of the heat and the flies, he wants to go home, or at least to somewhere colder and northern. He misses the snow"

Alex smiled at the big corporal. She took his giant hands in hers.

"I want to thank you, thank you both for such a staunch and resolute help you have been to me since we escaped from Bryant's palace"

Lanscki smiled "we know...but we're still coming with you, then we'll split up and make our own way back north...we can look after ourselves too you know."

"That you can...very well, pack your kit, we leave tomorrow at first light, straight back to where we started...then away for good"

At dawn the old Beechcraft lifted off into the early dawn sky and eight hours later came into land on the top of the mountain at Angouri. Nothing appeared to have changed. A few of the guards looked at Lanscki and Januscz but said nothing. They were all afraid of the big corporal anyway.

Alex asked some of them if they knew what Bryant had done with her yacht. One of them said that it was still moored on the coast. There were some plans to bring it to the lake but it hadn't happened.

"But you'll need to speak to the big chief....he's taken over operations since Bryant was killed"

Alex wondered who it was but as she had her personal protection squad with her there was little danger, and she could arrange transport more easily.

They climbed into an electric jeep and set off down the tunnel, back to the main palace complex. It all looked familiar. Then to the elevator and out into the side of the central courtyard. Alex stepped out and saw several of the black robed women sitting in the shade to the side and the sound of children playing in the gardens. Some older boys came over. Alex looked at them. "God they look exactly like Edward,... or Bryant" she thought

She stepped over to the hallway at the edge of what had been Bryant's main entertaining room and stopped short.

A man was standing watching her. He was dressed in a flowing cream djelaba, on his feet Algerian babouche slippers.

"Jerry!" Alex's shocked tones made the party stop in its tracks.

"Hello Alex, good to see you again."

But something was not quite right. Jerry Bradman stood there but the hairs on the back of her neck made her stop. There was something about the voice, and the words, Jerry would have said 'hello Colonel'.

"Henry?"

Bradman doubled over with laughter and came up as quickly, laughing.

"Damn...I thought I had you there, ...well what do you think" and he held both his arms out as if very pleased with himself.

Alex noted a silver ring.

She turned to Lanscki "Keep away from that ring he's wearing, it's deadly" Lanscki un-holstered his gun.

"Oh now let's not get off to such a bad start... bygones are bygones eh?...look at this.."

He used his hands to display his new body "Not quite as tall as I was ....but he's got a bigger dick... I quite like it...maybe I'll do some genetic mods to my next clone."

Alex's brain couldn't quite get used so quickly to talking to her old Jerry, whilst recognising that this wasn't him. Bryant's mind was inside.

"How did you...."

"Well I've told you...at least once I had reviewed all the security footage of your last visit anyway....I had some gaps as my backup mind transfer file pre-dated our last meeting but I've caught up with most of it. They tell me I was killed by my own black jaguar....still had that not happened...and there just happened to be an empty human.." he waved his hands down his body theatrically again "I could have been put in some local Arab boy...who knows....but if I hadn't been killed I wouldn't have known that my system works!" he looked so pleased with himself.

"Weren't you two of my guards?.." he scanned Lanscki and Januscz "I seem to remember your faces vaguely"

"Before we get into any more pleasantries Henry please remove that ring"

"So untrusting Alex...very well....just don't have me killed again...it's just so inconvenient"

Bryant slipped the ring off his finger carefully and laid it down on one of the tables.

Alex picked it up and gave it to Lanscki "One for you...it could come in handy"

"I know, I've seen him use it once or twice" Lanscki slipped the ring onto one of his fingers.

"...And keep away from any suspicious looking arches"

"Alex, Alex, please....don't you think it's fantastic!...that I can do this?...the King is very pleased too as you might imagine" he stopped as he realised he might disclose too much to the two guards.

"I'll leave you in peace Henry....you know it was not my intention that got you killed ...but I want my boat returned and I want transport to the coast...I'm not staying here longer than necessary"

"Well of course you do...but please stay for dinner, it's late anyway. Better to go in the morning....oh and I have something to show you"

"We're leaving Henry...no more of your tricks..."

Bryant clapped his hands and asked one of the women that Selisha should bring her children to the courtyard.

"We're leaving Henry...just lend me one of your cars to get us to the coast and we'll be gone..."

"Wait, wait" his voice excited.

Another black robed woman appeared holding hands with two very young children. Two girls. There was something familiar about them.

"They're you Alex...your daughters...well clones actually...but seeing as you can't have any children of your own...." Bryant was grinning and trying to make the little girls smile but they slipped behind their mother's robes and hid.

" Daughters for you Alex...or maybe in a few years time I could transfer your mind into one of them and you could be a normal woman again....like magic!"

"You know Henry, I'm not sure you're not actually mad...in the insane sense...and your manners leave a great deal to be desired" she added.

Bryant's face dropped a little and he had a strangely unpleasant look in his eye. "My manners are perfectly intact....it's your reality that isn't....get used to it Alex...by the way Edward is really not pleased that you have abandoned your post you know...I think you've well and truly used up any brownie points you once had with him"

"Good...then we're all square, now if you'd be so kind as to order up some transport we'll be on our way....where is my boat moored?"

Bryant shrugged his shoulder "Where you left it I suppose...in that harbour ...Cavallo? Some local shit-hole anyway...probably been stolen or stripped by now...I didn't keep track of it."

Lanscki spoke to Januscz in Polish. "I've told him to get us a car...he knows where they are."

"Good, well Henry it was an unpleasant surprise to say the least, but let us part as old comrades....as you said...bygones are bygones...I have no need for enemies" and she held out her hand to him.

Bryant said nothing but took her hand and nodded. His palms were sweaty but he had Jerry Bradman's rough skin from hard labour. It hadn't worn off entirely.

" Actually Henry as I don't trust you an inch you can come with us until we're on a clear road outside of the palace complex...just in case"

She un-holstered her gun and told him to take them outside.

"Of course if you shoot me I'll just come back

again you know"

"No need to shoot you as long as you're a good boy…move"

So they took one of the cars and were let out of the main gates onto the coast road, into the North African night. It was getting chilly. They travelled a short distance, no more than a mile then let Bryant out of the car.

"Goodbye Henry"

He didn't respond but began walking back to his own gates.

Lanscki knew better than to ask about the girls or how Bryant had managed to reappear as Bradman. Not his business.

Januscz drove with a seemingly happy expression on his big, ungainly, unshaven face.

Alex's mind turned over all that had happened. Bryant was alive and well. His bullshit about mind transference wasn't bullshit…apparently. There were two clones of her….did she want children?…she shook her head silently, it was another bloody mind game and she'd had enough. She drifted into an uneasy sleep in the warmth of the car.

It was after midnight when they hit the coast. Alex had a good memory and quickly located the small fishing harbour where she and Jerry had landed years ago.

Incredibly, there was her boat, in the moonlight, riding at a fixed anchorage just outside the harbour entrance, bobbing gently in the night swell. Maybe the locals were superstitious about stealing someone else's boat she thought.

There were a couple of tatty old fishing vessels tied up on the jetty. They stank of fish and diesel.

Lanscki turned to Alex "Is that it?"

"Yeah, can you get me on there?"

"Corporal Januscz here spent his early years on a boat out of Gdansk...didn't you chum?"

Januscz grinned "Ja Ja"

Januscz jumped down into the outer boat and, after some fiddling, the diesel engine coughed into life. They cast off and steamed over alongside the yacht.

Once she was aboard she realised that much of the gear had been stripped out including the batteries, and the solar and wind chargers, all the satnav equipment was gone, although that wasn't necessary. Her sextant and compass were gone which was more of a blow. The sails had been removed but she found the old torn and repaired sails in the forward stowage. The halyards and the sheets were still intact though and when she looked in the bilges she found her tins of long life food still down there. If she was desperate. And there were no leaks. The engine remained but the diesel tank was gone, but the water tank was intact. Some of the cleats were gone but not all of them. Basically it was being used as a donor as parts were required by the locals, as and when.

In short it was capable of sailing, albeit for small distances, and in daylight. She figured she could find a better port along the coast. She had plenty of gold and silver to buy, or find, the necessary equipment. The thing about those who live by the sea is that they keep to themselves so she was sure that even in Algeria...or Morocco... or somewhere along the coast there would be enough places to acquire the parts and rebuild her floating home. She had done it all before.

She came over to the side of the boat where it was tied to the old fishing boat.

"So this is it then lads...once again I thank you... what will you two do?"

Lanscki smiled up "We'll head for a better port than this...and acquire ourselves a decent blue-water boat that can take us back up to the Baltic and back to Gdansk...then, who knows?"

"Good luck boys"

Both men waved as Alex cast them adrift and off they puttered, out to sea and along the coast.

Alex went below and pulled out her old sails. It took her over an hour to get them back into position and hoist them up the mast.

She unhooked herself from the floating buoy. Her boathook was gone. She began to make a mental list of all the things she would need to recover.

The sails caught the wind so she swung the

wheel hard round and the boat turned out to sea. She wouldn't take it far out, just enough to avoid any contact with the shore for now, wait until daylight and then head down the coast to start getting things ready for the open water. Then sail west, probably the Caribbean. Find a small quiet island where it would be unlikely to have any 'Edwardian' influences. "Free at last" she said to herself. It had been a long time.

But it would not last.

Gaunt tossed and turned in an uneasy half-sleep. The weeping black sores on his legs and body continued to grow and cause pain. He was taking too much opium. How long could he continue like this. At least Bryant had shown that his system of mind transfer actually worked at long last. He had seen his clones. Strong, growing boys. They would turn to men soon. He could put all this behind him. He would need all the energy that youth had in abundance, but took for granted.

Levine sat in his chambers, reading a small Torah. Mumbling to himself. Leave it alone. He knew that, but he was an intelligent man. What the hell was going on that he didn't know about? Careful...careful. His leg stabbed him with pain just to remind him.

Simon Brevard sat with the Chieftains in a large tepee. They would work with him and restore their great lands. The buffalo herds would return in their millions, they would have the space to roam unhindered. They could make war with the tribes, live as free men. Brevard smoked his cigar and smiled at them.

And in China, the Emperor studied a small, green, oblong tin with European writing and wondered what it was....... The DC3 stuttered. One of the engines coughed and stopped.

XXVII
France

The pilot, Saunders, sat in his seat staring ahead. They had been flying for several hours but he couldn't remember why, nor where they were heading.

His thirteen passengers sat in two Rows of canvas seats down each side of the fuselage. Their faces blank, he looked out of the window. The sea beneath the aircraft was flashing past at speed. Now there was land beneath them. The wind continued to blow them east as it had been doing during the entire flight. Saunders would have corrected for this but for some reason he had not.

The port engine coughed and, as the starboard engine had done, it stopped, silence swept the aircraft save for the sound of the air rushing past.

Something was keeping the nose up. And also slowing the plane. Out of habit Saunders looked out of the window towards the rear of the port wing. Something was attached, a tube of some sort. He didn't know what it was but it must be heavy as it was trimming Plane as it fell in a free glide.

His co-pilot, Johnson, he thought that was his name, sat staring out of the cockpit, a completely blank expression on his face. Saunders tried to remember why he was there. Something about parachutes, but his mind wouldn't focus.

The land below was getting very close now. He should do something but he couldn't think straight. The aircraft was slowing. He thought that was quite nice for some reason.

A moment later there was a crash as dust and dirt flew up over the cockpit windows. Straw flashed past the side window and then the plane seemed to spin round so that they were traveling backwards. It spun again and then came to a complete halt. No one moved.

Saunders looked backwards. His passengers were still in their seats but there was now a large hole at the rear of the aircraft where once there had been a tail-plane. He knew that, somehow, but now it was gone. He thought he should go to look for it so he unbuckled his seat belt, more by instinct than conscious thought.

He swung himself out of the seat and walked to the rear of the plane.he stepped outside. Two men were running towards him. He waved to them. They came up to him and were speaking to him but he couldn't understand a word.

One of them switched to broken English

"Ok? You ok? .....English?"

'Hello I'm ....er ...sorry...."

Saunders voice tailed off. He couldn't think of anything to say.

The two men peered into the plane and talked

to each other before stepping inside and tried to speak to the men in the seats who just sat there looking at them.

The Frenchmen signalled for them to get out of the plane which they did. They stood around silently .

'They're stupefied"

"or drunk"

"not drunk....there's no smell of booze...drugged maybe. We'd better take them to the farm.maybe they'll come round soon."

It was only in the evening of the second day that the men began to get back their wits.

And many questions

Where are we? How the hell did we get here?

They looked to Scarman for answers.

'We're in France lads, but you all know that. Somewhere in France. I don't know how we got here but I'll wager my last shilling on who did it...bloody Levine. He must have slipped something in our drink...that's what I think. Then he put us all on that plane and he probably hoped we'd be in the Atlantic by now....feeding the fish."

The farmers came in to the kitchen where they were standing or sitting and said something in French but none of the men could speak it. Connor had some schoolboy French and said it was something about the aero plane. Connor said "nous visite?" He pointed to the door. The frenchies led. Him along with all the men out into the field to see the wreck of the plane.

Saunders peered into the fuel tanks.

"not just empty, they're bone dry. We must have been running on fumes for a long time, lucky I think, we could have been burnt alive if any of the fuel was left in the tanks when we crashed....what a bloody mess...and she had survived all this time"

'We're lucky to be alive" said Scarman

'Not so bloody lucky sarge, we've got no money... where's all that loot from the tunnels?"

'Your mate Levine has robbed us as well as try to get us killed...what a bastard"

'Aye well we'll sort him out eventually, meanwhile we've got some assets to trade...haven't we Grimson?

'What...I haven't got a bean, like the rest of you...." Grimson looked anguished but Scarman knew his man.

'Grimson stop pissing about....we need some cash to get us started again...and to pay these fine frenchies for feeding and watering us...they could have left us be and who knows what would have become of us.....I know you Grimson...you've got cash on you somewhere so let's be having some of it..."

The rest of the men were looking at him in silence while Grimson pulled every face then very reluctantly slipped his finger into the side of his shoe and pulled out a gold Napoleon.

'Thought so...you're a damn fine thieving little toerag, but you do have your uses.....right, Connor, tell these frenchies that we can pay them with this but we need horses and supplies, and a map....I've got a plan...and don't worry Grimson, you'll get your money back as soon as I get hold of Levine and squeeze his balls until he gets our loot back and more....ok lads?"

The men cheered up...they would trust Scarman to lead them back home and sort out the mess....even Grimson.

XXVI
Shipwrecked

Alex Rheinhart was back on the water, somewhere away from people and pressures of life on the land. The sea, the wind and the sun gave her all she needed to thrive.

However the boat needed many things before she could return to her nomadic life. The desalination plant for one....and all sorts of spares to recover from emergencies....and fishing gear....and cooking gear....all sorts.

As she sailed west but then had a better idea so sailed north and east towards Malta, where the rich keep their boats away from the taxman.

The boatyards in Malta were largely in ruins. The sea and the weather had taken their toll but there were few people available to maintain the wealthy boats which lay unattended, dirty, and in generally poor shape. But there was plenty of decent equipment to be plundered ....so Alex plundered.

She left Malta with a properly equipped and provisioned boat. She could have taken one of the other, bigger yachts but she felt that her little steel Aussie sailboat had brought her through some terrible seas and she trusted her instincts.

She headed west out of the gap of Gibraltar without incident, but once in the Atlantic the seas took a turn for the worse.

Huge storms churned up giant Atlantic rollers into

killers, and the wind blew consistently from the south west making it impossible to stay on course. She was being steadily blown and pushed North and East. A huge freak wave hit the boat and dragged everything under. She had fastened herself to the safety rail and managed to cling on while the badly damaged boat righted itself. The main mast was gone and most of the sailcloth. Worse still she couldn't feel her right leg and blood was now flowing.

John Chappel was taking a break from the farm. He was a 50 year old man but he still looked much younger, partly courtesy of his thick black hair, a legacy no doubt from a Spaniard liason in the 16th century after the Armada was wrecked off the Cornish coast and several survivors making it to the shore. There was plenty of that in Cornwall. He was a fit man. He had spent his life working outdoors and farming the land as well as a bit of tin and lead mining in old disused commercial mines.

He climbed steadily upwards from the valley until he was standing on the overlook to Prussia Cove, staring out to sea. The recent storms had passed and he wondered if anything useful had been washed up on the shores.

In latter days there had been plenty of shipwrecks along this coast. The nature of smugglers in Cornwall was deeply ingrained, and wrecking had been a notorious pastime. Men would light lamps on the shoreline at night luring in ships that thought they were harbour lights until they were grounded and wrecked on the rocks and their ships plundered.

Something caught Chappel's eye. A torn sail and a boat mangled into an almost unrecognisable heap lay on the mix of gravel and sand of the beach…the battered hull rocking slightly as the waves pushed and pulled it over the granite outcrops…and then….a figure sprawled on the sand. He quickly ran down the slope of the overlook down onto the beach where the tide was beginning to rise.

The figure was a woman…and she was alive, but unconscious.

She was wearing a sailor's waterproof coat, so he grabbed the collar and dragged the unconscious form up the beach to where the tide would not reach. He could see blood, and her right leg appeared to be at an odd angle. He would need help to get her back the farm…or the local King's camp, further up the river… so he set off at a fast trot and reached the farm… before getting hold of four men and within an hour returning to the beach with a makeshift stretcher.

The woman remained unconscious though as they got her on the stretcher she let out a deep groan. The men carried her back to the farm.

"She'll need a doctor…Ben, take one of the horses and fetch the doctor from the camp….Simon, best get Meg as well."

Ben set off and returned an hour later with the man they knew as the camp doctor, Dr Mortimer.

Chappel, Meg, his wife, and Mortimer stood over the increasingly feverish form.

Mortimer took her pulse. "She's very weak, …lost a lot of blood by the looks of things….I'm going to cut off these jeans to see what is going on with her leg"

He pulled some scissors from his bag and sliced

through the sodden denim to reveal the extent of the damage.

It was bad. The bone had splintered and come through the flesh just above the knee. Worse still there was a bad smell ...."Gangrene" said Mortimer as Chappel and his wife wrinkled their faces and Meg put her hand over her nose.

"This leg will have to come off I'm afraid, but she seems to have done a running repair with this tourniquet" pointing to the strip of canvas tied tightly round her thigh. " probably saved her life ...so far"

He put his hand across her forehead " yes, hot,...she's running a fever...I need to get her up to the camp as quickly as possible. He quickly pulled open her shirt to check if there were other injuries. Despite a few bruises and minor cuts she seemed to be unharmed except for the leg break.

Meg spoke " I'll get the cart out of the stables and I'll drive her up there with the Doctor myself....Ben" she shouted " Get the cart hooked up to the horses please , I need it straight away"

The camp, The King's Horse, Mounts Bay, is located in Acton Castle, an 18th century fortified house taken over by the Kings men during the war, not far from the bay and virtually adjoining the Perranuthnoe farm. Several timber out-buildings now lay in the grounds including stabling and barracks for the men and the women who made up the main local community. The farm provided food and the King's men provided the services for daily life in the area.

Jim Mortimer had been the local doctor, he and his wife and sons joined the camp during the war. His wife Sally acted as his nurse. He had built a reasonable surgery inside one of the castle rooms including an operating theatre. Much of the equipment had been retrieved for a nearby hospital which had been abandoned.

Meg and Ben brought the woman into the surgery where Sally stripped off her clothes and quickly set about with a disinfectant swab to clean around the gaping wound. Dr Mortimer took one of the small glass phials of morphine, snapped off the top and jabbed the small syringe into her right thigh immediately above the injury.

Surgical sheets were placed above and below the wound site and with skill learned from hard experience Mortimer removed her right leg and sewed up the stump. He injected some anti-biotics into the leg,

"Take this and put it in the castle furnace Sally" she nodded, taking hold of the amputation. She noticed a small tattoo on the outside ankle...a kind of upturned anchor. Or maybe a pick on a green background. She wrapped the leg in a cloth and went down to the basement where there was a large furnace fuelled by local coal. Bill, the furnace man was there.

"Open up Bill will you," and she pushed the leg into the blazing coals. Bill shut the furnace door and nodded grimly, he'd seen this before, too many times. " Poor bugger" he muttered to himself.

It was the pain that brought Alex back to consciousness. Her leg was agony. She was lying in a strange bed, in a strange room, not on the boat. Her last memory was of being washed ashore after the boat grounded on rocks and she knew she must crawl onto the beach despite the agony in her leg. Had she dreamt it?...no....even though she knew by then that she was going in and out of consciousness there was no doubt she had pulled herself out of the sea onto some strange beach before passing out again.

She felt light headed, tried to reach for a glass of water by the bedside to quench a raging thirst but knocked over the glass onto the floor. A moment later a woman came in .

"Ah...you're awake!" she said.

"Where am I?"

"You're in Acton Castle in Cornwall, in the King's Camp hospital, we found you on the beach after your boat was shipwrecked. I'm Sally Mortimer, I help with the nursing here."

"England?"

"Well yes but don't say that too loudly round here, the Cornish are the Cornish, not English.......how are you feeling?"

"How long have I been here?"

"We found you 10 days ago but you have been near death for most of that time. You had very serious injuries and infection…you're still very poorly but I think you're a tough lady and now that you're awake I think you're going to be fine…we've done our best with what resources we have here but even so…with what you've been through…you're going to take a long time to fully heal…what's your name...we didn't find anything with your name on …. "

"Alex….Alex..Hart….my leg? It was badly broken in a storm out at sea …has it been fixed?"
Sally's face dropped, she hated this part. "I'm very sorry Alex but we had to amputate your right leg, the infection had gone too far… you would have died."

Alex looked down the bed from the pillows on which her head was resting. There was a cage over both legs to keep the sheets away from the wound….but she knew …it didn't feel right…even if it hurt like hell… she knew it had gone.

She said nothing , just closed her eyes, then she said "Thank you for rescuing me, and for saving me…I…"
Sally leaned over, try to rest, you're a long way from being well yet. I will look after you. Are you hungry? …"
Alex weakly shook her head, " some water please"

"Of course, I'll clear this up and bring you a fresh glass and help you with it"

Alex lay back. The morphine was wearing off and the pain was intense. When the nurse came back she injected another batch of morphine into her side and Alex drifted off into a narcotic sleep.

When she woke two days later Dr Mortimer was removing the bandages to check the wound and there was another man standing in the room looking slightly uncomfortable.

He was scrawny, dressed in heavily soiled clothes, his hair unkempt, his hands bruised and calloused.

"Ah, you're awake....I'm just changing the dressing and having a look at the wound...he frowned, well we'll have to have a go at some of our homemade anti-biotics...just mould scraped from jam....but it sort of works....hmm..."

He could see that Alex had a fever, her skin was white and waxy with a thin film of sweat.

"Oh this is Nev" pointing to the man " he's our blacksmith...at the camp...very clever with metal he is". Mortimer tried to sound jolly.

"He's going to measure you up so that he can make a leg to fit on the stump...he's a magician when it comes to making all sorts of things...aren't you Nev...."

The man muttered "aye" and took a few tentative steps towards the bed, his eyes fixed on the mess that was the stump of her leg.

"Its quite swollen at the moment but that will go

down in a week or two so you can estimate the size at least…" Mortimer again trying to sound cheery but neither Ned nor Alex looked in any way cheerful.

"In return, Ned would like your permission to salvage your boat, he says there's good metal and timber which he's always in need of…oh and Meg has found some of your clothes…she's washing them in the river to get rid of the salt…should be as good as new…"

Alex nodded faintly and Ned took that as a yes.

He took some measurements, mumbled "aye " again, nodded to the Doctor and disappeared from the room.

Mortimer wrapped fresh bandages around the stump as gently as he could. He mixed some odd looking powder into a small glass of water and made her drink it. It was foul.

"There, more rest for you but I'll be back tomorrow… ah here's Sally with some soup" and he too slipped out of the room.

Over the next weeks and then months Alex gradually grew stronger. She had managed to get up and move about on a pair of crutches.

She left the castle and went down to the farm to help where she could.

Ned returned with a wonderfully crafted aluminium leg with soft leather padding, and assorted straps. Even the knee joint had a large spring which could be latched or unlatched whether standing or sitting. The foot had one of her trainers on it. With some help from Meg she got it on, then pulled on some oversize jeans and her other shoe. She tried to walk with the crutches but the stump was incredibly painful. She knew it would be, she'd seen many soldier's wounds.

But she saw herself in the mirror and realised that she was standing up. Unless you knew then it was as if her proper leg was there...at least until she tried to walk...which was another thing altogether.

Still, she thought, back to being a farm girl...and no-one knows who I am....I'm amongst decent hard working people...self sufficient...food on the table... the only problem was that she couldn't really recount her story when they all sat round the fire in the evenings...she had to be economical with the truth... but as long as they thought she was just a farm girl, swept out to sea on a doomed attempt to go fishing.

John Chappel would give her a sideways look now and again as if he suspected there was more to her than met the eye. There was also the occasional slip in the dialect to something akin to South African....and there was the gun he had found in the bilges of her wrecked boat, along with the charts indicating a much larger journey around Africa. But it wasn't his business so he said nothing, but he might have a word with one of the men who kept in contact with Levine, just in case. These were strange times after the devastation of years back. Lots of strangers, all trying to survive. Like him.

XXVIII
France

Scarman held up the gold Napoleon in front of the two French farmers. Connor was translating as best he could.

"We need horses, a rifle and two shotguns with some ammunition....an axe and some knives...and a container for water..."

The Frenchmen looked at Connors who was trying his best. They replied.

"What are they saying Connor?"

"I think they're saying they can't eat gold.....it's no use to them...wait...something about the plane... I think they're saying they would like the plane..? ...er plenty of metal and Rolls Royce engines...and something about putting the animals inside it during winter?...

Scarman hadn't considered the plane as technically they already had it, and it was not as if they could carry it back to England...but if that was the case?

"Tell them they can have the plane in return for six horses and all the other stuff..."

The Frenchmen smiled.

"Two horses they say..."

"Four..."

"Three they say...." Scarman could at least count in French but he just nodded...

"...and the rest?"

The Frenchmen shrugged their shoulders as the French do. "Viens..." and they pointed to follow them.

A farm lad came round with three decent looking horses. Scarman had lived with horses all his life and soon realised these were good animals. All three were saddled and reined. The lad tied their reins to the post outside a large barn

They were led into the barn and after some searching around the frenchies began putting some items on a table...an old rifle, probably German, no sights and rusty, a shotgun in slightly better condition, then three large knives also rusty, and a rusty axe. "voila!"

Scarman picked up the rifle and removed the breach section. The barrel looked rusty but probably only surface rust. "Ammo?"

One of the Frenchmen pulled out a box of suspiciously old bullets.
"Collins, take this outside and see if it fires straight"

Collins took the rifle and one of the bullets then disappeared outside. There was a loud report of the gun then he returned.
"It's ok sarge, a couple more rounds through it will clean the barrels good but it works and it hit the tree over there about 300 yards."

"Shotguns?"

"only one it seems but he says its fairly new and he'll give us two boxes of cartridges."

Scarman took the gun out himself and shot a pigeon flying overhead. The dead bird cam down nearby so he picked it up by the neck and walked back to the barn.

"Bon!" he said, and everyone laughed as he handed the pigeon to the first frenchie.

"Phillips, see that grindstone wheel over there, give those knives and the axe a good sharpen will you....and find some oil to give these guns a bit of an oil and polish."

"Water bottles?"

"Ah oui!" and the second frenchie poked about in the back of the barn to produce a couple of five litre plastic bottles with lids."

"Grimson, get those washed out will you, they look like pesticide containers and I don't want to be drinking any of that "

Scarman stepped over to the Frenchman with a smile on his face "Bon.. merci..le plane is yours...." He held out his hand and shook hands with both men who seemed pleased.

"Connor, tell them we leave tomorrow at dawn, and thank them again for their hospitality"

The farmers signalled for them to go back to the

house.

As evening fell all of them sat around the kitchen table eating the most wonderful pie, with potatoes and vegetables.

"Chicken and pigeon pie!" they all laughed.

Good French red wine was handed round liberally, and the farmers presented Scarman with two bottles of French brandy, and two chickens in cages...."Eggs!"

"Thoroughly decent fellows...for Frenchies"

As the dinner finished, Saunders came up to Scarman.

"I don't wish to undermine your authority Scarman, nor the apparent loyalty of your men, but I'm a Captain, and Johnson here is a colour Sergeant so we both outrank you"

Scarman sat down in an armchair, the wine making him drowsy but he kept both eyes on Saunders, who continued.

"I've looked at those maps and my view is that we would be better to head for the West coast, it's a lot nearer and a ship north should be relatively easy to come by. Straight up the coast, and then across to Jersey or Guernsey and we're home pretty quick, well as near as dammit. What do you say?"

Scarman looked at him steadily wondering if the drink had given Saunders the courage to speak about his leadership of the men, after all Saunders and Johnson did not have the long-term bonds that had tied the Devon men together.

"Well, Captain..." he let the phrase linger for just a moment longer than was necessary. " As you say you outrank me so it's your call whether you go west or come with us...but I have already looked at the maps and decided that the sea is the more dangerous option here....I don't know whether you've actually been in the Bay of Biscay on a small boat but I have...and there are plenty of lost souls who thought as you do only to end up drowned. Also I'm not sure you're right about the speed. The wind and the currents out there make it damned difficult to beat northwards. More often you have to hold up in some French port along the coast for days or sometimes weeks, and that's assuming you're not blown onto the rocks, they're just below the surface in most parts, or hit by one of those big Atlantic rollers if you go into deeper water. Then there's the issue of paying someone to take you. You'll have noticed that apart from Grimson here we've got nothing. So you'll have to steal a boat, crew it yourself, you and Johnson and what will you eat and drink? Steal that too I suppose, and hope the Frenchies just let you walk away? For me...and I think I speak for all my men, we would be better taking a bit of time, eat and drink off the land, plenty of game about and some decent streams, plenty of dry wood for fires...good luck trying to pull a fish out of the Bay...so you see I've given it plenty of thought and that's why we're going north by land."

Saunders smiled at Scarman, I'm very glad we have you on our side Sergeant...and for what it's worth we'll,... that is colour sergeant Johnson and me,...will join you if you will have us"

"Of course Captain Saunders...and you never know ... we might find an aircraft along the way..."

"Meanwhile, Captain, does the aircraft have a ditch kit?"

"Yes, for landing on water you mean?"

"Aye"

"Well yes but why would we need that? It's pretty heavy."

"There'll be rivers we may need to cross, and we may not be able to find a boat handy....get it out and give it to Murray, he's a strong lad he won't mind the weight...also get all the parachutes as we can use them for tents and ground sheets, spread them amongst the men....are there emergency blankets?"

"Yes, we have some survival gear..."

"Get those out as well and spread them round...and if there's anything else you can think of, or see, bring that out too ..."

Both men smiled, Saunders headed off to the downed plane with Johnson to gather supplies before heading to one of the barns to get some sleep. Scarman dropped off in the very comfortable French armchair.

At dawn they were up having retrieved some straps from the DC3 to hang the chicken cages, the water flasks and brandies over one of the horses.

Collins had also made straps for the guns and the axe which were carried by Scarman, Phillips, Grimson and Connor.

Scarman led the party walking his horse, and Phillips walked the other two. He put,...actually he asked Saunders and Johnson to act as rear guard which they were happy to do.

"we spread ourselves out a bit so that if we get jumped or whatever we'll have some of us in reserve....Captain Saunders, I believe you have your pistol?"

"Aye Sergeant and so has Sergeant Johnson...I've also

got the flare gun from the plane"

The sun was rising in the east which made it easy to head north through the fields and valleys of the Dordogne.

Grimson spoke, " a bit odd really..."

"Scarman looked at him "What is?"

"Well...two Frenchies...two men....no women to be seen or heard...didn't look like farmers to me.....and they just hand over what we ask for ....more or less... and ask us for the plane instead of that gold coin ....and send us on our way...it's odd that's all."

Scarman nodded "Aye...I felt something wasn't quite right there but couldn't really put my finger on it....my guess is it's not their farm...they're either vagrants or travellers...or running from something... or someone, and just wanted us gone quick in case we drew attention from somewhere...so they gave us other people's stuff."

"Maybe they killed the previous farmers and would have done us in as well?"

"Maybe you're right but they'd have to be damn good given there are nine of us...plus one look at your ugly face they would have seen trouble!" Scarman laughed

"Yeah Sarge..that's me!" and Grimson laughed too.

They had figured out from what the frenchies told them that they were somewhere west of Perigeux in Northern Aquitaine, with the sea about 100 miles to their left.

Scarman had studied an ancient map that he found buried under a pile of papers. He reckoned they were a good 800 miles from the Normandy coast. He would head towards Cherbourg and then get hold of one of the local fishermen to take them over the channel to Blighty. He wondered if they might head for the nearer coast in the west and get a boat from there but he knew that the waters were difficult in the Bay of Biscay. He was a man of the land and so were the rest of them, so landward it would be.

He worked on the basis that they could make an average of twenty miles a day, 30 on a good day, 10 on a bad one, depending on terrain and weather. So 20 miles a day, that's 100 miles per five days, so 40 days if they travelled every day. So probably 50 days or within two months, as long as they weren't hindered.

This was, of course foreign country, so they would avoid any towns and villages, keep to the countryside and the woods where possible. Post night watchmen. Keep themselves to themselves and they should be fine. The rifle and the shotgun would give them meat and birds. The hens had already laid a couple of eggs and Stuart was put in charge of feeding the chickens and not letting them escape when they were feeding.

They came across many streams. If the horses drank then the water was ok so they could fill their flasks.

There were plenty of dead tree branches and the weather was fine so at night they lit a fire and generally ate very well.

The brandy was rationed out very carefully by Scarman in a tiny cup that he made from the lid of one of the water bottles.

Outside of the big cities, and particularly towards the centre, France remained largely unmodernised with a way of life that hadn't really changed much in centuries. There were woods and open fields everywhere, plus lots of small discreet cart roads.

They had been on the road for about two weeks and were making good time. Phillips went in front, about 50 yards ahead, as a scout.

The road rose steadily in front of them and crested out around 100 yards away.

Phillips stopped. "Sarge, better look at this."

Scarman signalled the others to stop, then stepped up to where Phillips was looking out over a beautiful valley.

Along the tops of the valley were deciduous woods and forest, but on the North Eastern slopes, facing South-westerly, a great vineyard stretched down the slope. On the other side a more gentle slope had a mixture of cattle and crops. Down the middle ran a small river with a water-mill and several thatched barns and houses. Smoke was rising lazily from a chimney on one of the larger barns.

They could see people moving about the vines, and in the crops, but most curiously they all appeared to be women.

Scarman searched the area visually but could not make out any men whatsoever.

"Do you think it's a convent or something Sarge?"

"You might be right Phillips but they aren't wearing nuns clothes...dunno....Hmm...well we can't go through there without being seen, and I'm not going to go all the way round...so only one way to find out...lets go down and meet them..."

Scarman turned to the others and explained.

"Sling the two guns on one of the horses, but keep 'em

handy just in case, no point setting off alarm bells if we can avoid it"

The party set off and were quickly spotted by some of the women. A bell started ringing and all the women stood still in their fields or vineyard to watch as Scarman and his men approached.

Once they reached the bridge over the stream beside the water-mill, Scarman held up his hand, palm first, fingers splayed, "we mean you no harm...we are travellers passing through."

There was a quick shuffling and some low talking in French, then one of the women stepped forward. She spoke in perfect English.

"If that is true then you are welcome to our little piece of heaven, but if you intend to turn it into hell we would ask you to leave....if you stay then we would be happy to share a meal with you to set you on your way."

Scarman nodded "That is kind of you, we mean no ill intent" and then for some reason he added "we are away from our homeland as you can hear...we are making the journey back to the north coast, but we would welcome a meal with you, and in return if there are any needs which might require the strength of men then we will be happy to help....my name is Scarman and these are the 'Ballast men'" pointing to his motley band of men.

The woman smiled. She turned and spoke to the others in French then waved the ballast men across the bridge.

"My name is Anne"

"You're English"

"Yes I married Jean-Paul and we moved here many years ago,...you are in the tiny village of Moulevre... we have...had, a small house here, he was the local wine merchant for the vineyard that you see here... then the war...or whatever it was happened...and we.." She pointed her arms to all the women dotted about the village and the fields " were all left as widows.

"All the men?"

Anne sighed and looked to the ground.

"There was a rugby match in Paris." She used the English pronunciation .

"The team from Cholet...a few kilometres north... our local team, were playing the much bigger Nantes in the Stade de France. It was the final match for the Coulet Trophy, a huge event as the team had never got to any final before. All the men, young and old took the coaches to Paris that day ....none returned. As you may know, the devastation began on that day and spread throughout France. Many cities are now death traps either from radiation, or more often from disease and decay."

"I'm sorry...." Scarman couldn't think of anything else to say.

A tear ran down Anne's cheek but she smiled..

"It was quite a long time ago now and we have all kept together...mourned, cried, and then decided that we must survive...a few of our older daughters went too ....I had two sons....." She sighed and looked up at the clouds.

"They look down on us now from their heaven to our little heaven here...we survive and we remember....and we keep things going as best we can, but we may take you up on your offer...there are some things where we could use some muscle...the water-mill in particular."

Scarman noticed that not all the women seemed that pleased. Many gave them dark looks and several crossed themselves.

Probably no wonder as they were a ragged scruffy looking company wearing the same clothes they had left England in, substantial beards and stubble, matted hair and no doubt smelled badly.

She turned to Scarman. "Evening is coming and we tend to eat together while it is still light. See that sports pavilion over there." She wrinkled her nose then pointed to a relatively modern building next to a big field which had rugby posts at each end . "there's a big rugby bath in there and the water should be warm from the solar heaters on the roof you can wash in there and join us in the big barn...there.., where Annette and Dorcas are preparing the food... you'll hear the bell when it's time. Then you can tell me about you and the 'Ballast men' ...what a curious name?

"It's a long story.."

"I bet..."

"You'll also find some of the men's clothes in there, might as well use them if you wish, then you can wash those rags you're wearing too...."and with that she went to speak to some of the other women before disappearing round the corner of one of the small houses.

"Alright men" said Scarman " we've been invited

for dinner by these ladies, so best behaviour...we're Englishmen remember, don't get too pissed and don't try anything on with these women...remember they're hot-blooded these Frenchies...a wrong move and they'll sneak in at night and cut your cock off if they don't like you." A few of the men grinned at Scarman's lecture " ...we don't know much about this place yet so keep your wits about you...meanwhile lets do what the lady says and set ourselves up in that sports pavilion.

She was not wrong about the water which came out of the bath taps absolutely boiling from the sunshine. The bath filled up as the water temerature cooled as the tank drained. They all stripped off and slid into and under the water. Everything was there which had obviously not been touched since the men all left on that day several years ago.

Grimson found a whole cupboard filled with the team strip including navy blue track suits and trainers.

By the time they emerged they looked like the rugby team that had once thrived in this little French hamlet. All dressied in confortable, matching blue track suits, their hair slicked back and most of them now clean shaven.

Several of the women gasped or put their hands to their faces when they saw them. It was as if their men had returned. There were tears.

The barn was well lit in the evening sunshine. There were long trestle tables laid out with jugs of water and wine, a sharp white, and a soft red. Bowls of salad leaves and walnuts were laid out at each place setting along with a knife, fork and spoon. Wine glasses completed the setting.

At one end there was an enormouse open fireplace

with a stone chimney leading up through the roof. Across the opening was a large mesh plate of steel and on half of the top was a thick steel plate. The fire was a mix of dried wood and bundles of brushwood. There were two women doing the cooking. One threw a bundle of brush wood onto the fire which almost immediately flared up in a gout of flame under the steel plate. The other was laying several large fish onto the plate which were almost instantly seared.

The women were taking their places and Anne suggested that Scarman's men split up to sit at assorted tables to meet the other women. Some of the women still looked at them with some hostility and shooed them away from their tables , but others seemed more accommodating and soon there was a general hubbub of talking and even some laughter.

The fish course came and it was delicious. Pieces of white flesh, seared over a brushwood fire with a light yellow sauce made from goodness knows what. Then steaks, cooked rare, with another sauce made from butter and herbs, and golden chips made in the way only the French can do. Followed by fruit and molten cheeses which you had to eat with a spoon.

Along with this were copious quantities of wine, and finally some Arminac brandies and coffee.

Scarman had not eaten as well as this in his entire life. His men must have thought this too because they were as well behaved as he had ever seen them. Conversations flowed between the men and the women despite some language barriers. It was as close to normality as he had witnessed since a long time ago.

Murray was deputised to take some food out to Cauldwell who was grumpily sitting with the horses, until Scarman made the decision that he should come in and join the gathering. He felt that they were not under threat. Maybe it was the wine.

He turned to Anne. " I've been wondering where you sell all this produce? The wines, cheeses, meats etc....you must produce a handsome surplus from the size of the farming that I've seen already?"

Anne looked down and smiled "We don't sell any of it....we give it all to the church...well to the monks who come to collect it...there's a huge monastery, the Abbey St Denis, not far from here...it's all men... monks, priests and the like...you have to hand it to the Catholic Church, they are extremely well organised. Any men that come here...Frenchmen anyway, end up as monks in the monastery, usually as labour for building more monasteries....all over France. I suppose they are offered eternal salvation... actually I have to be careful what I say as many of the women here are devout...they don't see it as I do...but then I'm CofE by birth at least and when I came here I converted for Jean-Paul's sake.

The following day, Scarman and the ballast men were given tasks including sorting out the water mill which had stopped working. Scarman called Cauldwell over to have a look.

"You're a joiner aren't you, what do you think?"

Cauldwell took a look round the wooden shafts and

great wooden blocks of gears.

"This one's buggered, it needs pulling out and a new set of teeth cut into it"

"...well go and find some tools and see if you can fix it"

Cauldwell disappeared and Scarman went out to check on the others, a few were helping the women dig up vegetables, and others being escorted by women to their homes to help repair some of the broken fixtures.

In the distance a small group of men emerged at the far end of the village all dressed in grey monks habits. They paused at the sight of Scarman's men, but continued uneasily up the street.

Scarman stood in the middle of the road, as if it was a gunfight at the OK Corral, one of the monks came closer.

"Qui e vous?

Scarman replied in English "we're travellers passing through, these ladies..." he waved his hand around ... "have been good enough to feed us and in turn we have offered some help ..."

One of the older monks came up as translator for the younger monk. He spoke briefly. Then waited to translate the reply.

The younger monk said a few word and the older man said " You are not welcome here, we have no need for Englishmen, you must go....in peace"

Scarman considered the words. He didn't want to antagonise things that might prove a problem for the women, so he chose his words carefully.

"I agree with you, and as I have already said, we are simply passing through. We will leave when we're ready, no more than a week and we will be on our way, meanwhile my men have skills which you probably don't have, so once we have given help, and we have rested from our journey, we will be gone, and no harm done"

The monk looked at him with undisguised disgust, so Scarman added " ...of course I will be happy to explain this to your Abbot if you wish....." he left the question hanging.

Scarman noticed that some of the women had come out of one of the barns and were pushing a heavy cart loaded with food towards the monks. Eventually some of the younger ones walked over to them and took over the cart before turning back towards the far end of the road, then stopped waiting for instructions. One of the women came up to one of the young boys, perhaps no more than 12 years old, gently put her hand on his face and smiled a mother's smile. He shuffled and must have said something because she stepped back and looked away before walking back wearily to the barn.

The monk said something to the translator who gave Scarman a weary look and said "My brother is not pleased ....but I will speak to Fra Michael or Abbot and he will decide, I will return with his message" and he nodded then walked away along with the younger one who spoke something to the carters and they were off back from whence they came.

Anne came over to Scarman.

“They’ll not be pleased “ she said “ though it is our custom...it has become our custom anyway... to send our boys to the monastery once they’re old enough....one of them you’ll have noticed was in the group...Beatrice’s boy. Some of them run away once they’re older but they can’t come back here...it’s the monastery system so they have to go far away and hide...God knows where.”

Scarman put two and two together. “I think we might have come across a couple of them. Two French lads hiding in a derelict farm where our plane came down. They pulled us out of the plane and fed us...gave us some stuff...very helpful they were.”

“Did you find out their names?” Anne looked concerned.

“No, I didn’t, but one of the men might know.

“it’s just that they might be from this village. We know that a few of our boys have run away, ...but oh what am I saying...they could be from a completely different monastery...they’re all over the place.”

Scarman asked around anyway but none of his men had

Scarman looked at her, but it wasn’t his business, and the last thing he wanted was to get tangled up in local disputes...if that’s what they were. He shrugged and said “ well, we’ll help you sort out a few things before we leave if you and your friends don’t mind feeding us for a few more days while we gather our strength, then we'll leave you in peace"

Anne smiled " I know, but in a way it's a shame....we are beginning to like having you men here...." Her voice tailed off and Scarman felt a pang. But they would leave, and quickly before he, or his men, started something that would end badly.

Later that day the old monk returned.

"Monsieur, my Abbot, Fra Michael has asked if you can join him tomorrow morning at the Monastery....the women will tell you how to get there..shall I convey your reply?"

"Thank you, I will be pleased to meet with Fra Michael and will be there tomorrow morning."
The old monk smiled, nodded and set off back to his monastery.

That evening Scarman called his men together. " We'll be leaving very soon. If any of you are thinking what I know you're thinking then there'll be trouble ...no doubt. So keep your hands, cocks and wits about you...do not get drunk...I will be going up to the monastery tomorrow morning and hopefully we'll get out of here before we get tangled up in the local politics....capice?"

The men smiled, nodded, then went across to the barn where the smell of cooking was wafting across the road.

The following day.

Scarman was shown into a small office where a monk dressed in an off-white robe stood to greet him. He was an old man, Scarman reckoned, perhaps in his eighties, but his eyes were as bright as a young man's would be, and he had a broad, welcoming smile. He spoke in perfect English.

"Sergeant Scarman, I'm Fra Michael, welcome to L'Abbe De St Denis" and he held out his hand. Scarman shook hands.

"Good to meet you Father Michael…you have perfect English?"

The older man smiled gently. " ..a long time ago I was a diplomat attached to the French Embassy in London...long before I took my vows...which was also a long time ago....please take a seat Sergeant Scarman…do you have a Christian name?"

"John…"

"Ah.." The abbot smiled again and sat in a simple wooden chair facing Scarman " Church of England? Or Catholic? "

"CofE…"

"Well at least you believe in God Sergeant" and he laughed a pleasant, humorous laugh.

" You have a military title…are you a military man?"

"I was a Sergeant in the British Army a long time ago…like you…but no more, but my men still call me Sergeant as a sign of respect"

"Ah yes…you're men answer to you…but who do you answer to I wonder?"

" A small Lord on a small estate in Devon…I'm his gamekeeper" Scarman smiled back.

"Hmm…and this small Lord answers to your King, no?…your King Edward the ninth?"

"I guess he does but we don't really have much to do with Royalty….only gamekeeping and ground maintenance…a bit of farming of course…" Scarman's left the sentence hanging. He decided not to go into detail with this man.

"Hmm…and how is your King..?, a Frenchman I understand…a Plantagenet no less!…thinks he's descended from Norman nobility I understand."

"Your King too if I'm not mistaken….I have no idea I've never met…well only once, very briefly."

"Hmm…" Fra Michael did not comment further

"Ah well…we have even less to do with Royalty…I answer to his Holiness, the Pope…in Rome, but tell me John Scarman…what brings you here to our little valley, and where are you going?"

"We will not be staying long…if that is you're question". Fra Michael smiled but said nothing. "We are here by accident, our plane crash landed about 250 kilometres south of here and I am aiming for Cherbourg or similar to find a boat to take us back to England."

"A plane crash Hmm?…but where was your destination? …not France you say"

"Our plane ran out of fuel…we were lucky not to be killed, and the wind blew us East so we landed somewhere south of Perigeux.."

"Hmm….I see…what sort of plane?…forgive me John Scarman but I have always been interested in aircraft since I was a boy…"

"It was an old DC3...a good aircraft..." His voice tailed away.

"Hmm...I see" Scarman could see the man's mind ticking away.

" And what will you do when you return to England?"

"As I said, I'm a gamekeeper, so me and my men will return to the land..."

" A worthy occupation....of course you could stay and join us...we are always recruiting new trainee monks to serve God here in our little heaven."

Scarman could hear the faint chanting of the monks at prayer. " Kind of you but no thanks...not for me, nor for my men."

"It will not be safe for you further north, the population may be heavily depleted but we hear of roving bands of mercenaries preying on travellers....on villages...moving from one to the next. And it is a long route home for you...many kilometres to the north coast."

"We can look after ourselves father Michael, if that is your concern, and we have nothing to steal, just poor travellers...like your Franciscans here."

Fra Michael smiled. "Well, perhaps I can help you return much more quickly."

Scarman sat quite still...he wasn't sure about this clever old man.

"We have a small Beechcraft King Air, quite old, but two of the monks are pilots and I am required to attend Rome to visit his Holiness twice a year. The catholic church is well organised when it comes to bringing the faithful to Rome ...to check up on us..." he smiled...

Scarman found his suspicion rising and said, "Again, kind of you but I think we'll keep to our plan...and to the land."

" You will be wondering why I could be so helpful... Hmm?...you see here we have a band of Englishmen, led by a Sergeant, who seems a very capable man, a Sergeant who has met a King. Kings only meet Sergeants for one reason and that is to thank them, for a service performed, a Sergeant with a handy group of Englishmen under his command...I wonder what service...what reward?...and then, this group of men are sent in a precious aircraft, no doubt with the King's consent...or, or maybe one of the King's senior courtiers perhaps, yes we have heard of Sir William Levine, the High Lord Chancellor, who would look to your small Lord to provide some men for a particular service, or operation...or operations."

Scarman sat quite still as this clever old man pieced together a story from his simple questioning...

"But then he sends you off on another mission, onto an old DC3, which has a probable range of less than 1500 kilometres, which runs out of fuel and is blown east into south-west France...but the only thing west of that is the Atlantic ocean, and our equinoctal winds are famous for blowing things inshore, boats...or aircraft....perhaps you were on your way to Spain, you might have made it to Northern Spain, but it is doubtful, and there is no landfall in the Atlantic that even the best DC3 could make...so perhaps you had been too useful and you were being sent to a watery grave?...but then God intervened and blew you to us...unharmed...and you now seek your revenge on whoever sent you?...so I will help you return to England..our old enemy...because I am not keen to have a tight English unit of the King, led by a capable Sergeant interrrupting our little system here, and because our enemies enemy is perhaps our friend...not very Christian perhaps but we French are also capable men, and practical too.."

Fra Michael smiled at Scarman, he knew he had painted a resonably accurate description of both Scarman's position and also his own even if the details were not entirely known.

All Scarman could do was smile back while he thought this through, he had visions of getting on the Beechcraft and somehow be thrown out at ten thousand feet, most likely into the Channel, finally he said "We have our own pilot, if you consent to him being the co-pilot, and that only your pilot accompanies us so that he can bring back your aircraft then we will take up your offer."

The old monk clapped his hands in pleasure.."Good, then we have a win-win situation Sergeant.. I will introduce you to Brother Christien, our pilot and he will fly you home...I hope I have your assurances that he will be allowed to return?...I don't want to have to explain the loss of my little aircraft to his Holiness..."

"You have my word"

"Good, well it is too late today to fly so I suggest you and your men meet at the air strip, just two kilometres up the road, tomorrow at dawn and we will say Adieu!"

XXIX

Cornwall and onwards

Despite the pain Alex continued to push herself to walk as well as she could, and to help on the farm. The people were kind. She tried to do things that had once been so easy for her but now ...the damned leg, not just the leg, the sweating, the pain like a constant devil eating into her.

Things began to take a turn for the worse again and the fever returned. Homemade antibiotics are no match for commercial pharmacy drugs and they were no match for the infection which began to spread thoughout her body.

Mortimer came and went. Meg mopped her with cold water to bring down her temperature, however it was clear that she was dying. She began to get delirious, unsure whether she was awake or unconscious. She could not see straight and began to lose her grip on what was real and what wasn't.

'Was that a Chinook flying overhead?....twin rotors? ....who were those men who came in?...soldiers? and another man who injected something in her arm? ....another man in the field....John Chappel?....so much noise then nothing. Was she dreaming she was now back in a Beechcraft? Flying...the man with the syringe? Then nothing...a strange dry dusty smell? Then nothing...in and out of consciousness.

She came awake. There was no pain. The room

was filled with light. A gentle warm breeze floated through an open window. A smell of flowers... Jasmine, and Honeysuckle. The walls were of soft honey coloured Tadelakt, smooth and polished with beeswax. She knew this. An Islamic arch, beautifully proportioned, the plasterwork, and the mosaic tiles.

She had been here before.

A woman entered the room carrying a tray of food. She smiled.

"where am I...?"

But the woman just smiled and waved her hand downwards as if to say 'stay put for now and get some rest'.

Something wasn't right. Her hand looked odd...and her wrist....her skin was darker as if tanned a light khaki....her hair was dark brown..she felt a strange sensation in her belly and crotch. Instinctively she put her hand under the sheet and between her legs. She pulled it out ...blood...she was bleeding... menstruating.

She pulled herself up and out of the bed. The woman frowned at her and tried to make her lie down again but she ignored her and stood up. Her body was not hers...it was that of a young woman...her skin smooth and taut, her breasts quite full but equally taut. There was a small mirror on the wall and with a shock she looked into it ...at a stranger's face peering back at her. Dark brown eyes...olive shaped, a fine nose and mouth...hair cascading down her face. Then she realised she was standing on her own legs and feet.

It was impossible to comprehend for a moment but then her training kicked in.

She had been in Cornwall...the shipwreck...her leg had been amputated...the fever....she had come close to death....the Chinook. She was in Algeria...in Edwards palace....Bryant !....she'd been transferred into a new body.

She sat back on the bed trying to force away a sense of panic. Her heart was beating hard and her breathing was coming out in short gasps.

The woman came over and put her hand gently on her back. She noticed the blood and drew her breath then went scurrying out of the room, returning in a moment with a bag of tampons which she handed to Alex with a light smile and pointed to the bathroom at the edge of the room.

How many years had it been since she'd had her period? ...she had thought that all that was behind her, but now. She looked at the bag and the tampons inside, then looked at the woman who smiled back.

It was really an auto response that she found herself heading for the bathroom...she turned on the shower and stood under it for what seemed like an age before stepping out and drying herself then slipped in a tampon.

The bathroom had a full-length mirror. She looked at the stranger peering back at her, her almost black hair dripping over her shoulders. The woman came in and towelled her down then pulled her damp hair back and tied it with a silk band.

Her body was soft and feminine, not hardened by

years of hard exercise. No muscle to speak of, just soft female arms and legs. She hated it all.

The maid pointed to the bedroom. On the bed were a set of clothes, cream silk pants and a camise, a long silk shirt and brown silk jacket. A set of brown, short leather boots.

She was retired Colonel Alex Rheinhart aged 47 now standing in the body of a late teens Algerian girl.

She dressed in the offered clothes, which fitted her perfectly. She had become a beautiful woman. She had been a good looking woman before but hardened almost like a man…but now….

She put her hands to her face and sat down looking at the floor…staring at it without seeing. Tears of frustration , anger, bewilderment welled up in her eyes.

She sat on the edge of the bed while to woman tidied up around her and then brought the plate of food over to her and sat with her. Of course this woman had no idea what had happened and was just being kind to a younger woman who had obviously encountered some trauma or other. She patted Alex on her back and again held out the food.

" What I need is a drink…Algerian brandy…"

The woman clearly knew what she meant but wagged her finger and shook her head. Algeria is a muslim country and drinking alcohol is a sin.

Alex stood up and smiled at the woman, then walked out of the room. She began to recognise her surroundings. She would find Bryant, who would have something stronger than tea…. and once fortified she'd rip is balls off.

She recognised the palace inner garden and headed over to where it joined the main reception room where she had last been almost a year ago.

She could hear voices, voices that she recognised, was that Edward?

Alex stepped into the garden room, the one she had found herself in several years ago when she first found Bryant.

A very tall, strong, black haired young man stood towards the table in the centre of the room, his back to Alex, facing an equally tall young woman dressed in riding jodhpurs black riding boots, a cream shirt tucked into the jodhpurs, and a tan suede short jacket. She was an extremely attractive woman with strong features and her long dark hair tied back in a ponytail, as if she had just come back from riding a horse. A riding whip lay on the table.

The woman looked over at Alex and a smile crept across her face. A cruel smile.

The tall man turned to see what had attracted her attention and the three of them stared at each other for what seemed like too long.

Alex spoke to the man "Edward?"

"Hello Alex"

"Well this is nice" the tall woman spoke "Old comrades re-united and not one of us in our original skin"

“Henry?”

“Well what do you think ?” the woman made a short twirl “ I think mine is better than yours …don’t you think?…and I rather like the female form, perhaps I’ll keep it instead of waiting for my clones to get a bit bigger.”

Edward spoke “ Despite Henry’s inevitable theatrics I’m glad that he’s managed to save you. You were at death’s door when we found you on that farm….and he’s put me in one of my clones due to my forthcoming imminent death.” He turned to Henry. “I must say I’m delighted to be free of the constant pain that has been my companion for so long, and it’s wonderful to feel the energy of youth once again.” He turned to Alex. “Same for you I imagine?”

“I..I cannot say how I feel right now…it’s as if I’m in some sort of living nightmare…and who gave you permission to do this to me?” turning to the Bryant woman.

“He did” Bryant pointed at Edward. Both looked at Alex but she turned away to stare into the garden.

Edward turned to Bryant, “Henry why don’t you leave us for a while, lower the temperature somewhat?” The Bryant woman nodded, smiled and walked off along one of the palace corridors.

Gaunt came over alongside Alex, “Let’s walk a while, and we can talk”

He gestured towards the garden and stepped onto one of the stone paths that wound through the palace gardens.

After a moments hesitation Alex followed.

"Why have you done this to me Edward? It didn't occur to you that I might have chosen to die...as myself."

Gaunt looked at her " It did occur to me, but I did not want to waste your life...and you and I are special, we have been all along, but I have never told you ."

"Special? In what way? We have already spoken about what you did to me in Afghanistan....that was not special...it was cruel."

Gaunt sighed gently to himself "Yes it was, but that's only the half of it...." Alex looked up at him.

"You are my sister...or more correctly my half-sister...we share the same father"

Alex continued to look at him, staring, wondering if he was mad, or was it her?

"What the hell do you mean?"

"Henry told you about my background, my father, descended from John of Gaunt via the French Capetian arm of the French royalty, who married my mother, an Ottoman princess.." he waved his arm around at the palace "This was her palace before it became mine....he was what would be described as a playboy, an idle waster, in the fashion of the nineteen fifties and sixties. He married my mother, she became pregnant with me but also picked up the pox from him, syphillus, the black lion, as it was known in some quarters. When she realised what he had done she came here and gave birth to me here. I was also infected from birth. Naturally she never forgave him and kept me away from him. But I was curious as I grew up, and I tried to contact him. Too late, he had already died, but I visited his Chateau in Gascony and met with his staff including his private secretary, Francois DeMeussier.

DeMeussier and I spent many days going over my deceased father's affairs, both financial, and personal. Apart from his many forays with various well known prostitutes, he had occasional affairs with other members of the so-called 'high society', including a Belgian Countess. The teenage Countess of Brabant. He got her pregnant and to avoid scandal DeMeussier arranged for her to stay at a convent in Gascony. The nuns looked after her until she had delivered a baby girl, and then made arrangements with an adoption agency to have the girl adopted. Something that the Nuns did on a fairly regular basis on behalf of the so-called nobility in return for a generous donation to the church. A Rhodesian farmer and his wife made enquiries as they had found themselves unable to have children of their own, Charles and Elizabeth Rhienhart."

Alex felt cold and despite the warmth of the day she felt nothing but cold...she simply put one foot in front of the other while Gaunt continued.

" DeMeussier said that it had happened twice to his knowledge, another girl, this time from a stable maid, and again the Rheinharts took her back to Rhodesia with them.

Probably there were others, bastard children, but either DeMeussier didn't know, or they were... terminated by the mothers. I don't know.

Years later, I heard of a remarkable woman, a rising

star of Sandhurst, the youngest female Captain in the Army, her name Alex Rheinhart, a South African some thought.

I made some discreet enquiries about you. So when Henry and I convinced the MOD to establish the Psych Ops unit, I suggested you as the female member of the team. The rest you know."

Alex was pale. Gaunt summoned one of the guards from across the grounds and spoke to him in Berber to fetch a bottle of brandy and a glass. He motioned Alex to a garden seat in the shade of a large Jacaranda tree, it's purple flowers set against the green of the grass and the blue of the sky. Alex was trying to process all this and her first reaction would be disbelief...however her inner voice told her it was true. Nevertheless she took a deep breath.

"How can you be so sure, there are quite a few Rheinharts in South Africa, German or Dutch German decent?"

" Well for one thing you had a certain look which I recognised in myself, ...but I also got a DNA sample of you...no need to say how...and that confirmed it. You are my half sister"

"Why am I pox free then?"

"Yes ...as I understand it, it's not always inevitable that it's passed on to the child as in my case...but I did have your blood checked at the time...and you are indeed free of it unlike me...or rather my former self...another advantage of Dr Bryant's very clever achievements."

"Is my mother...my biological mother still alive?"

"Yes I believe so... though I have never made contact myself."

"If your father was a waster as you say, how could he afford the lifestyle of the playboy...let alone pay for Nuns and so on?"

"My mother was the one with the money, that's why he married her. Even after she left him she was an honourable woman and paid, I'm sure begrudgingly, a monthly allowance to him. Never enough, ... he left behind many debts which, through DeMeussier, I arranged to have settled finally."

The guard re-appeared with a bottle and two glasses.

"Only one glass...for the lady....I am a good muslim" Gaunt said to the guard who smiled and handed the glass to Alex.

"I cannot be seen drinking Alcohol in my own country" he said to Alex after the guard had left. "But here..." and he poured a large shot for Alex.

She stared at the glass for half a minute and then downed the lot without so much as a shiver.

"Christ!" she stared ahead. " I don't know what to say or how I feel. To think that I have known you all these years and you kept this from me until now... and this" she wave a hand over her body " ...this body change...all at the same time...you really are the bastard....not me."

After a while she turned to Gaunt.

"What have you done with my body?...the one-legged one."

"She's in the mortuary awaiting your instructions."

"I want to see her" she filled her glass and drank it back in one.

This new body was not used to alcohol and Alex found herself swaying slightly. She took a glass of water from one of the maids.

Gaunt called for one of the Chinese doctors and he led her down into the clinical research corridor which she remembered from her 'tour' with Bryant. They turned into a cold room with wall refrigeration cabinets.

The doctor pulled out one of the drawers, a flat slab of steel on which lay a body covered by a simple cotton sheet.

She turned to the doctor. "Please give me a moment..."

"Of course" and the doctor stepped slowly from the room to wait outside.

Alex lowered her head, how could this have happened..and yet it had. She raised her head and pulled back the cotton shroud to see her cold face lying still on the slab. She put both hands to her mouth but kept staring at the face. She pulled the sheet off completely and looked at the haggard, naked, cold white, faintly blue body. The stitched up sewing of the stump of her leg looked black against the rest of the flesh. It was a lean hard body, her body, but all the abuse it had endured in life remained fixed in the flesh and bones of the corpse. Her tattoo still visible, but pale, and now apparently irrelevant. She wasn't Rhodesian at all, she was French Belgian with royal blood in her veins. No, not even that anymore, she was an Algerian girl with no more royal blood in her than anyone else. Enough to drive anyone mad just thinking about it.

A corpse, that's what she now was. Her corpse, naked and cold and dead. And yet here she was, alive, in a beautiful new, young body, able to look down at her old corpse. Something no-one would have done or thought possible...except of course Henry Bryant had , no doubt, done exactly that, and now Edward.

She felt a terrible weight on her...a pain that could not be cured...her eyes began to stream with tears....her whole body convulsed and great wailing sobs came out of her. She sank to the floor and hoped it would swallow her...she had no thought... just insane grief....not just for her former self....the whole story of her life stuck in her throat and she could barely breathe....the rapes and murders... the betrayal and deceit by Gaunt and Bryant...and Brevard....her parents...not her parents....she was an orphan again...and now she was living in some ridiculous female body...not hers...never hers...she hated herself...everything.

She lay on the floor, not aware for how long. The doctor came in and made a gesture that he was about to say "let me help you...you need rest" but the old Alex returned and she stood up slowly. "No...I'm alright" she wiped her new face with her hands

"I'd like you to cremate her and make arrangements to send me the ashes in due course, Dr Bryant will know where to send them"

The doctor nodded. Then she said to him

"Are Dr Bryant's and the King's bodies here too?"

The doctor considered for a moment, he was unsure about the protocol, but as the King had brought her to him he felt she would be allowed to know.

"Yes, we have Dr Bryant's last two bodies here, but not the King's yet."

Alex puzzled for a moment then realised that the first original Henry had died at Makhalo, and he'd transferred into Jerry's body, so two, which meant that Jerry, or what was left of him, was dead too. When will it end?.

XXX
Langley Castle

The smell of gangrenous flesh and superation hung in the air. William Levine stood by the King's bed trying not to breathe too deeply, as if the miasma in the room might penetrate his own flesh.

The King stirred, his eyelids rose slowly and his gaze drifted across to his Lord High Chancellor.

Outside, mist and fog swirled around the castle grounds. Damp and cold dripped from the branches of the surrounding woodlands.

Langley castle was in the border country where, traditionally, Scotland and England merged together, The boundaries shifting back and forth over the centuries. The castle built in the 14th century along with several others across this stretch of the country to keep the Scots in check as numerous Jacobite rebellions came and went.

The King was dying. He'd been dying for years as his body gave way to the erosion caused by his syphallytic condition which he'd had all his life.

'You have called for them?"

'I have sire"

"You will also be getting a couple of visitors, strangers to you, let them in"

Levine bowed his head.

"And the men, they're ready?'

"Aye sire, a big army, tucked away, surrounding the castle.'

The King lay back.

Levine stepped out of the room, relieved to be away from the rotting stench.

He stood outside the castle gate. A few of the guards

nodded to him, he nodded back but knew their fate so didn't stop to talk.

The light, such as it was, drifted slowly over the day. Rain began in earnest. Soon it would be mixed with much blood.

He stepped back inside to stand near the fire set in the castles great hearth.

As evening began to fall, two strangers appeared on horseback, accompanied by Captain Farrell who had the watch.

A tall young man, perhaps no more than 16 or 17 years rode at the front, he rode with ease. Levine had never seen him before but for some reason he looked damned familiar. Behind him, riding side-saddle, a woman, striking in her appearance, foreign features and a dark olive complexion. She wore a great velvet dress in red silk with fur trim. Her hair, jet black, she wore a strange expression, a smile as if she knew something and was keen to tell.

Levine was about to speak but the young man spoke first 'Chancellor Levine, how fares the old king?'

Levine was somewhat taken aback. That voice he had just heard was the king's voice, but with the strength of youth'

'He is dying.....sire'

Levine decided to play safe. This was no ordinary stranger.

'...and the Lady..?'

'The lady is with me....'

The young man jumped down from his saddle and handed the reins to one of the guards who had stepped forward to assist. He was dressed in a tight leather jerkin over a red silk shirt. His woolen hose was a dark green and he wore brown and black riding boots. All this of seemingly very high quality. At his neck hung a bottle green riding cloak, fastened with a pin which looked like a piece of broom. A Plantagenet.....or Robin Hood, Levine thought.

God he was tall and fit, well over six feet in height and not yet fully grown.

'Yes sire, he is expecting you'

'We will speak with him alone at first. I will call you when we're ready....the Dukes et al are here?'

'They are sire'

Levine shuffled, how the hell did he know this?, who is he?

The Lady was helped down from her horse. Shorter than the young man but quite tall for a woman. She carried herself as no other woman he'd met save perhaps Colonel Rheinhart.

The young man strode into the castle, followed quickly by the woman, straight up the staircase and towards the kings chambers as if he knew.

Levine struggled to keep up, his leg almost giving way half way up the stairs, but he managed to stay upright.

The two soldiers posted as guards to the king stepped forward at the sight of the two strangers and raised their weapons. Levine managed to catch up in time to tell the soldiers to stand at ease and let them through.

'We will see the King alone. I will call for you William when we're ready and you may bring the court into the King's bedchamber.

Levine noticed the use of his first name but simply nodded. In his mind he feared the sound of swords and death coming from the room but instead he heard absolutely nothing.

Edward Gaunt, last of the Plantagenets, King Edward

IX, lay in his bed with his eyes half closed. He had heard voices outside, so when the pair entered his room he sat up slightly and ushered away the medic who was sitting patiently in a chair at the back of the room with a wave of his hand. The medic left.

Gaunt looked at the young man, then his brow furrowed as he saw the woman.

" Who the hell are you?"

"Well I might just be your new nurse Edward..." the woman laughed and made a small courtesy with a wicked grin on her face.

"You're Henry !, for God's sake..."

"Oh, is it that obvious...well do you like it?" and she gave a small theatrical turn..."I

The conversation was as if they had been talking for hours.

Gaunt looked again at the woman. 'Given the circumstances Henry you could have shown some restraint'

The woman spoke 'why? You forget that I'm a wanted man in England, I came in disguise!....in any case my clone is not as old as yours yet...what do you think of him, ...that is, ...you?'

The young Edward answered "it is everything I could have wished for, I am young again, with the strength and vigour of youth, and the mind and experience of my 70 years...I am very pleased indeed. Look at my broken and wasted body there'. He pointed to the King 'I have held on to this old and diseased body for too long...it is a great relief'

The old king looked at him ' so there are two of us now, ... I can die now which means the succession is secure....at last. You will know that I, perhaps I should say 'we' have decided that the court should know you as my son. It would be better that way. But that you will continue to be known as Edward IX.'

The young king spoke 'I have had further thoughts on the matter and it would seem odd if I retained the same name...as your son. I should become Edward X.'

'This might prompt our enemies to launch their attacks if they think the old king is gone. But let them, they will attack anyway, as we're about to see with the Scots...'

'Speaking of which, Levine tells me the Scots are massing just north of Berwick, various inns have been supplied with large quantities of strong spirits and wine. They'll be as drunk as monkeys by the time they get here. Sykes will have all on to control them once they're let loose. He tells me that Sykes has brought the German princelings with him so we can kill two birds with one stone.'

'Captain Farrell brought us through one of our camps to the south. I kept my counsel but it looks like we have deployed well to the south, the east and the west....and the bait lies ready...' the young Edward looked at the King. '

'Tell the Chancellor to come in, it's time he knew, and then he can bring in the rest of the court.

William Levine was summoned......

'are Brevard and Rheinhart here?"

"Rheinhart is here but Brevard isn't....we have had no reply from him as yet." Levene scanned the, as yet, strange assembly.

The king looked up. 'William, I have some good news for you, meet my son and heir prince Edward, shortly to become King Edward X.....'

Levine looked at the young Edward.

'So..'thought Levine, 'at last a succession plan'

He knelt before the young king, 'my lord, I pledge my services to you for as long as you will receive them, as I do for our King'

'Arise William, perhaps, you will be Sir William, yes that would be good...and the ...Lady here is ... Dr Henry Bryant...someone I think you have been looking for, for sometime?'

Levine looked mildly shocked.... 'I am pleased to meet you Dr Bryant, I confess I had imagined you as a man....so it is a pleasant surprise to find you as you are'

'Such a charming man Lord Chancellor' and she held out her hand for him to kiss.

...and the king began to laugh... 'William stop....Henry behave yourself...

....so to matters in hand. Why is Brevard not here? The king looked at Levine.

'The straight answer is that we don't know. He received the command to attend here, I sent an emissary. He hasn't returned and we have not had a signal from Jamestown. It's possible that he has been delayed en route but I'm suspicious. When we last spoke he mentioned some trouble with the confederate army generals. I believe there's a Frenchman, Lafayette who Brevard suspected of treason.'

'Then William I want you to go there, find out what's happened. It's too late to delay the succession....but go quietly, you know what I mean,....if there's trouble in the colonies....." he left the sentence unfinished.

The King began coughing and the young King went

to him but he raised a hand to stop him

"It's alright…where is Colonel Rheinhart?… and does she know you in you're…disguise?"

The young King "She's here and she knows everything…I told her…we told her"

The old Gaunt lay his giant frame back on his pillows, he sighed "Yes… all for the best."

"Henry please leave us, I want to speak with William."

The Bryant woman left the chamber and disappeared into Castle.

"William, come"

Levine walked over to the King's bedside and the young King pulled a chair over for him to sit.

"William, you have been more loyal to me than I could have ever hoped."

Levine began to speak but Gaunt held up a hand to stop him.

"…more loyal that I could have hoped and you must now forgive me and my son here for not telling you all that you probably should have known, but I did it for your benefit. There are things that I know you have suspected for many years, and you probably have guessed some of it but not all. I will tell you all now, I have not done so previously, not because I doubt your loyalty for one second, but because knowledge is a dangerous thing, and you know that better than most. These few secrets I have held from you are of fundamental importance to the realm, to me, and to my son. If they were to fall into the wrong hands then much would be undone. I cannot risk that, you keep many secrets for me, and I know that you will keep these safe as well. But you do a lot of my dirty work, as I'm asking for you to do again. It requires you taking risks and if you were to fall into enemy hands you know they could extract everything you know sooner or later. But if you are to go to find Brevard you need to be aware...so these are the pieces you have been missing..."

Gaunt laid it all out and Levine sat listening intently.

After a while Levine looked at the King. "You are my King my lord and I am your loyal servant always, as I will be for your son and heir....you are right that I will be taking some risks soon and I appreciate that you have trusted me now with this most precious of secrets...I now understand....If I fall into enemy hands well ...it'll be my own knife for me ...." He let the sentence fade away.

"Meanwhile Major Sykes and his army now approaches so I will do my duty to bring him here as you have commanded. I hope to carry on my journey north, and west, and will do my best to locate Governor Brevard if he's still alive....Farewell my Lord King"

Levine lifted the King's hand and kissed it, then rose and knelt by the young King and did the same to him. "My Lord King" He rose and with a final look back left the Kings chamber for the last time.

"The pieces are laid ....you have the control?" said the young King.

Old Gaunt lifted the bed sheet revealing a trigger control in his hand. A metal grip with a red cover over a simple trigger.

The young Gaunt nodded. Then let us move back to the Cheviots and keep an eye out to the north.

He walked towards the open door.. "Well I suppose it's fitting to say goodbye...even if it's not..." Both men smiled and the door closed shut

.

Scotland

An early morning mist hung in the air making everything damp and gloomy.

Sir William Levine looked at the castle one last time then took the reins of the large Destrier from one of the stable lads, and with some effort managed to swing his gammy leg over the saddle, then pulled himself upright.

"Good lad" he said to the stable hand, "Now get yourself down to the Cheviots with the others as quick as you can lad" The boy nodded. He loved horses and he loved the big Destriers. It was like the books he read about knights of old and tournaments. But here it was just a stiff old man climbing aboard a big horse in the damp fine drizzle of a border-country early morning.

Levine swung the horse around and headed out of the West gate of the yard and out along the tracks on the field edges. He was planning the use General Wade's military roads. A continuous track laid in the 1700's by the English to move large armies north to deal with the Scots uprisings. He would pick up Wade's road at Crieff but even so he had a journey of over 250 miles to cover before reaching Fort Augustus on the southern shores of Loch Ness. Levine reckoned on a seven day ride if he was lucky, faster if the weather held, or longer if not.This was to be his destination, but he knew from his intelligence reports that Sykes was bringing his army down the same road. He was also aware that Syke's army had already crossed the border at the River Sark, heading south and east towards Langley. He estimated that they would be past Longtown by now, east of Gretna Green, then head east along the old Hadrian's wall. Levine kept the wall, or what was left of it, in sight on his left as his big Destrier trotted along at a reasonable speed where the paths allowed.

He reached the edges of Longtown in the evening, but there was no evidence of the Scots army as yet. It was dark so he looked for any lights on at the edge of town and found a small farmhouse with a single chimney and a barn at the back. He tapped on the rough wooden door and an elderly man came out holding an old shotgun. Levine calmed him and gave him some food as payment for resting him and his horse in the barn for one night.

It was a pitch dark night but no rain. He found a ladder and climbed on to the barn roof and found what he was looking for. The light of many camp fires, probably no more than 20 miles away to the North.

He slept with the horse and was up before dawn, took his ablutions in the farmhouse, the man gave him a cup of strong tea. With that he mounted the Destrier and was away northwards.

Around mid-day he picked up the forward scouts of Sykes army and let himself be taken to the command group knowing that Sykes and his generals would all be together somewhere in the middle of the formation. Levine saw that it was a large army, possibly more than 10,000 men and perhaps the same again in the rag-tag support wagons that follow along after every army in the world.

The columns had halted for the noon meal and Levine was brought into a large canvas tent. Sykes was standing with some other Kilted and armed men when he turned in surprise to see Levine in captivity. Two teenagers with pale faces sat in a corner eating some fruit.

"Well well, Here's a fine gentleman, no less that his majesty the Lord High Chancellor, William Levine, and the pretender's right hand spy-master."

The assembled men looked at Levine in his dark blue navy cloak and muddy boots. He had left some straw attached to cloak and his trousers. He looked like he'd slept rough in a barn, with his horse.

One of the Scots captains moved closer to Levine and drew his sword "One less to deal with don't you think....kill him now?"

Sykes smiled. "Not yet I think Caister, I want to know what he's up to first...why is he here, apparently travelling alone on our road where he knew he would meet up with us most likely. He's a canny one this fellow and I'm gai suspicious."

"Well?...what have you to say man?"

Levine took a step towards Sykes and they all began to draw their swords. But the Highlander scout who brought him shouted "He's unarmed! Do ye think I would have brought him here without a throrough search by God!...he's got some food and a bottle of Scotland's finest in his pack though...and a fine horse with him...here.." the scout threw Levine's saddle bags onto the table and pulled out a bottle of pale single malt whisky.

Levine smiled at them " I'm heading north to Fort Augustus if you must know Major Sykes, to see my older brother John Levine who has been at Loch Ness these past 60 odd years."

"It's General Sykes if you don't mind Levine and what mischief were you planning if you got to the Loch..Hm?"

"I haven't seen my brother for more than 10 years and I'm planning to stay with him"

"He's joining us !" one of the men shouted and they all began to laugh. Levene just smiled but said nothing.

"Aye as canny as a snake in the grass" said Sykes "Angus" this to one of the men, "...you've got some men from Augustus, go and get one will you."

One of the men stepped out of the tent and went to find his men.

"So...off to bonny Scotland are you Wiliam?..to see your long lost brother mind...and leaving the King to dangle no doubt without your expertise by his side?"

Levine said nothing.

"Nothing to say eh? Perhaps we can loosen his tongue for him?"

"No!" Sykes spoke "not yet at any rate...here we have one of England's top men riding towards his enemy, on his own...unarmed, and he wanders straight into our army marching south, no co-incidence surely..and yet he looks like a vagabond. He's left the dying Gaunt...oh yes we know all about him and the syphillus which has been gnawing at his bones for many a year now, ...Is he dead already?"

Levine said nothing but looked down slightly...

Sykes continued, he liked to consider himself to be

smarter than the rest and he'd always enjoyed the sound of his own voice. "No not yet…we'd have had word by now…but we know he's abed in Castle Langley, which is where you were until a few days ago I believe..so he's at deaths door and you've decided to get out of the way before the inevitable happens…he has no heir…the kingdom fails and it'll be a bloody mess when all those Dukes and Earls start fighting one another…that's it lads!…we can just sit and wait while they slaughter each other and then walk in through an open door!."

Levine spoke "He's not dead and there'll be no open door…not for you at any rate" Levene liked to sow doubt in the minds of his many enemies and in this he was a master.

"What?…not for me..then who?…don't tell me he's nominated one of his thugs to take over already?… and let me guess, the first order of the day will be to kill all the previous generals and spymasters before they cause trouble?….oh very Machiavellian"

Levene said nothing but gave Sykes a sour look. "so if you don't mind I'll have my bags back..and the present for my brother and I'll leave you to get on with your business while I get on with mine."

Sykes stood back for a moment, with a scowl on his face but then the sarcastic smile returned.. "…taking whisky to a Scot as a present…who'd think it…not the other way around!"

His men smiled but one said "agh..! what are we waiting, for let's take off his head and get on with what we came here for,…all this talk is not going to change anything…let's get the men up and going… we've wasted enough time with this shit…and we've got some more miles before we can fight…the men are restless to spill some English blood…not this …

this Jew!...take off his head and be done with him"

One of the Highlanders drew his enormous Claymore and stepped towards Levine.

Sykes turned on him. "I'll be the one to give orders round here...Captain..."

At that moment the man called Angus returned with another dressed in tartan from head to foot, with a great ginger bristling beard. The man must have been nearly seven feet tall.

"This is Douglas MacLean, one of my men, from Fort Augustus, he says he knows John Levine and that he's a fine Scot."

MacLean spoke in a surprisingly high voice with a typical far highland accent. "Aye I know him well, what's he got to do with all this?"

Sykes leant forward and pointed at Levine "This man says he's John Levine's brother...does he look like him?"

Maclean leaned forward and looked down into Levine's upturned face.."My God! He's the spitting image!...who is he?"

Sykes ignored the question but said "Douglas, how long have you known John Levene and what does he do?"

"Johnny Levine is a boatman on the Loch...runs a small boat yard and does the tourist thing...or he did before the world went upside down...he's a fine man except he's only got one arm and one leg...served in the Highlanders for years and got himself blown up in some god forsaken hole abroad...I've known him all my life...and I'm guessing this must be Billy, his younger brother?...Johnny said you might be coming to live with him, help him out with the boats...he's getting on a bit now."

Sykes stepped back. "Thank you Douglas, that'll be all for now.."

Maclean stood upright "Aye well" then turned to Levine "If you're headed his way then say hello from Dougie MacLean for me…tell him I'll be back to help with the boats as soon as I can.."

"Thank you Maclean…that'll be all..thankyou" Sykes tried not to sound irritated. Dougie said "Aye " and left the tent with a nod to his captain.

"The snake tells the truth it would appear…and if he's going to Loch Ness then we can keep an eye on him and .." he looked over at the two teenagers "…He might actually be useful to us once we've reclaimed the throne with the rightful Princes….the Lord High Chancellor here knows too much for his own good but Gaunt found him invaluable."

"Are ye mad!" one of the Captains stepped forward "kill him…and let's be off"

Sykes turned to the man "back off Fifer…I've already said it's my decision..and my decision is to let him on his way…but he'll be accompanied by you, and that ginger giant to keep an eye on him…any trouble then you can have your way..but if he makes it to the Loch then you come back here and ginger can stay with him and his brother."

Some of the men muttered but decided now was not the time to question their General's wisdom…"No English blood for you then Georgie!" one of them said to Levine's escort.

"Pah! " Georgie stormed out of the tent back to his men.

Sykes then gave the order to Angus to take Levine and his horse to the rear of the column and send him on his way north with Dougie MacLean.

“My saddle bags if you please..”

Sykes picked them up and put the whisky back in one of them…”We’re not barbarians Levine…”

But he stopped, he had to have a look for himself in the bags. Pieces of bread, probably Choler, some cheese, a water bottle, some raisins and dates and assorted small cakes. Then his eye caught on a small leather bag at the bottom. He opened it and pulled out a small prayer book. He looked at Levine who said nothing, at the bottom of the bag was a large signet ring. Sykes pulled it out and Levine shuffled slightly.

“What’s this…slinking off with some Royal loot are we…if I’m not mistaken this looks like the King’s royal seal to me…well, well , so he really is at death’s door and you’ve pinched one of the great seals of England …what?….a memento of happier times William?”

Levine didn’t answer. Sykes held the ring and turned to look at the teenagers at the rear of the tent. “Well this belongs to us now….we’ll be keeping with the proper traditions once this is settled…I’ll keep this” He turned to Levine who gave him a sad look.

Levine was led out of the tent, and Maclean was summoned. Dougie Maclean looked quite relieved when his Captain told him to accompany Levine back to Fort Augustus. The Fifer was nowhere to be found so the two were led back to the rear of the column past many men and women who all looked slightly worse for wear. ‘Scarman did his job well’ Levine thought. He also gave a silent thanks to the Goldsmith in Hexham who, a few weeks ago had made up a lovely gold ring that was for all the world like a great seal that might belong to a King.

Dougie helped him up into his saddle, strapped on the saddle bags then climbed on his own horse. It was sightly comic as Dougie was probably bigger than the horse. The poor beast sank in the middle. The Destrier nuzzled the other horse, glad for the company.

The two set off north bound, and as it turned out Dougie knew all about the General Wade roads so within two days they had gone past Crieff and were heading North.

The only problem was that once Dougie began talking he couldn't stop. "It'll be grand to get back home....I'm not alone in that...there's already been a few desertions...more each day...not all of us are convinced that Sykes is the right man...and even less that we can take on an English army equipped with so much hardware....Aye we're a proud people but I canna see that this will end well...and even if it does and those two teenagers take back the throne...well they're not Scots either....to me...and many of us... it'll just be the same as before after a while. We're better off tending our own and be damned to the English as long as they leave us alone...actually no... we've always had good relations with those across the border...a bit of trade and the like...and they've helped us when times have been hard...so ..." Dougies voice tailed off , he looked down into the fire lost in his thoughts.

Levine looked at him though the firelight. "Dougie, I've grown to like you a bit...even though you talk too much...."

"Aye...It's been said before"

Levine continued. "your friends...those men are all going to die...and the women and children tagging along behind...you may think I'm a twister, and you'd probably be right but on this occasion I'm telling you the truth."

MacLean gave him a look.

"Ride back to the camp, I doubt if they've moved yet...from what I saw they'll need a couple of days to finish the drinking before they'll march....go back and tell them they'd be wise to turn round and head home before it's too late....I can't tell you why I'm so certain , but I am....I will wait here for you and we'll carry on our journey together. Bring back as many as you can along with the women and children...at least get them walking north...then ride back to me. Take my horse with you as long as you bring it back."

Dougie gave him a hard look.

"How can I trust you....maybe Sykes was right... you've been sent to muddy the waters...but I'm thinking you're probably right...agh I dunno...why are you telling me this?"

Levine looked down "...because I don't want to see good Scotsmen die..."

Dougie looked down in thought.

Levine lay down and wrapped his cloak around him.

He woke late in the morning to find Dougie had gone. He'd also taken Levine's horse. He put fresh wood on the fire and blew it back to life as the Scottish weather was closing in. He made a simple cover using a dead fir tree, then he covered it with fir branches and leaves. He moved the fire back in front of the shelter. He packed several dry fir branches and leaves onto the floor so that he was insulated from the ground. Then he collected as much dry wood as necessary to pile up in the shelter. He found some food in his bag that he'd taken off the horse the previous night. Then he sat back and read from his little black book...

muttering to himself.

It was night on the third day before Dougie returned, bringing himself and five others with him...one riding Levine's horse.

Levine was sitting inside his small shelter but the light of the fire was easy enough to spot.

"Well that's set the cat amongst the pigeons!" Dougie wasn't smiling but he sat down next to the fire to warm his hands. The others followed after tying the horses.

"I found my brother, Jimmy Maclean, and we had a chat with a few others. It looks like Sykes is losing more and more by the day, so it wasnae difficult to pass on what you'd said and it really didn't take much to get several of them to agree to withdraw.....I reckon the word has spread so there'll be more coming this way before long."

"Did they try to stop you?"

"Oh aye....a few of the captains were all for stringing me up but I can look after myself you know... spreading discontent amongst the troops and all that...one of them called me a traitor...an I'm no traitor....but he's dead now...so let's not dwell on it anymore ...I'm keen to get away now...probably better we move now...the Ware roads can be travelled at night and I'd like to get as much distance as possible in case Sykes sends out a hunting party for us...especially me."

Levine picked up his bag and climbed on his horse with help from one of the men.

"Dougie, you lead the way..."

"Aye, you and me will be heading into the far highlands but these men will be soon be going different ways and some will be waiting for their women and Bairns to catch up before they get off the road."

Levine nodded and set off behind Dougie leaving the others to take advantage of his small shelter and fire as best they could.

Forlorn Hope

Lieutenant Drummond pushed his hands into his back but it was no good. His body was wracked with pain from the cancer. He stood as straight as he could in front of an equally uncomfortable group of men.

The Forlorn Hope. A name given to a group of soldiers who, for one reason or another have little time left. Those who are in pain and suffering who wish to die as honourably...and as quickly as possible volunteer for the 'Hope'. In times past these were the men who would be first into the breach. Once the cannons or petards had brought down the walls or gates of a town or city, and the defenders poured their fire into the attacking soldiers, the 'forlorn hope' would run towards almost certain death in order to try to overwhelm the defenders, to get inside the walls and kill as many as possible before succumbing to the inevitable, but would give time and diversion to the next wave of attackers who might get through the breach intact and gradually take over the town. This has been a formula in many of the English wars in the past, particularly during the Napoleonic wars, commanded by Wellington.

"Men...I'm honoured to lead you...this forlorn hope....in protecting the King for one last time against our enemies who are now approaching. You all know now what this group is, and you all know that it is certain death. For my part I am ready to face eternity with what strength I have left, and to feel that I have honoured my oath to King and Country." He stopped as another sharp pain spread through his body. He tried not to wince.

"Any man who does not want a part of the 'hope' can

leave now. You have volunteered and I will not force any of you to meet your maker if that is your wish. Go now with Godspeed.

No-one moved, they had all volunteered. Some form incurable pain, some who had lost everything and just wanted their life to be over. Whatever their reasons they all stood as best they could.

"Very well.." Drummond smiled " You know your positions, I want four of you out on the corners to give the signal as soon as you see even a glimpse of tartan" some of the men smiled.

"The others into and around the castle, six of you inside and two outside the King's bedchamber. When the enemy attack I want you firing until you're out of ammo, then get bayoneting...make sure your bayonets are fastened before you start shooting. You may charge the enemy ranks at will once they're in the castle grounds.....Let's show these bastards how an Englishman will look certain death in the face... and charge towards it!"

There was a cheer from the assembled group.

"Alright men of the Forlorn Hope...take up your positions and here's to God, King Edward, and St George!"

Another cheer before the men dispersed to their stations to wait.

It didn't take long for a shout from one of the outliers in the grounds, followed by a shot then a keening sound as the Scotsmen came forward. They were surrounding the castle. The war cries began in earnest now. Big men in kilts charging across the open ground firing their semi automatic rifles at the English. Several went down as the 'hope' fired back. The ammunition of either side didn't last long before the swords and the bayonets started their grisly work amidst screams and howls from both sides.

A group of Scots ran forward to the Castle's main door and pinned a large petard onto the front, then dived for cover as the door disappeared in a huge flash and a cloud of smoke. More Scots charged in and were shot down by the men inside the castle. But more and more came. No-one really knows the strength of Sykes force but it numbered several thousand, against perhaps one hundred English so the castle was soon overrun. As the firing and bayoneting receded, Sykes led a small party towards the gate on horseback including the two Princelings trying to look as royal as possible amid the carnage and destruction. Sykes led them through the arch and into the main building before dismounting. He knew the layout of the castle by heart so he led the royal party up the main staircase, up two floors towards Gaunt's bed chamber where his spies had told him.

Several scots were on the landing standing over two dead men lying in pools of their own blood. Sykes nodded to the Scotsmen then signalled the royal party forward and into the chamber.

Fifty miles away, Gaunt and his court of Dukes reined up on the top of Langdon Pike, a hill around seventeen hundred feet above sea level, giving a relatively good view of the northern pennines, more importantly, a clear line of sight towards Langley castle, now over the horizon.

It had taken less than two days to ride slowly away from the castle with the aim of moving on to Durham Cathedral and its ancient hillside location, seat of the old English Prince Bishops.

One of the signalmen with the party had spoken to

Gaunt to advise that the Scots were now closing in on the castle so the royal party of Edward X, sat astride their horses and looked north.

Edward Gaunt, Edward IX, King of England, and all her Dominions lay silent in the bed, his head propped up on pillows, his great mane of hair stuck to him with sweat from the pain of his deteriorated condition. A light gold crown sat on his head. The place smelled rank with gangrene, blood, and pus. No amount of herbs or lavenders could mask the stench.

Sykes out his arm round the shoulder of the boy. "You must take the Crown of England your majesty, take it from him, and you must kill him with this." Sykes produced a thin bladed knife with a jewel encrusted hilt. "Cut his throat and take the crown..."

The boy prince was shaking, perhaps not with fear but with dread of the deed. They had spoken about it for some time but now this old man was in front of him he wondered if he could go through with it.

Gaunt broke a smile. "Here boy..." and he raised his chin to reveal more of his neck.

Sykes frowned but said nothing. He had said what was needed. Action was now required...and it had to be done by the boy...his own King, his true king who would unite the royal houses of England and Scotland.

The boy stepped closer. Gaunt broke into a short laugh. "He's not going to do it Sykes...you'll have to oblige your new master I think..."

Still Sykes said nothing but his frown remained.

"Let me ease the tension Sykes...and ease your passage." Under the bedclothes he flicked off the safety cover on the trigger. Sykes saw the movement. The King gave him one last look and squeezed the trigger. There was a fraction of a second delay then everything went white....

On Langdale Pike the horses stomped. Gaunt shouted "Close your eyes!"

A blinding flash turned everything orange under the eyelids of the watchers, like looking directly at the sun. The horses staggered and began to fret and had to be steadied by their riders. The ground trembled beneath their feet and a hot wind rose up from the north and into the clouds. They could see that above Langley the clouds had gone and a large circle of blue sky was expanding rapidly. Under this blue sky a familiar mushroom cloud of dust began to rise into the heavens.After a few moments the westerly wind blew away any warmth. It began to rain.

No-one spoke for a few minutes. Transfixed by what they were seeing, then the realisation that the old King was gone, along with a large Scots army, vapourised in a second along with the castle and surrounding forest. Black smoke now rose in isolated patches far away signifying the fires that would consume everything that the blast did not.

Alex Rheinhart was the first to move, she spun her horse around. "It's done Lord King, let's move on to Durham before nightfall". The King smiled at his half sister, "Come then...to Durham...and new beginnings..."

Loch Ness

Levine felt rather than heard or saw the explosion. He and Maclean had left Crieff after a brief stop for supplies at one of the farms.

He turned his horse and looked south. There was a faint sliver shine in the clouds far south. He may have imagined it but he was sure he felt a tremor in the earth. His horse became skittish for a moment. Maclean's horse whinnied but stood still.

"What is it?" Maclean was looking at Sir William.

Levine pondered the question "...Death....the King....and sadly a lot of brave but foolish Scotsmen....plus your General Sykes and his so called royal charges....all gone."

For once Douglas MacLean was silent.

Levine turned his horse back north and they headed up towards a deep valley. The Scotch mist fell but they had a while to go before nightfall.

It took another few days, riding gently, to reach the southern shores of Loch Ness, that great body of troubled, sinister fresh water that lies in the Great Glen. Dark and deep, with odd currents that swell up and then subside back into the inky blackness of the water. No wonder the popular myth. The great looming sides of the hills surrounding the loch with their almost vertical sides disappearing down into the depths, a sinister and maybe unnatural environment with no regard for humans, indeed.

However at the south end the hills drew back as the loch emptied its waters down various rivers and streams. There was a short beach of stones and mud. Alongside, a boatyard cut into a slope on the west of the hills, with a decaying selection of boats and tourist platforms for those that would venture onto the loch for whatever purpose they had in mind.

A figure was standing outside a small office, next to a larger warehouse, or boat yard repair facility. He waved at Levine and Maclean.

"Oh aye there's your brother look." Maclean waved back at the figure. Levine turned his horse and they both rode up and into the hard standing in front of the office.

Levine dismounted. He winced as he got off.

"...Should have had it off like me" said John Levine "You've got too much shrapnel in that leg than's good for you William"

Levine smiled "Hello John" and the two men shook hands warmly.

"I see you've brought a big strong lad with you to help me manage the boats" John turned towards Dougie Maclean. "Good to see you back Dougie, and Mandy will be very pleased your back and safe too"

Maclean smiled "Aye well I'm looking forward to seeing her too, now that I've dropped off my charge here." He nodded towards Levine.

"Thank you Dougie and Godspeed to you now, I daresay John and I have a lot of catching up to do, or will you join us for a bit of supper first?" Levine held up two brace of Partridges which had been given to him by a local farmer en route.

"Good of you both but I'll be off to see my dearest Mandy, so I'll say farewell for now. I daresay we'll be meeting up again if you're around and about the loch."

"Well take her these two birds anyway" said Levine, handing him the brace "..as we ate yours last night"

Dougie trotted away.

"Come on in man..." John Levine beckoned him into the office. "It's been a while but great to see you again and still in one piece." He tapped his artificial leg, and swung the artificial arm as far as he could.

"Yes it is John, and lovely to see you too again even if there's less of you now..."

The office was in fact a house with and office attached to the front. A curtain and a door separated the two and John pushed open the door, leading the way into the parlour at the back.

"How's business John?"

"Oh can't complain...I mean there's no tourists but plenty of traffic down below. There's a couple of Aussie officers up in the warehouse right now. You'll meet them soon. Will you join me in a glass?" He waved a bottle of whisky.

The two sat down and raised a toast to the Navy. Both had been senior officers in the Royal Navy. William, a Commander, and John a Vice Admiral. Both had taken serious wounds in several operations. John had lost a leg from flying ships's shrapnel, William had been hit by fragments but had kept the leg and the pain that went with it. An unusual incident where both brothers had happened to be on the same ship at the same time during one of the intermidable wars in the Gulf.

John, lost his arm from a ship's propeller while diving to remove a cable that had trapped the prop shaft. He got it off and saved the lives of his crew, but the arm was gone.

Both brave and experienced men. They talked for an hour before two men came through the door dressed in civilian clothes but with a distinct military air.

John introduced them to William. The Captain, and

Executive Officer of a joint US/UK/Australian boat. Jim Fairey, and Colin Stroud, both from Sydney. They knew who he was and what he was so William chatted to them and shared some of his brothers whisky with them while John plucked and roasted the birds, along with some fried potato, oat and onion cakes, and some turnip green tops. Submarine commanders are quiet, calm types, they have to be, so talk is short and to the point, and kept at a steady low volume.

After they had eaten William asked them where they're headed.

"We're heading back to Sydney once we've re-supplied here, should be underway in a couple of days....the Chief Engineer is sorting out a problem with the de-salination plant, and he's doing a full test of the electrics, otherwise we'd be gone tomorrow. Where do you want us to drop you off?"

"If you don't mind a detour I'm heading for the US, East coast,...Jamestown River most likely if it's still there."

"No good for you...Norfolk has gone, just a big wet pool and the river has held on to the nuke dust....no navigation north or south until you get to Wilmington. We could stow a small sail boat and let you off about 20 miles off the coast which is deep enough for us....shouldn't be too bad a crossing and you can get rid of the boat in one of the dunes there. Plus the roads are just about ok for horse traffic. I know because we dropped off one of the King's men there a few months ago"

Levine looked up with a quizzical expression.

"Can't tell you his name as he never gave it, one of your couriers we were told"

"Ah yes, I recall now"

"Well Wilmington it is then and I think we have just the boat for the job."

John nodded "The Tideway 10 I think you're referring to....it's just been repainted but I'll slap on a coat of black so it shouldn't be too visible."

The ExO said he would get the men to bring it on board tomorrow night when it's dark.

"...well now, would you like to meet the Adelaide?"

"Yes that would be good, ...how many crew?"

"Thirty five right now, more than enough to sail her"

The two officers rose and led Levine through the house to a panel in the bathroom. There was a code pad under the sink unit. Stroud keyed in the code and the panel unlocked to reveal a heavy steel door not dissimilar to a ships watertight bulkhead door. He spun the locking mechanism and the door opened onto a long corridor rising upwards at a shallow angle. An electric golf cart stood at the edge of the wide corridor and they all climbed in.

" A great tribute to the engineers that made this I always think when we get in here. Said Jim Fairey.

Levine knew all about the tunnel and what was housed here.

The Americans built it shortly after the second world war after one of their sub captains had discovered the huge caverns that lay under the tectonic plates that made up the great glen.

Around 400 million years ago the Laurentia and Baltic plates collided to create what we now see as Scotland. They slid together and whilst the fault is largely inactive today, though still slipping occasionaly, the northern side heading north east, the southern plate heading south west. During the last ice age part of the upper crust of the Glen was carved out leading to the creation of several Lochs along it's path, but underneath the visible surface their remains a vast collection of caverns filled with sea water. The salt water being heavier than fresh water avoids the mixing of the two, except at the barrier level deep below

Captain Chuck Arnott of the US Navy Sub, the Detroit, had torpedoed a German frigate but was being chased by a Destroyer off the North East Coast. He took the sub beyond it's recognised operating depth to avoid the depth charges and found himself in a huge salt water cavern. Sonar indicated that they were actually under land. The batteries were running low by the time he reversed out and surfaced later that night. He reported his finding to the Navy brass, and to the British Admiralty. He volunteered to take a sub with more batteries on board to explore the extent of the undersea caves using very basic sonar and radar. To everyone's surprise he surfaced in Loch Ness. Fortunately at night.

A later expedition, shortly after the war and with more advanced navionics found that the caverns continued on past Ness and out into the Irish Sea. The whole venture became highly classified. It is believed that it is only known to a select number of sub captains. Even many of the crew are unaware that they are passing under a huge land mass, nor where exactly it lies.

Over the ensuing years a few 'kinks' in the channel have been smoothed out and at the same time a totally underwater naval base was built into the mountain on the East shore of the Loch utilising one of the existing underwater caverns. The base is named Laurentia House to avoid any interpretation of its location.

The golf cart ran upwards for a while before levelling out and then started to descend before reaching a sharp bend downhill. Levine recognised the smell of water ahead. At the end they emerged into a huge man-made cave where the water level matched that of the Loch outside. Sitting in the water was the HMS Adelaide, a Dreadnought class nuclear submarine, built in Barrow-in-Furness. The boat made small rises and falls as the water moved about from the currents in the loch. The coating on the hull reflected no light, it was as close a match to the surrounding water as it could be though Levine knew this was a deliberate part of the boats camouflage both visually and sonically.

On the far side was a hotel and restaurant to provide for the crews who could not venture outside. Only the Captain and ExO were allowed topside, unless there was a specific reason, such as bringing in a small boat to be stowed in the top hold. Even then it was done inside the main warehouse, out of sight of any public, and brought down the service ramp.

No-one knew about the great nuclear leviathans lying deep in the hills, nor when they emerged deep under the lake to sail into the depths of the undersea canyons and out under the open seas.

None of the crew paid Levine any attention and he only spoke briefly to them whilst he was given a tour of the boat. Fairey spoke to the deck officer and arranged for a cabin for him. Levine asked that he eat in his cabin on the voyage which was also arranged.

Outside the missiles had been carefully unloaded and were being serviced by experienced men. There were no women aboard. The desalination plant had been taken apart on board but Levine met, and was introduced to the Chief Engineer briefly.

Food trucks were at the quayside, brought into the warehouse and driven down the service ramp. Boats like this could stay underwater indefinitely. The only restriction was the re-supply of food for the officers and crew. There was no alcohol.

Levine left the men and set off back up the tunnel from which he'd come, back into his brother's home. John Levine was sitting reading a book.

"All good?"

"Yes thanks John, just one curious thing, who was it that they took over to America?...'one of your king's men'?"

"Yes I noticed that...well if it was then he didn't start here. Either he was already on the boat when it docked, or they picked him up en route"

"Ok ...perhaps it's nothing, maybe one of Gaunt's emissaries to find Brevard ..."

"You'll be heading into dangerous waters William so best get some proper sleep while you can...I could never sleep properly on a sub."

John Levine got up and made him a hot toddy with Whisky and hot water. "Here's your room, get some rest...they won't be ready for 48 hours so no need to rise early this time.

"Aye thanks John....I'm sorry I can't stay longer this time but...well you know.."

"Aye a restless King and his Lord High Chancellor....."

"Something like that...well goodnight."

He slept for over 12 hours in the end, but didn't feel any less tired for it...but he ate some eggs and toast then the brothers talked for hours as brothers do.

He slept again but was woken in the early hours.

John shook him awake."The boat will be underway in a couple of hours."

So Levine got up, showered and dressed in some of John's clean clothes. Took his satchel that he carried and said his goodbyes to John.

Get rid of the horse and tell Dougie Maclean that I've gone east to the continent....'in exile'...yes say that to him...I like Maclean but he talks too much and there's no point arousing unnecessary suspicions."

"I've been doing this longer than you William... I'll sort it out...Dougie and anyone else he's already told....you've slipped away in the night for a boat out eastways"

"Also please signal the King to advise that I've departed Laurentia..."

"Thanks John...well hopefully we'll see each other again when I come back...."

Levine slipped past the bulkhead door and away on the cart.

Commander Fairey and Exec Officer Stroud gave him the salute and he was welcomed aboard. The Tideway and her sails all stowed. The hatches were closed. The checks done, then the order to submerge. Straight and level down inside the underwater cavern, then out deep into the Loch, then into the west appsage of the undersea caverns and out under the Irish sea, north to the Atlantic, and heading for America and what might await there.....

Printed in Great Britain
by Amazon

33008572R10225